MW01126928

Craft Circle Cozy
Mystery Boxed Set

Books 1 - 3

By
Stacey Alabaster

Table of Contents

iv

Introduction

Thank you so much for buying my book. I am excited to share my stories with you and hope that you are just as thrilled to read them.

If you would like to know about all my new releases and have the opportunity to get free books, make sure you sign up for our Cozy Mystery Newsletter.

FairfieldPublishing.com/cozy-newsletter

Stacey Alabaster

Steps From Death

Chapter 1

"Sorry, no dogs allowed in the house."

I stopped, my high heels just about to step onto the polished hardwood floors of the house I was hoping to become the new owner of. "Really?" I asked the real estate agent. She was blonde, with red-painted lips and a permanently-fixed smile. "Surely if I buy the house, I can have as many dogs inside the house as I like." I stood up straight and flashed her a bright smile. "And I certainly intend to!"

She glanced at the hardwood floors and made a 'you can do whatever you want, crazy lady' face. "If you purchase the house, that will be an entirely different story of course. But until then, sorry, no dogs allowed."

A whimpering noise came from my ankles. I looked down. "Sorry, Jasper. You're going to have to stay outside." I held up my hands. "Not my choice! Don't shoot the messenger."

The real estate agent made another face. *Okay...so,*

this lady talks to her dog. She's one of those people, I could see her thinking.

Jasper looked up at me with sad eyes.

The agent shifted uncomfortably, clearly ready to get on with the tour. She laughed a little nervously while I tied Jasper's leash to the front door and told him not to run away. "Maybe you should leave him at home next time," was her not very helpful suggestion.

I shot her a wink and followed her into the house. "Oh, I take him everywhere. Abandonment issues," I said with a knowing look.

"Right."

I could tell she wasn't a dog person.

I didn't know much about Jasper. I'd only had him for two weeks, the same amount of time I'd been living in Pottsville. Before that, Paris. Yes, from Paris, a city of over two million people, to Pottsville, a town of seventy-five hundred, give or take a few. Pottsville, with its small town charms, full of artists and crafters and painters and antiques collectors, seemed like the perfect spot for me—for now.

I hadn't met many people so far. But I had met Jasper. It had been love at first sight, though he had a naughty streak and a few behavioral issues. We could work on those.

The rescue shelter hadn't even provided me with the right birth certificate for him. It said he was twenty pounds, when he was clearly closer to forty, and it said his coat was red, where really it was black and white.

He was a border collie, I knew that much. You could tell just from looking at him, but also from his intelligence, typical to that breed. They are the most intelligent breed of dog. But I didn't know how old he was, or who his previous owners had been, or what had caused them to abandon him. I only knew that he didn't like to be left alone. One could hardly blame the poor fellow!

"Nice bangle," the real estate agent commented. She used the kind of ambiguous tone that wasn't clear whether she was being genuine or sarcastic. Or just making small talk. I decided to take it as praise though, swirling the large bangle, with its blue and yellow balls, around my wrist.

"Thanks!" I exclaimed. "I made it myself."

"Oh?"

I nodded. "I'm a bit of an arts and crafter...and a jewelry maker. A bit of everything, really."

I could see her eyes glaze over. I could tell from her expensive suit that she wasn't exactly a 'homemade' kind of gal. The kind of chunky, loud, handmade jewelry I was wearing, not just around my wrist but around my neck and ankle as well, was definitely not her style. Still, I decided to have some fun with her.

"I've opened up a new store in town. George's Crafts," I said to her. "You should come in and look around some time."

She frowned. "Who is George? Your husband?"

I had to stifle a laugh. I got this all the time. Shaking my head, I explained it to her. "George, short for Georgina. Most people call me George."

"Oh," She looked a little embarrassed. "So, what do you sell there?" she asked, cringing and trying to be polite.

"Bit of everything. It's a bit ramshackle, just like myself! Paper, of course, crafting tools, beads, jewelry supplies—basically anything you need to make your D.I.Y. dreams come true!"

She looked a little pale at the idea of 'do it yourself.' "Okay," she said, fixing her smile back to her face. "What do you think of the place then?"

The house was beautiful. Large, four bedrooms, two bathrooms, glass windows all around the open plan kitchen and dining room, with a view out to the woods and lake behind. Something like this in Paris would have taken me a few lifetimes to pay off! But in Pottsville, it was suspiciously cheap.

I narrowed my eyes at the sprightly young real estate agent, my long upper lashes brushing against my bottom ones.

"So why is it so cheap?" I asked. "There's got to be a catch, right?"

"Haha," she laughed, uneasily. "No catch as far as I can see. The owners left Pottsville in a hurry, they are just ready to sell."

I pursed my lips. "No one died here, did they?" I saw the look of shock on her face, so I let out a loud laugh to let her know that I was only joking. "Don't be so serious," I said, waving my hand. "I love the house."

A sudden shriek came from the front of the house.

"Umm, sorry about that, I'll be back in a second," she said, almost tripping over her heels as she ran to see what the issue was. I decided I'd take the chance to check out the backyard.

I wandered around. The yard was large, full of luscious green grass before it backed onto the woods. Perfect for Jasper. He was an intelligent dog—too intelligent, I sometimes thought—and he needed space to run around and play. Too much time cooped up inside and he became bored, turning his attention to destroying furniture and items of clothing. The month-to-month rental I was in was far too small.

The yard would be good for him.

And the house would be good for me. I closed my eyes and breathed in the fresh air, so different from the sooty, meaty smell of city air. I'd miss life in a big city, of course, but there was no use in dwelling on it. Life had been fun before. Fun, and messy, and disastrous at times. But now it was time for a change. Pottsville and this new, beautiful, far too cheap house were my homes now.

The real estate agent ran back into the yard. I expected an apology to come from her lips, but it was she who was demanding an apology from me. "That dog of yours got loose and got into the neighbor's yard, destroying the rose bushes!"

That explained the screaming then. I made a face. Whoops. Looks like I'd made an enemy of the neighbors already and I hadn't even moved in yet.

I could see Jasper in the distance, dirt around his mouth and paws.

"Come here," I called and he ran over, wagging his tail. "Good boy." I straightened up and gave him a very serious look. "So, Jasper, do you think this is our new home?"

His tail wagged even harder in answer. "I guess I'll put in the offer, then." I grinned at the agent, who was looking down at Jasper's muddy paws in horror. "How soon will we be able to move in?"

* * *

A smashing sound came from the back of the craft store. I closed the magazine I'd been lazily flicking through and straightened up. "Jasper?" I called out. Yikes. Maybe it hadn't been such a good idea to let a border collie loose in a shop full of glass items.

An irritated looking woman peeped her head out from behind an aisle. "Sorry," she said, creeping out, a broken glass tile in her hands. "I knocked it over with my purse. I will pay for it of course," she said, sticking her hand into her purse.

I waved my hand. "Don't worry about it. I've got plenty more." I winked at her. "They only cost two dollars each! Price of doing business!"

I'd expected a bit of gratitude from her, but she straightened up and pulled a 'just sucked on a lemon' face.

"This is no way to run a business!"

"I'm sorry?" I said.

She came stomping over to the counter. So much for timid. "Just what is this place, anyway? I can tell you're not a serious crafter."

"I..I...Erm." I was not often lost for words, but this lady had me stumped.

"You've got too many different things in here!" she said, clearly having taken the gravest offense at this, for some reason. "It's all over the place. Baskets, beads, picture frames, jewelry items..."

"Yes," I answered. "It's a craft shop."

"Some of this stuff isn't even for crafting, it's just junk!" She narrowed her eyes at me. "And don't think I didn't see that display in the back, trying to sell your own jewelry. Is this a crafting supply shop, or just an excuse for you to sell your own junk?"

A bit of both, I wanted to say. I tried to not laugh at her, biting my lip. "I take it you didn't like my jewelry then," I said, returning to my magazine.

She pulled two dollars out of her purse and slammed it down on the counter. "I insist on paying for what I broke. And if you are any sort of business woman, you will insist on making people pay for items they break!" She shook her head before she stormed toward the door. "You have a lot to learn about this town, young lady!"

Young lady? I raised an eyebrow, unsure of whether to be miffed, or pleased by the compliment. At forty-three, I wasn't old by any stretch, but I was no teenager. That said, I'd always had a youthful way about me that made people mistake me for being far younger than I was. Men, especially, seemed to make this mistake.

The woman was just about to leave. "Make sure you come back tomorrow night for my first craft circle meeting! It's going to be a lot of fun!" I called to her, trying to stifle my laughter as she stomped out, shaking her head.

I looked out the window as the woman hurried

down the street.

Surely there had to be some more likeminded people in this town? I mean, sure, I knew I'd moved to the middle of nowhere. That was part of the plan. The middle of nowhere was where I wanted to be. But I'd still thought there would be a little excitement, from time to time. At least some women my own age that I could make friends with.

I turned my head to the side and examined the sign I'd put up in the front window. "Craft Circle. Meets every Tuesday at 6:30pm. Refreshments provided." It had a sort of homemade charm to it. Totally appropriate for crafting group, right?

But I'd only had three sign-ups so far. I sighed heavily and raised an eyebrow at Jasper, curled up in his bed by the window. "You'll come along tomorrow night, won't you, Jasper?"

He gave me a sleepy look and returned to his nap.

Maybe not.

* * *

I'd thought a small, informal gathering of local

crafters was going to be a chance to chill out, drink some wine, have a laugh, and make some new friends. I was wrong. These crafters turned out to be the more serious type. Crafting in Pottsville was clearly a serious business.

When the middle-aged woman from the day before with the broken tile walked into the shop at 6:30 on the dot, I couldn't wipe the look of surprise off my face.

"My name is Brenda," she said, with a tight-lipped smile. "I thought I'd come along and see how you run this thing." She took a very stiff seat in one of the chairs I'd set out.

"Wonderful."

There were only two other human members of the group that night, though Jasper was sniffing around as well. A nice, smiley man named Billy who had an interest in soap making, and a bright-faced woman, around my age, named Amanda, who was already keeping me sane. "Don't worry," she'd said, leaning in to whisper to me while I carried the cheese platter to the center of the room. "You're not the first person to be on the end of Brenda's wrath."

I grinned at her. "I'm glad to hear that!"

She let out a laugh and took a piece of brie off the

plate, popping it into her mouth. She was wearing a bright floral dress with a rose decal. "I love my rose bushes," she said. "And flower arranging. Anything flowers. Anything loud and bright, really."

I shot her another grin. "Sounds like we have a lot in common." Thank goodness Amanda was there.

"So I thought for the first meeting, we'd keep things light and breezy," I said with a smile, flipping my hair over my shoulder, my large bangle flashing for everyone to see. Maybe I'd get some jewelry buyers out of this, at least. But Brenda just scowled at my wrist. "Anyone want any wine?" I asked, reaching over to open a fresh bottle of pinot noir.

Brenda pursued her lips. "So you have no intentions of this ever being a serious crafting circle?"

"We can be serious and still drink wine, can't we?"

Brenda glared at me. "I'd rather talk about my paper mache, thank you very much."

I caught Amanda's eye. She was trying not to laugh. I was doing the same.

"What's so funny?" Brenda demanded to know.

"Nothing," I said quickly. Suddenly Jasper ran over to Brenda and jumped on her, his paws on her lap, licking at her face while she screeched and pushed him away.

"What are you thinking, letting a filthy dog in here!" she yelled.

Billy stepped in to my defense. "Come on, Brenda. Georgina is new in town. We can at least try to be friendly to her." He called Jasper over to him and ruffled his head. "And to this gorgeous boy."

I smiled gratefully at him but Brenda had already had enough. "I'm leaving," she announced, making a show of brushing herself off before she left. "And I don't think I shall be returning."

Amanda and I looked at each other and burst out laughing. We took the rest of the hour to chat, introduce ourselves, and consume plenty of wine and cheese. Billy had to leave a little early, but that only gave Amanda and I a better chance to bond. We both loved dogs, flowers, handmade jewelry, and a good glass of red. Finally, someone I actually got along with in this town!

"I'm glad you moved here," Amanda said, picking up her purse when it was finally time to leave.

I waved Amanda goodbye. "I'm glad you're around, too," I said with a wink. "This town would be dead boring without you."

Chapter 2

"Jasper!" I screamed, watching the trail of mud he left as he dashed from one end of the hallway to the other. "No!"

Maybe the real estate agent had a point about no dogs in the house. First day, boxes still sitting unpacked, and I already had a huge mess to clean up. I glanced over my shoulder at the new hole in the front yard. What I needed to do was break his hole-digging habit.

I placed the box I'd been carrying down in the hallway--the last one--and stumbled into the kitchen. I hadn't unpacked much but I had unpacked the kettle. I'd invited Amanda over for afternoon tea, the very first in my new house. We hadn't had a chance to talk since the craft circle five days earlier and I was looking forward to seeing her again. I put the kettle on the stove and checked the time. She was ten minutes late. Oh well, I wasn't exactly the most punctual person myself!

I heard my phone ringing and looked around to see where the sound was coming from. *Oh, don't tell me I've packed it.*

Eventually I realized it was coming from my coat pocket. "Hello, George here," I said brightly.

There was no response for a second. Then, a male voice spoke up. "Georgina? I-I'm sorry to say, Amanda won't be making it to your appointment today." The voice on the other end sounded eager to get off the line.

"Oh," I said, disappointed. "Did I do something wrong?" I asked. Then I thought to ask, "Who is this, by the way?"

"My name is Officer Mathews."

My stomach dropped a little. "What's wrong?" I asked. "Is Amanda in some kind of trouble? Has she been arrested?"

"No." The voice on the other end of the line was quite matter-of-fact about the next part. "She's just dead."

So much for life in Pottsville being quiet and boring.

* * *

I was stunned. Shocked. But I managed to wrangle a

leash onto Jasper's collar as I walked the half-mile to Amanda's cottage by the lake. I still hadn't bought a car since arriving in Pottsville. I'd had to rely on an over-priced moving company to move my boxes into the new house, and knew I needed to get a vehicle soon. The walk to Amanda's seemed to take forever.

I'd never been to her house before, but I could tell it belonged to her at first sight. "Sit, boy," I murmured to a nervous Jasper as I looked at the bright blue cottage with the rose garden in front. I stood back a moment and surveyed the scene. There was a police car out front.

There were two officers wandering around the front, taking notes. Two uniformed officers. Hmm. Probably not a murder then. Still, there was an uneasy feeling as I approached the cottage.

"I'm Georgina Holt," I said, introducing myself to one of them—the one who seemed to be in charge. "We spoke on the phone, I think."

I tried not to look at the red roses outside the front window. I could see how much pride and care Amanda must have taken in them. They were perfectly pruned, tall, red, no rotten leaves or brown petals.

The officer was cute. Far too young for me—

probably, who can really judge these things—but cute.

"Sorry, miss," he said. I was pleased to hear 'miss' instead of 'ma'am.' He gave me an apologetic smile. "You can't really be here."

"I was her friend," I said quickly, shooting him my best smile. "I'd just like to know what happened. Please."

He looked at me skeptically, but there was a little twinkle in his eyes as he spoke. "Her friend?" he asked. "Really? Because I thought I knew everyone who lived in Pottsville, and I've never seen you around her, miss."

Again with the 'miss.'

"I'm new to the area," I said calmly. "Amanda and I hit it off, though. We'd become friends in a short period of time."

He seemed more interested in speaking to me now as he moved closer. "Well then, maybe you won't mind answering a few questions."

I suddenly felt as though I was under interrogation, but I tried to stay calm. He was just a local policeman, not the FBI. Plus, I'd faced worse than him in my travels. "Why don't you tell me what your name is first, Officer?" I asked, flashing him a bright smile.

"Officer Mathews," he said.

"Your first name."

"Ryan Mathews."

"Great. And may I call you Ryan, then?"

He looked a little taken aback by the request. "I suppose that's fine, miss." He got a notebook and pen out and tried to concentrate on what was in front of him.

"So you said you and Amanda had become friends?"

"Yes. Very good friends."

"And had she been acting strange lately?"

Well...I'd only met her the one time. I furrowed my brow as though I was really thinking about it. "Er, not that I really noticed."

"You were friends, though?" He was still skeptical.

"Yes, of course we were."

"She hadn't been acting depressed, hadn't seem down at all?"

Well, she'd been desperate enough to turn up to my craft circle of misfits and weirdos. Was that really something I should say, though?

I shook my head. "No, she didn't seem down at all." She'd been anything but down the night of the craft circle. She'd been bright, bubbly, and full of life. And now she was so not full of life. I leaned over a bit so I could peer around his shoulder. "Can I just go into the cottage for a second?"

"No," he said firmly, looking astonished that I'd even asked. "That's where the body is."

"Oh dear," I said, making a face. "Just lying there, is it?" I was still trying to catch a glimpse in through the door. Ryan stepped in front of me, blocking my view entirely. Darn.

"Bit strange that they've sent you, isn't it?" I asked.

"What do you mean?"

"Well, a uniformed officer, to the site of a murder," I said, trying to act natural. "Would have thought they'd send in the detectives."

"Murder? Who said anything about a murder?" Ryan looked shocked. "Amanda—Miss Jennings— simply fell."

I raised my eyebrows. "Fell?"

"Fell and hit her head," he said plainly, before snapping his notepad shut. "Can I give you a ride

22

somewhere, miss?"

I glanced down at Jasper. "Are dogs allowed? In your police car, I mean."

He shot me a little smile. "I'll make an exception this time."

"Great," I said with a grin. "You can take me to work, then. I own the new craft shop in town."

* * *

Ryan stopped the car right in the front of the craft store. The ride had been too short. I needed to spend more time with him. So I could figure out what really happened to Amanda, of course.

"Come on, Jasper," I said, calling him out of the car.

Ryan climbed out as well. "I'll walk you to the door," he said.

"Oh!" I said, hitting my forehead with my palm like I'd just remembered something. "I just realized I need to go to the supermarket."

He glanced back at the car, a little unsure. "Do you want me to give you a ride?"

I shook my head. "It's just down here," I said, pointing down the road. "Can you walk me though? I'm feeling a little shaken after the death of a good friend."

He shook his head slowly, but there was the hint of a smile on his face. "Come on then," he said, getting his notebook out of his pocket again. "I'll go over my notes again. Maybe you'll even remember something this time."

I grinned and pulled on Jasper's leash, but I made sure not to walk too quickly. "Do you really think she just fell?" I asked Ryan.

Ryan flipped his notepad shut. "Yeah, I do," he said with a drawl. He had sort of a southern accent, but clearly he hadn't lived there for a while. "She was found at the bottom of the staircase. Seems pretty obvious what happened."

"Hmmm," I said, deep in thought as I wondered if that really was so obvious. Or was he just leaping to conclusions?

"What's the hmmm for?" Ryan asked, mimicking me a bit. "There's no 'hmmm' about it."

"Just wondering..."

"Wondering about what? There's nothing to

wonder about."

I stopped walking and turned to him. "How does it happen?" I asked. "How does a woman just die like that, in her own home?" I started walking again. "Without anyone even knowing about it for days."

Ryan shrugged. "She was single, in her forties, lived alone, owned a dog..."

"Hey!" I said, taking a little offense. "You're pretty much describing me you know." I raised my eyebrows at him and shot him a little wink to know that he hadn't wounded my pride fatally. It was just a little injured.

He made a face. He looked a little surprised, or maybe that was just in my head. "I didn't know you were in your forties. Had you pegged as much younger."

"You don't need to flatter me," I said, noticing that there was more of a spring in my step now as I bounced along beside him. How old was he? Geez, to look at him, you'd think he couldn't be much older than twenty-five. But I was terrible at guessing the ages of people, especially those younger than me. He could be older. Did I hope he was older? I didn't want to ask in case he took it for flirting. Which, of course, it would have been.

"Still," he said with a little shrug. "You look younger.

Act like it as well."

That was true enough, I supposed. "I've never been the settle down and get married type," I said breezily. "Well, that's wrong. I have been married, three times, actually." I caught the look of surprise on his face that he quickly tried to hide. "So I suppose I am the marrying type! Just not the settling down type."

We'd arrived at our destination. The small supermarket gleamed in front of me.

"I guess this is goodbye, for now!" I said with a wink.

"Bye, Georgina," he said. He started to walk away, but stopped and added something over his shoulder. "And don't go worrying yourself, all right? It was just an accident."

I nodded and watched him walk away. "Come on, Jasper," I said, pulling him back in the opposite direction. I didn't really need to go to the store.

* * *

All day, I thought about it. "It was just an accident." I tried to go back to work, tried to focus on my shop. Still,

I was a little rattled by what Ryan had said earlier. About the victim—Amanda. I had to keep reminding myself that she was a person, and for a brief moment my friend—fitting a certain profile. The very same profile I had.

We were similar. Too similar. A shiver ran down my spine and I tried to shake it off.

By the time I got home, it was dark, and I felt even more unsettled. The sight of unpacked boxes everywhere didn't exactly help that feeling.

"You'll protect me, right, Jasper?" I said, taking a heavy sip of wine while I petted him with my other hand. "You won't let that happen to me, right, boy?"

He made a little whimpering noise and bounced up and down. He wanted a treat. I reached into one of the boxes that I had cut open and produced a doggie biscuit.

Something didn't feel right. Maybe it was just the wine talking. Maybe it was the new, strange environment I was in. But I just couldn't shake the feeling that Amanda's death was not an accident.

I'd always trusted my gut. I'd always trusted my feelings. Sure, they'd gotten me into trouble plenty of times before, but they'd almost always been right.

I didn't believe that Amanda's death had been a simple fall. I had a bad, strange feeling that there was someone out there somewhere who'd targeted a woman just like Amanda.

A woman just like me.

* * *

I knew I shouldn't really be there. Okay, no 'shouldn't really' about it—I definitely wasn't supposed to be snooping around a crime scene. And Jasper was hardly making me look less conspicuous. It was dark, but he had a way of garnering attention. I just hoped he wouldn't bark.

He was sniffing around Amanda's rose bushes. "Don't!" I scolded him. "Sit. Be a good boy." I tried to keep my voice low as I peered in through the front window.

Ryan might be cute and charming enough, but these local cops hardly seemed like the sharpest tools in the shed. I was worried they'd jumped to conclusions too quickly, seen an accident where something more sinister was at play.

If they caught me snooping, I'd just tell them that Jasper had pulled me in this direction. "He has a mind of his own, I can't control him!" I'd say with a laugh. Didn't make me sound like the best dog owner, but I wasn't the one who had raised him after all, was I? He was badly trained due to someone else's bad raising of him.

Too late I saw that Jasper had ignored my instructions and was digging through Amanda's rose garden. Not just digging, destroying.

"Stop digging! Jasper!" I called. "Naughty dog." I tried to chastise him, but it came out like I was praising him and he started waggling his tail even harder, thinking he was about to get a treat! I had trouble being firm enough with him.

I shook my head and placed my hands on my hips. "Jasper, there's no treat, okay? You've been a naughty boy." I looked at the ruined rose garden in dismay. I supposed there would be no one around to care about it now, but it still didn't seen right. I knew that Amanda took pride in her rose bushes. I should have been looking after them for her now that she was gone, not responsible for their ruin.

"Jasper, stop!" I said again, but he was digging like

crazy.

He was sniffing wildly and began to bark at me, trying to get my attention. There was something in his mouth.

"What is it, boy?" I asked, leaning down to see what was in his teeth. "What have you got there?"

I pulled it out of his mouth. A note. Covered in mud.

Chapter 3

"What was that?" I spun around and saw lights flashing in my eyes. Police lights? I ducked and covered my eyes, blinking rapidly due to the fact that I'd almost been blinded. "Jasper, come here," I said, pulling his leash so that he couldn't get away and cause more havoc. He put one of his muddy paws up on my knee. Great. I was wearing white jeans of course. "Thank you very much," I whispered.

I squinted to try and see what the lights were. There was a long stream of light, moving erratically from place to place. Not from a cop car, I realized. From a flashlight. There was someone creeping around on the other side of the road. Were they looking for me? At me? Or did I just get caught in the cross hairs?

"We've got to get out of here, Jasper," I said, shoving the note in my pocket and trying not to think about how muddy it was on the inside of my white coat. What a night to be wearing all white. I crept down on my hands and knees, crawling in a way that I hadn't done since I was a toddler.

I tried to stay close to the cottage, begging Jasper to

stay quiet while I crept away, hoping that the flashlight wouldn't shine its deadly light on me again. I wasn't even sure what the punishment was for snooping around a crime scene. Was that what it was? A crime scene?

Once I was sure we were in the clear, I stood abruptly and started to jog. "Come on, Jasper, it's time for your exercise. You like going for a run, don't you, boy?"

The flashlight suddenly turned off and just before I ran, I caught a glimpse of the face that had been holding it.

Brenda.

I shook my head and ran off, Jasper in tow. *I should have guessed.*

* * *

Rain started to fall right before we reached the house, causing Jasper to coat the floorboards with yet another layer of mud. I shook my head. "Remind me to buy a mop next time we're at the store," I said, hanging up my coat.

I sighed and walked over to him, but he was barking and nodding in the direction of my coat. I turned around, confused. "You want to go back outside?" I asked, thinking that was what his interest in my coat was. "We can't go back out. It's raining. Plus, it's dark." And suddenly, Pottsville wasn't the quiet, safe, town I'd thought it was when I arrived.

But Jasper kept barking at the coat. "What? Oh, right! The note!" I exclaimed, slapping my forehead. Sometimes, I can be really absent-minded. "Luckily, I have you around to keep me in check," I said to Jasper, before digging into my pocket.

The note was soggy as well as muddy, and folded, roughly, into fours. I pulled it open carefully, trying not to rip it as the page stuck to itself.

"Darn," I said, sighing as I tried to make it out. "The ink is running."

Jasper, of course, was no help in that regard. If I had a dog that could read, I'd pack up the craft business and retire to be a millionaire.

I straightened the note and placed it under a lamp so I could make out the writing better. I gasped. "No, that can't be right!"

Jasper's tail wagged a little. He was interested now.

I gulped. The note was addressed to...me.

"Dear George..." it read in smudged letters at the top. "At least, I'm pretty sure that's my name," I said, squinting a little. I tried to read the rest of the note, but it was so smudged that I could only make out a few random words throughout. "Don't. Careful. Watch."

I shook my head and took a few breaths. Why did Amanda write me a note when she knew we were meeting later that week? Was she intending to send it to me? Deliver it in person?

And most importantly, what the heck was she actually trying to tell me? Was she trying to warn me about something?

About someone?

I blinked a few times, looking at the note. Was this evidence? Should I have been turning it over to the cops?

"What do you think?" I asked Jasper. "After all, the note was addressed to me. Amanda wanted me to have it, right?"

He gave me a look that said 'don't ask me, lady, I don't want to wind up in jail.'

"It's okay for you, dogs don't go to jail," I said,

scratching my chin as I looked at the note.

"It's probably nothing. Probably nothing important to the case, anyway." Uh-oh, I just realized I'd referred to this—whatever this was—as a 'case.' Had I been reading too many detective novels? Or was there really something more sinister going on here?

I also realized that I'd already decided, for better or worse, that I was keeping the note.

"No," I said, looking to Jasper for support in this little crime of my own. "I think this is a note best kept to myself. For the time being, at least. Maybe when it dries, I'll be able to make out the writing better." I shrugged, picking it up carefully. "Or find some kind of expert in reading smudged writing. There's enough eccentrics in this town—you never know!"

I pegged it to a flower pot on the windowsill and opened the window just an inch so that it would dry before I hid it away later. I shivered. Not a great night for an open window.

"Now don't go touching that," I warned Jasper. "And no more getting into trouble tonight, either. I think it's time we both got some sleep. I do have a store to run, you know."

* * *

But the next morning, I decided that opening the store was going to wait. I checked my large, loud, bright red clock. Hmm, 9:30. I'd missed opening time already by half an hour. What would another half-hour matter? Besides, if you can't keep a relaxed, sleeping schedule in a town like Pottsville, where can you keep one.

Jasper seemed to be pulling me in the direction of the store, but I led him in the opposite direction. The way that just happened to lead to the Pottsville Police Station. On the other side of the street, though. I was trying not to be too obvious. If I saw someone, or didn't see someone, that would just be a coincidence.

I needed to sniff out some more information. I was going to have to make this look as casual as possible to not raise suspicion.

As soon as we reached the location opposite the police station, I slowed a little, letting Jasper know to slow as well, though he still tugged on his leash. There was a uniformed officer just exiting the station, about to walk to his car.

Ryan! I fluffed my hair up a bit and glanced at myself in the reflection of a shop window before I hurried across the street, Jasper in tow.

"What a surprise to see you here." I flashed him my best smile.

"Well, you know, small town," he said good-naturedly. Then, he added, a teeny bit more sarcastically, "Plus, this is right outside where I work."

"Oh, I was just walking past," I said breezily as I followed him to his car. Then I decided to go for a slightly different tactic. "Though, maybe my coming across the station wasn't a total accident."

He paused with his car keys in hand. "No?" he asked in surprise.

I shook my head. "Maybe subconsciously I was feeling like I needed the protection." I let out a heavy sigh as Ryan straightened up.

"I hope everything is okay." His face creased in genuine concern. He cleared his throat. "Here, let me walk you back to your store, then."

"Thank you, Ryan." I then put on my best damsel in distress act. "I suppose I just feel a bit scared, you know, all alone in that house of mine, after what happened." I pouted a little. "I mean, I do have Jasper, but he's just a sweet little puppy, he wouldn't harm a fly."

"Mmm-hmm," Ryan said, glancing down at Jasper's dirty mouth and paws.

"Rose garden," I explained. "He can't get enough of them."

Ryan looked at me a little more seriously this time. "I can't say I blame you, actually. Especially considering the house you live in." He turned and started to walk slowly. "I mean, not that I believe in ghosts or anything like that."

Uh...what? I shot a look at Jasper as we both started walking to catch up to him. "Ghosts? Huh? I'm sorry, Ryan, I think you might have lost me there at some point."

No damsel in distress act now; I was genuinely confused.

He stopped walking again. "Sorry," he said. "As I say, I don't believe in them or nothing. I shouldn't have said that."

I frowned. "But you mentioned something about my house. I'm afraid that bit went a little over my head."

Ryan looked a little uncomfortable. "I'm sure you're totally safe," he said, looking anxious to get away from the conversation. "And you can call me any time you need me."

I liked the sound of that, but he still hadn't told me what I actually needed to hear. "What is wrong with my house, Ryan?"

His eyebrows shot up a little. "You really don't know?" he asked me, searching my eyes a little. Was he trying to see if I was lying?

I shook my head slightly. No, I didn't. And I didn't like this feeling of not being in the know.

He looked around almost like he was making sure he wouldn't be overheard in the street.

"There was...there was an incident a year or so back," he said slowly.

"Incident? What kind of incident?"

He really, really didn't want to talk about this, that was clear. He let out a heavy sigh.

"A woman was killed."

I waited for the next part, already knowing what he was going to say. Already dreading it, but needing to hear it nonetheless. I leaned forward, waiting for it.

Finally, Ryan said the words I knew were coming:

"In the home that you live in."

I crossed my arms and closed my eyes, nodding slowly. "Of course. I should have known it. This kind of thing can only ever happen to Georgina Holt."

Well. That certainly explained why the house had been so cheap.

* * *

"Thank you," I said. "You didn't need to walk me all the way home. It's well out of your way."

The sun had started to set. After a busy day at the store, I'd accidentally—really accidentally this time—bumped into Ryan just as I'd been leaving, and he'd very kindly offered to escort me home. Of course, I hadn't objected.

I wanted him in my home. And not for the reason you might be thinking. I needed to know where it had happened.

"I felt like I needed to," Ryan said, then caught the look on my face. "Not because you are demanding or anything! I mean, I just wanted to walk you back, make sure you were safe...after everything."

I smiled at him casually as I opened up the door. "Would you like to come in for some tea?"

He looked around me, making a strange face as he looked inside my house and hesitated. Maybe he really did believe in ghosts.

"Come on, it's the least I can do," I said. "It would be impolite not to accept."

"Sure. Why not." He started to take his shoes off but I told him not to bother. "You'll see why in a minute."

He raised his eyes at the muddy paw prints as we headed down the hallway into the open-floor space and I headed straight to the kettle to put it on the stove, telling Ryan to make himself comfy while I boiled a pot of peppermint tea.

"Watch out, it's hot," I warned him as I handed him a steaming cup a few minutes later.

He took the cup gingerly. "Really? I was expecting it to be cold," he teased.

He definitely had a sense of humor about him. Too bad he was far too young for me. I like a guy with a sense of humor, especially a sarcastic one.

"So," I said, raising my cup of tea to my lips. "Where did it happen?"

"Where did what happen?" Ryan asked, taking a sip.

"The murder. Where was the body found?"

He almost spit his tea right back out. He stared at me once he'd gained his composure a little. "Do you really want to know?"

I nodded. "Of course I do." I waved my hand around my newly purchased home. "I live here, don't I? I should know what happened in my own home."

Ryan took another sip of tea, more settled now after the shock of my question, and raised his eyebrows at me. "Does anyone else ever really know what has gone on in the homes they've lived in? Most of the houses in Pottsville are a hundred years old, at least. They've all got a history. Arguments, tears, births, deaths..."

I gave him a wry look and tilted my head. "Yes, you may have a point. But this is something that happened recently. A murder in the very house I am living in!"

He cast me a sharp eye. "It wasn't confirmed as a murder."

I crossed my arms. "Just tell me where it happened, okay? Or I'll have to take that cup of tea back."

He held it upside down. "All finished."

"Fine. If you don't tell me where it happened, I will

have to take my friendship back then."

"We're friends?" His eyebrows shot up in a little dance again.

"For the time being. So, spill."

He sighed heavily and stood up, a little reluctantly. "I was only called in when the body was first found, I didn't work on the case or anything," Ryan said in that drawl of an accent I couldn't quite place. "I'm not a detective."

"But you were here. After she died. You saw the body."

He still looked unsure whether or not he should answer. "Yes."

"So," I said. "Show me where it happened."

He began walking to the edge of the room and I followed him. I suddenly knew where he was heading. And I knew what he was about to say, without him needing to say it.

"At the bottom of the staircase," I said quietly. I gave him a slow look. "Hmmm."

Ryan looked a little uncomfortable. "It ain't the same..."

I narrowed my eyes a little and looked up the stairs. "Tell me, was the victim, say, a woman...forty something...living alone?"

Was Ryan turning a little red? It was hard to tell, he had quite an olive complexion. He was definitely heating up, though.

"Yes, she was," he admitted. "But, Miss Holt..."

"Oh, please, you must call me George," I insisted. "None of this Miss Holt stuff."

He nodded. "George then. You have to realize what happened here had nothing to do with what happened to your friend Amanda the other day."

I shrugged and looked at him wryly. "I never said it did. You're the one saying that, Ryan."

He looked even more nervous. "And I ought to make this clear, it wasn't ever confirmed it was a murder," Ryan said nervously. "We never found out who did it. Or didn't do it."

"Well, that's reassuring."

He looked a little embarrassed. "It was supposed to reassure you, actually. I don't want you to feel afraid in your own home, George."

"Ah, I'm made of stronger stuff than that," I said

with a wink. I smiled at him to make sure he knew that I really wasn't scared. That he hadn't done the wrong thing by telling me. Hey, I'd wanted to know, hadn't I?

He still looked guilty. I hadn't meant to make him feel bad. I wondered if maybe he wasn't only feeling guilt about telling me, but maybe also guilt about the case never being solved.

It wasn't Ryan's fault, either way. He just would've been the one called out on the first day when the body was found, then he'd be the one left behind to clean up while the detectives worked on the real case. Or, didn't work on the real case. Ryan might have been trying to reassure me, but after our conversation, I felt anything but. I knew he meant well, though.

"One last question," I said, right before I showed Ryan out the front door. "Did she have a dog?"

Ryan thought about this for a second and shook his head. "No. She was a renter and the last owners were strict about having no pets in the house."

"Huh."

Ryan shook his head, just about to head out into the night that was now black, the sky starless and overcast.

"I can't believe your real estate agent didn't tell you,

45

though. Isn't that against the law or something?"

I gave Ryan a look. He was standing right there in front of me wearing his police uniform. "Well, you're the one who ought to know, aren't you?" I asked teasingly.

He laughed a little. "I better double check that. You want me to go speak to her?"

No, I didn't want Ryan to go and speak to my young, attractive real estate agent. "I'm not sure she even knew, to tell you the truth." And I wasn't lying. I thought back to that day. She'd seemed nervous when I'd questioned her about the price, but not necessarily as though she was trying to cover something up. Ryan was right, that sort of thing was supposed to be disclosed, and she'd be in big trouble if it was proved that she hadn't. I didn't want to get her in trouble, either way.

"All right then," Ryan said, turning to leave. "Keep safe, George. And call me if you need anything."

I watched him walk away and sighed. I had a feeling I would be calling him sooner rather than later.

Chapter 4

Three days had gone by since Amanda's body had been found. There was talk of a funeral happening on the weekend, but I wasn't sure I was invited. Had we been good enough friends?

Jasper and I were taking a casual stroll to work as I mulled the situation over.

"I know, Jasper, I am investigating her murder. I have every right to attend her funeral." I felt as though I had a responsibility to attend. In a small town, it might be inconspicuous to not attend a funeral. It might also put me in people's bad books; I could be shunned! And I needed to be making friends, not enemies. With Amanda gone, so far I had one friend, if you counted Jasper. Well, two, if you counted Ryan.

Jasper whimpered. "Yeah, yeah...maybe three," I said, thinking about Billy from the crafting circle. He'd actually texted me during the week, using the cell number I'd put on my business cards and asking me if I'd like to go for a drink. I was a bit hesitant. He was friendly and loved dogs, but he was also a bit old for me. Anyway, I don't like texting, so I was letting the matter hang, waiting until I saw him in person again to decide whether to say yes or no.

Besides, there was another man I needed to see that morning.

I quite literally had to see a man about a dog.

I tied Jasper up outside the police station and told him to sit and be a good boy for five minutes while I went inside. He pouted but sat. "Hello again," I said as I glided through the glass doors. Ryan was standing behind the desk, just finished with a phone call by the looks of it. "You must be growing tired of seeing my face every day."

Ryan shook his head. "Never," he said with a grin. "What can I do for you today, George?"

"It's just that I remember that Amanda said she had a dog," I said. "I only just remembered—I can be scatter-brained like that, I'm afraid. Anyway, I'm just wondering what happened to the poor thing? I don't remember seeing it at her cottage on that..." I stopped. I'd almost said 'night.' The night that Jasper and I had been snooping around. "Day. The day she died," I said, choosing my words a little carefully.

Ryan came out from behind the desk and led me back out the front door. "Where are we going?"

"Look," he whispered once we were back out on the street. "I'm not really supposed to be working on this case."

"So it is a case?" I whispered back.

He shook his head. "No. Not a..." He let out a heavy sigh. "You know what I mean. I was told to just leave it alone."

I frowned. Interesting. Very interesting.

I looked at him, completely innocently. "I'm just asking about the dog," I said quietly. "Not about the case."

He gave me a slow look like he wasn't sure whether to believe me or not. "Okay," he said quietly. "But that's all I can tell you about. I've already told you more than I should have," he said, glancing around. "That was wrong of me."

"So what happened to the dog then?" I asked, as Jasper tried to get free behind me.

"She got taken to the shelter."

I reached down and untied Jasper. "Which shelter?" I asked.

Ryan blinked a few times. "There's only one in town, I think," he said. "We've pretty much only got one of everything in Pottsville. Anyway, it's right on the edge of town, next to the llama farm."

I knew the place. I'd been there before. I glanced down at Jasper. "Looks like we're taking a trip back to where you came from, boy. But don't worry," I said. "I'm not going to leave you there."

* * *

Jasper refused to go anywhere near the building. His abandonment issues were real. He whimpered at the sight of the shelter and refused to budge even when I gently tried to pull on his leash to move him forward.

"Well, what am I going to do, leave you alone out here practically in the woods?" I asked. "That's hardly going to help your abandonment issues, is it?"

It had taken us a half-hour to walk to the shelter and I had no intention of just turning around. At least, not until I saw that Amanda's dog was really there and that she was okay.

Jasper sat down firmly on the dirt road and refused to budge. I dropped his leash and placed my hands on my hips. "It's okay, boy," I said. "I'm not going to adopt another dog. Is that what you're worried about? I've got more than enough on my plate with you. I don't need another dog to worry about."

Jasper didn't look convinced. "Come on," I said, picking up his leash again. "Sometimes in life, we've just got to do things we don't want to do. Dogs included."

Jasper reluctantly followed me into the shelter.

"Hi there," I said to a short, plump woman with short, brown hair standing behind the front counter.

She glanced down at Jasper, who was still whimpering, pulling on his collar, and trying to escape. "I'm sorry," she said anxiously, holding her hands up. "We don't have room for any new dogs right now."

"Oh, heavens, no!" I said quickly, worried that Jasper might be able to hear and understand. Of course, I don't truly believe he can understand what I am saying—I'm not a total Crazy Dog Lady—but he is intelligent enough to understand a lot of things. Especially body language. And he clearly had a very good memory of his own time in the shelter.

"No, this is Jasper. I actually got him from this very shelter two weeks ago. And I don't want to return him," I said with a wide grin, bending to give Jasper a pat on the head. "He can be a bit of a handful, true, but I wouldn't trade him for anything in the world."

Jasper seemed to relax a little after that. The woman nodded, but she still looked a little unsure. "Okay then, miss." I love being called miss! "Can I help you with something today, then?"

I nodded. "I was just wondering if there was a dog brought in three days ago." I had to blink a few times, trying to remember what breed of dog Amanda had owned. I was sure she'd told me that evening at the craft circle. I scratched my head. "I think it was a small breed. She might have been brought in by a police officer."

The woman—Bobby, I noticed her name tag said— suddenly nodded. "Ah, yes, I know the dog you are talking about." She suddenly looked a little sad. "Poor little thing, doesn't know what's happened to her."

I suddenly felt a horrible sick feeling in my stomach, thinking about Amanda's dog locked up here, wondering where her owner had gone, wondering if she was ever coming back for her again.

She wasn't coming back. "Can I see her please?" I asked softly.

Bobby nodded and led me down a hallway to where

a cage sat in the end. There was a very small dog huddled in a plastic green bed.

She was nothing like Jasper. She was tiny, white, and looked utterly terrified when she turned around to glance at us, eyes bulging out, way too big for her tiny body.

Bobby stood quietly beside me. "Her name is Casper."

I burst out laughing.

"Something is funny?" Bobby asked.

"Jasper and Casper," I said with a grin. "Just perfect." I looked into the cage. "Amanda and I really did have a lot in common," I murmured.

Bobby cleared her throat. "She does need a home, you know. I'm not sure how long we can..."

I glanced down at Jasper and could have sworn I saw a flicker of disapproval in his eyes. Ah well. I had to interrupt Bobby.

"I'll take her," I said. "Thank you."

* * *

Jasper sulked for a little while about having to share his affections with a new, very small, bundle of competition, but after putting them in the yard to play together for a few hours, they soon became good friends. Casper wouldn't leave Jasper alone, running after him with her tiny legs every time he tried to escape her, and snuggling up together when they finally tired.

Jasper had also instilled in Casper a few of his bad habits, such as digging, and destroying all plant life. I glanced at them out the window, wondering if I should scold them, but I had work to do inside. At least they were getting along.

I'd gotten my big old whiteboard out of storage, along with a couple of markers, and set it up. I didn't have any photos of Amanda, nor of the woman who'd lived and died in my house—Julia, her name was—so I'd had to make a couple of rough sketches. I wasn't a bad artist, if I do say so myself, but there was something a bit grim about drawing the faces of two dead women in the middle of my living room. Well, I supposed the whole thing really was rather grim, wasn't it?

Underneath each face I wrote a list of the things I knew about them, and the way they had died.

There was a frantic scratching at the window. "Okay okay," I said, looking at Casper's paws working like crazy, trying to scratch right through the glass. "You can come inside." I pulled the sliding door open. Jasper ran in after her and I fed them both before setting them up in two beds: Jasper's large and green, and Casper's small and pink.

"So," I said to the two dogs who were both curled up now, finally exhausted from a day of playing (and by a day of playing, I mean a day of destroying everything). I returned to the whiteboard and studied it. "What do we have here, exactly?" I looked over my shoulder at them for any answers they might have.

Some people might find it strange that I talk to dogs, yes. But they are the perfect sounding board. They give you their undivided attention, they don't contradict you, and they offer unconditional support.

I turned back to the board and sighed. Maybe unconditional support wasn't what I needed right then, though. I needed someone to help me with the puzzle in front of me. I could see the things that were obvious, but there was something that just wasn't properly clicking in my mind. And Jasper and Casper couldn't be much help in that regard.

I looked over the board, tapping my marker in my hands. We had two victims, both found at the bottom of a staircase. Amanda, and Julia.

"They were both forty, both single, both lived alone." I furrowed my brow. Those were similarities, sure, but nothing more than coincidental, really. I tapped the marker again and looked at the board. There had to be something else. Something that linked the two women.

Casper whimpered a little. I raised my eyebrow at her. "I know, girl. Would be helpful if they both owned dogs, wouldn't it? But that's not the link here; there's got to be something else to it."

Casper gazed at me with her big, bulging eyes. They looked a little watery, so I put my marker down and walked over to pet her until she snuggled back into her bed. She was probably missing her owner and wondering what on earth had happened, how she had wound up in my home instead of Amanda's.

"Don't worry, girl," I said softly. "I'm going to find out what happened to Amanda, you have my word on that. You're safe here now."

* * *

I stood on the edge of the main street of Pottsville—the only street, really—with my arms folded across my chest and my high heel tapping on the pavement. Dogs couldn't speak back; they don't have a knack for gossip. But I was pretty sure I knew someone in town who would know everything that went on in Pottsville, and have a pretty loose tongue as well.

Brenda.

I hadn't seen her since the night she'd almost blinded me with the beam of her flashlight. She'd been avoiding my store, which wasn't that surprising, but what I was surprised by was the fact she hadn't approached me to ask what I was doing that night.

Either she hadn't seen me, or she had something to hide.

Either way, she must have known something. She lived across the road from Amanda. Maybe she'd seen something suspicious the day she was killed. Maybe she'd seen someone enter the cottage and leave again, out the back, having just shoved Amanda down the stairs.

But that actually wasn't what I wanted to talk to her about. She was a church-goer, I knew that, so I was waiting at the end of the main street where the small, white-painted church was, knowing that she would turn up for Sunday service at some point.

"Brenda!" I said, giving her my best grin as she walked closer. It was too late for her to turn around and pretend she hadn't seen me.

Her face looked like a prune as she stared back up at me. She was definitely a short woman, probably just five-foot tall and wearing flat shoes, and I, at five-foot-eight plus heels, seemed Amazonian compared to her.

I showed her my wrist. "You like my latest addition to my collection?" I asked. The beads were strung along in alternating colors of white and hot pink. I thought they complimented my flowing white shirt nicely. White and pink are always a good combination.

"No one is ever going to buy your junky jewelry," she said. Never too early in the morning for Brenda to attack my jewelry, was it? "People in this town have a bit of taste, you know." She tried to move past me but I stepped in front of her.

"I haven't seen much of you around, Brenda, not since Amanda died," I said, raising my eyebrows at her.

Her face reddened. She tried to hurry past me again, her face down.

Again, I stepped in front of her to block her. "She was your neighbor, right?"

"That's none of your business," she said quickly. Had she seen me that night with her flashlight or not?

I wondered if I was wrong about Brenda enjoying the occasional piece of gossip. Or rather, far more than occasional.

I decided to test her.

"Hey, Brenda," I said, then I waved my hand. "Oh wait, you probably don't know anything about it. Never mind." I started to walk away. "I'll let you get to church."

"Wait one second," she said, stopping and turning around. "What don't I know anything about?" She stood up straighter, which only added about half an inch to her diminutive stature. "Nothing goes on in this town without me knowing about it, thank you very much."

Hmm. Maybe some things did. Anyway, I took a step toward her and brought up the topic I really wanted to talk about.

"The woman, who lived in my house before me."

There was an immediate flicker of interest in her eyes. A light lit up in there. "Yes, you've moved into the house with all the glass windows, the one that backs up onto the woods down on Hazlewood Avenue."

I'd never told her where I lived, but that just confirmed it for me: nothing happened in Pottsville without Brenda's beady little eyes seeing it.

"That's the one," I said.

"I'm surprised you took that house," Brenda said snarkily. Then added, "No, actually, I'm not surprised." She looked me up and down. "A freaky woman like yourself probably likes living in a place like that."

Boy, Brenda really didn't like me much, did she? I had to try not to laugh at what she clearly thought was an insult. 'Freaky woman.' I rather took it as a compliment.

"I don't really have a problem with it," I said plainly. "It sort of adds character to the place."

Brenda scoffed. "Ha! I'm sure you didn't know about the incident before you moved in, though. You do seem like the gullible type," she said. "Didn't you wonder why the house was so cheap?"

I stood up straight so that I was towering over her even higher. I didn't like the suggestion that I was gullible. "In fact, Brenda, I knew exactly what took place in that house, before I moved in," I said firmly. "I just don't let things like that scare me out of a good deal."

Brenda shook her head. "Well, I wouldn't be caught dead in that home."

I bit my tongue to stop myself from saying that was just as well, because there was very little chance I'd ever be inviting her over.

"Julia," Brenda said quietly, looking furtively at the church to her left. "That was her name."

I frowned a little. "You knew her?" I asked casually, knowing very well that Brenda would have known her, the same way she knew everybody in this town.

"Of course I did," she snapped back. "She was a crafter."

I suddenly felt my blood run cold. That was the link. "She was a crafter?" I asked, just to be sure.

Brenda nodded. "She was a big fan of paper mache, just like I am," she said, a strange tone to her voice. "It's a shame. We actually got a long quite well. We were friends."

She must have been the first and last friend of Brenda's.

I was having trouble forming coherent thoughts at that point, though, let alone any speech. I found myself gazing off into the distance, trying to make sense of this, while Brenda stood and waited to hear if I had anything left to say.

"Boy, you really are a space cadet, aren't you, Georgina Holt?" I heard her say, before she shook her head and hurried up the path to the church steps.

"Thanks for your time, Brenda," I called out softly.

Well, I'd gotten the information I thought I'd wanted. That's the problem with snooping and asking around about stuff though, isn't it? Sometimes you hear something you really don't want to hear.

* * *

The walk back to my house passed all too quickly. I realized that I was not in a hurry to return to it. Things had changed. If it wasn't for the two dogs inside, waiting to be fed and walked, I would have really taken my time returning.

I wondered if I would have actually purchased the house if I'd known a woman was killed there. I've lived in dangerous situations before, sure, and had my fair share of adventures, but I've never lived in a house where someone was killed. I shook my head. Surely I could handle it when I'd handled so many other things in my life.

I nodded as I turned onto Hazelwood Avenue, firm in my decision now, deciding that I would have taken it anyway, even if the real estate agent had been entirely up front with me. It was no big deal after all, right?

But when I entered the house again that evening, a chill ran down my spine. Casper ran over to me, jumping up and licking at my face as I knelt down to pick her up while Jasper jumped on me for attention as well. But even the company of two boisterous dogs couldn't warm me.

I put Casper back on the floor and walked over, slowly, to the whiteboard where I'd scribbled a giant question mark between the two women.

I knew what the link was now. Single, forty-something women who were crafters.

I fit the bill exactly.

Chapter 5

I glanced out the window and sighed as sleet started to come down. "Do you think I should just cancel, Jasper? I doubt anyone is even going to show up this time. And I don't blame them."

I'd decided to switch things up for this week's meeting of the craft circle. First, I'd pushed it to the end of the week, to Friday evening, and second, I'd decided to hold it at my house. There was more room than inside the shop, and I thought it might be more conducive to a relaxed atmosphere.

Jasper jumped out of his bed and ran to the window, barking and wagging his tail. I sat up and looked at what he was barking at. Did I actually have a visitor? No one had RSVP'd. I'd been about to pack up the wine and cheese and call it an evening.

Jasper barked loudly in excitement. It was clearly someone he was happy to see. *Not Brenda, then,* I thought with a giggle as I headed to the door to open it.

"Billy!" I said brightly, standing up straight. "I'm surprised to see you back again."

He was holding a bottle of red. My favorite. "Good surprised, I hope."

I smiled at him. "Of course." I took the wine from him and nodded, impressed at the brand and year. "We'll have to open this one, far better than the one I had planned," I said, heading to the drawer for the corkscrew.

Billy looked around the foyer. "Your house is beautiful. I always wondered what this house looked like inside."

"I really like it," I said, proudly looking around. "I have a lot of ideas. Sometimes at night, my mind goes crazy coming up with different paint colors and artwork to hang on the walls."

Billy laughed. "I bet it does! You're a creative person. I bet this place won't even look the same in a few months."

I kept the conversation light and breezy, hopelessly aware that I had never replied to his text message. It was the elephant in the room, though, and once the cork was popped, I felt like I had to address it.

"I think you sent me a text during the week?" I asked, handing him a wine glass. I waved my other hand. "I'm hopeless with all that...texting...phones..." I took a quick gulp of wine. It really was a good vintage.

"Don't worry about it, there's no need to apologize," Billy said kindly, taking a seat on one of my kitchen stools.

I hadn't been aware I was apologizing. More like trying to wriggle my way out of the whole situation. Still, I did feel a little guilty for not replying.

"There's been a lot going on this week," Billy said. "So I can understand you're not getting back to me right away. Are you going to the funeral tomorrow?" he asked quietly.

I took another sip of wine and placed the glass back down a little too loudly. "I will be," I said, taking a deep breath. "Though I'm afraid I won't know anyone. I might feel like a bit of an outsider."

"You'll know me," Billy said, brightening up a little. "We could go there together, if you like. Maybe we could grab a coffee afterward or something."

"Umm, let me think about that, Billy, and get back to you," I said, flashing him my brightest smile. "Meanwhile, why don't I pop into the wine cellar and find us another bottle; we are going through this one at record speed!"

Jasper followed me into the cellar, his claws clicking on the hardwood floors as he hurried to keep up with me. I heaved a little sigh of relief to be away from the conversation with Billy.

I suppose I felt a little sorry for him, though. There was nothing wrong with the guy. Actually, it was just the opposite—he was entirely appropriate for me. Maybe that was the problem

Jasper shot me a look while I rummaged around the wine cellar, like he knew what I was thinking. "Don't judge me," I whispered sharply. "It's just that he's a little older than what I usually go for, okay?"

Jasper was still staring at me with what I took to be very judgmental eyes.

"Okay, okay," I said. "So he's about my age. Maybe even a year or two younger. That's still older than what I usually go for, Jasper." I picked up a random bottle of wine. "I need someone a bit younger and spritelier...someone who can keep me on my toes."

Jasper gave me a knowing look.

"Yes," I whispered with a sigh. "Someone like Ryan." I shook my head. "But that's not important right now."

I heard a knocking coming from upstairs. Jasper's

ears pricked up as well. Footsteps sounded overhead and I heard what must have been Billy walking over to the door and pulling it open. "Hello there," he said.

I looked at Jasper. "Don't tell me that's Brenda," I said with a little groan. It wasn't that I wanted to exclude her from the craft circle, I really didn't. That would be mean and childish for one thing, and for another, I couldn't really afford to be choosy about members at the moment. It was just that after the week I had, Brenda was really the last person I wanted to see.

At least she'll provide a barrier between Billy and I, I thought, trying to look on the bright side. Maybe I wouldn't even have to answer his question about him accompanying me to the funeral tomorrow. Maybe I could avoid the subject entirely now that Brenda was there. Putting up with her sour prune face would just be the price I'd have to pay. "Come on, Jasper," I called out. "Let's go back upstairs!"

Right before I reached the top, I took a deep breath. "Be still, be calm, be loving. Be light and breezy!" I told myself, preparing myself to see Brenda, shaking off any negativity with a wild shake my shoulders, causing my homemade bangles to clatter. Brenda was going to love that.

"Hello, B..." I started to say as I walked back into the living room. I stopped. That was not Brenda standing there in my doorway. It was an older woman, maybe fifty-five, with hair that was well styled, still more blonde looking than gray, and wearing a pink dress suit that was clearly expensive.

"Oh, hello there," I said, shaking my head a little as I tried to readjust.

She offered me a bright, polite smile. "You must be Georgina," she said, extending a hand for me to shake. "My name is Prue."

I took her hand. She had a rather weak handshake. "Everyone just calls me George," I said. "So please feel free to use it as well."

She looked a little unsure about whether she should use a man's name on a woman, but I could tell she was far too polite to question a woman's preference for what she liked to be called.

"Okay, then, George," she said a little nervously. "Where would you like me to sit?"

I glanced around at the wide circle of chairs I'd laid out. I'd been optimistic, despite fearing that no one would show up. Very me. "Anywhere you like is fine. So tell me, what kind of crafting do you do, Prue?"

Maybe I shouldn't have judged, but she just didn't look like a crafter to me. Of course, all kinds of women—and people—craft, but there was just something about her uptight manner, and her expensive clothes, and the way she sat straight in her chair that made me wonder.

I shook my head and offered Prue a glass of wine. *You're just being overly suspicious lately, George.*

She took the glass and started drinking from it quite quickly. I shot a look at Billy and he gave me a little shrug. "Do you know her?" I mouthed covertly, trying not to let her see me. He shook his head "no" very lightly, so that she didn't see, then gave me a second little shrug.

Interesting. I could have some fun with this.

"So, Prue," I asked, settling in to my own chair. "What sort of crafting tickles your fancy?"

She looked a little unsure as she played with the string of pearls around her neck. "I really enjoy paper mache," she said.

I narrowed my eyes. That was funny—the third paper mache fanatic I'd heard about in the space of a week. I hadn't realized it was such a popular hobby.

In fact, I was fairly sure it wasn't.

"Right," I said, bringing my glass to my lips. "And what kind of things do you enjoy making out of paper mache, Prue?" I let the question sit for a moment while I watched her eyes dart back and forth, trying to think up a response.

"Elephants," she finally blurted out.

I leaned forward a little. "Elephants?"

She nodded and squeezed her wine glass. "Yes, elephants."

I leaned back again and pursed my lips. "Seems like they would be rather large to wrap the paper around."

I caught the look of shock on her face so I laughed to let her know I was only kidding. "It was a joke, Prue. I'm sure you find very small elephants to paper mache." I shot a look at Billy, who was also trying to contain his laughter.

Prue sat her wine glass down on the rug at her feet and cleared her throat. She was just about to say something when there was a scratching noise at the window. "Oh, Casper!" I said, jumping up. "She was having so much fun out there I didn't want to bring her in," I explained to the others before quickly moving to the sliding doors. "But she clearly wants to come in and join the party!" Haha, some party, I thought, hoping that Casper might actually liven the event up a bit. She was certainly in the best mood she'd been in since I'd gotten her from the shelter.

Expecting her to want to jump into my arms, I leaned down ready to scoop her up, but instead she bypassed me completely and made a beeline straight toward Prue—or rather, straight toward her feet, knocking the wine glass over and spilling blood red wine onto the rug.

"Casper!" I yelled in dismay, watching while the rug soaked up every last ounce of wine. I shook my head and walked over, not registering that Casper was clawing at Prue, tying desperately to get up onto her lap, scratching and licking at her like her whole body was made of dog treats.

Prue squealed. "Get that dog off me!"

Too late, Casper managed to jump right onto her lap and started licking at her face. Prue only squealed louder and pushed at poor Casper, almost knocking her right off! I jumped over and picked Casper up before she fell to the ground.

I glared at Prue. "She was only excited to see you," I

said, my mouth in a stern line. Though for what reason Casper was excited to see this woman, heaven knew. "There was no reason to try and hurt her."

Prue stood up, her mouth set in an even straighter, firmer line than mine was and returned my glare. "You ought to learn how to control your animals."

I opened my mouth, about to say, "she's not my animal, I've only had her a few days," but I just shook my head slowly instead. Casper was mine now. I was all she had. And I wasn't going to let this woman near her again if that was her attitude. Instead I said, "Maybe you should learn how to be a little nicer to animals! Or you won't be welcome back in this house again any time soon!"

"This was a waste of time," Prue announced, her nose in the air as she flounced out the front door. I put Casper down and she ran straight for the door, even once it was slammed shut, trying to scratch her way through it to get to this woman, for some unknown reason.

Billy stood up a little awkwardly and brushed himself down. "Perhaps I should go as well," he said.

"Oh, you really don't have to," I said. "Don't let what happened with that woman make you leave."

He smiled at me and headed for the door. "Maybe I should just meet you at the funeral tomorrow, George."

Right. Okay then. "Sure," I said quickly, opening the door and seeing him out. "Take care, Billy." I closed the door quickly and looked at the mess left behind. So it looked like Billy's offer of a date was retracted before I even had a chance to reject it myself. Hang on, can you even have a date at a funeral? I leaned back against the door for a moment and mulled it over. Yes, it was definitely intended to be a date, I decided. And I had definitely been rejected.

"Well, that was a total disaster," I said to a tired looking Jasper as I took a swig of wine. "I'm starting to wonder if I should just give up on the idea of ever making friends in this town! They all wind up being criminally offended by me." I made a face. "Or dead."

Jasper stood and came running up to me, asking for a pat. I leaned down and petted him. "I know, I know, Jasper. At least I have you. And Casper too!" With Prue gone, Casper had dropped down onto the rug and was already in a deep sleep. I looked at the ruined rug and sighed. That would have to be a problem for later. Maybe a problem for the garbage. White rugs and dogs do not mix.

I flicked off all the lamps and light switches and headed for the staircase, ready for bed.

The staircase. With the lights off, it suddenly looked far more sinister.

I gulped.

"Come on, Georgina Irene," I said, using my full name like my mother used to do, a very long time ago. "You are made of stronger stuff than this." I forced myself to take a step. But then I made the mistake of looking up at the landing, wondering what it would be like to fall off the top, down the long flight. What it would feel like to be pushed off.

I shook my head and made another step, grasping the banister.

I stopped, and then decided I needed back up. I didn't usually let Jasper sleep in my room, but on this night, I pulled his dog bed up the stairs and into my bedroom so that it was on the ground next to my king-sized bed. I called for Jasper to come upstairs and within moments, he had bounded up the stairs and made himself comfy on his bed next to mine. There. Now I felt a little safer. And Jasper thought he was king of the world, getting to be the special one upstairs sleeping in the bedroom, while Casper was downstairs.

"It's just for tonight, you hear me? We won't go making a habit of it."

I closed my eyes and tried to sleep. All I could think about was the funeral tomorrow, though. Very hard to sleep when you are obsessing about caskets and dead bodies and holes in the ground.

And staircases that lay just outside your bedroom.

"There's nothing to worry about, there's nothing to worry about," I kept repeating to myself, and finally I began to drift into a deep sleep.

I don't know how long I was asleep for, whether it was minutes or hours, but the sound of scratching brought me straight back to the land of the living.

I bolted upright.

"Jasper?" I asked. "Was that you?"

I flicked the lamp on and looked at the dog bed. Jasper was still lying on it, so it hadn't been his paws scratching against the floorboards that had been making the noise. But his ears were pricked. "Did you hear it too?" Jasper jumped off his bed and ran to the door, sniffing at it and trying to use his head to budge it open. Finally, he let out a sharp bark.

"Jasper?" I whispered. "What is it? What is it, boy?"

My heart was beating faster. "Is there someone there?" I gulped, picturing the staircase on the other side of the door.

Jasper let out another sharp bark. I closed my eyes and took a deep breath. It was probably nothing. I crept over to the door and Jasper ran through it, taking off straight down the stairs, barking wildly.

I ran after him and turned on every light in the house. "Who's there?" I called out. Jasper ran to the front door and barked at it, so loudly that all the neighbors must have heard him. I stood very still, trying to control my breathing. There was someone there. There was someone outside.

There was the sound of something smashing. A glass potted plant.

I looked around for something to grab, something I could use as a weapon if the intruder decided to come in. I hadn't realized that Jasper was such a good guard dog. I'd never seen him like this, so protective, but I was still pretty sure that he wasn't actually capable of hurting an intruder or of being truly vicious.

Unable to find a weapon, I reached for the phone instead and dialed. "Hello, Pottsville Police station."

Ryan's voice. I let out a small sigh, feeling just the

slightest relief while Jasper barked loudly at the door.

"Ryan? It's George. You said I could call any time. Well, I need you now. There's someone here. Outside my house."

Chapter 6

Ryan stepped over the broken glass carefully and wrote something down in his notebook.

"And you didn't see anything?" he asked.

I shook my head wildly. "No."

He gave me a look and then quickly looked away. He'd done that a few times now. He seemed embarrassed almost, careful not to let his gaze linger on me for too long. I glanced down and realized for the first time that I was wearing a rather sheer nightgown! Ryan had arrived so quickly after my phone call that I hadn't had time to even think, let alone dress. In any case, his arrival had scared the intruder right off.

"Excuse me, I'll be right back," I said, trying not to run too quickly upstairs before I grabbed my robe from behind my door.

By the time I had returned, covered, Ryan seemed to be finished taking notes. "Looks like someone tried to break in."

I stared at him. "I know that," I said. "They were breaking in, to get to me."

He shook his head. "We've had a few break-ins in the area. The thieves have only taken jewelry, things like that. No one has actually been hurt." He shot me a sympathetic look. "Do you have any expensive jewelry?"

I glanced at a dish lying on the kitchen counter that contained some of my homemade bangles that I'd discarded before bed. "No," I said. "Nothing expensive." I sighed. "Nothing that anyone would want to steal, at any rate."

Jasper was still whimpering a little and nervously looking out the open door.

"I'm sure it was nothing to worry about," Ryan said casually.

"Nothing to worry about?" I stood up straight and crossed my arms. "You do realize what has happened in this town recently, don't you? A woman was killed. I'm going to her funeral tomorrow!" I exclaimed.

"Are you?" Ryan asked. "I suppose I will see you there, then."

"Oh." I was surprised to hear that he would be attending. "I suppose I will."

Ryan let out a deep breath. "Look, what happened

here tonight had nothing to do with your friend's accident."

Oh, right, 'accident.' That was what we were calling it.

He stepped over the broken pot and into the house, still making notes in his notebook. "I'm glad you called me," he said with a smile. "Even if it was nothing."

I sighed and pulled my robe around myself tighter. He was trying to be reassuring again.

"Even if it was 'just' someone trying to break in, that's still not nothing," I pointed out.

"You've got Jasper here. He'll look after you. It looks like he scared the intruder right off."

"I'm not sure. I don't think the intruder left until you got here." I didn't want to admit it, at least not out loud, but I didn't feel safe, not at all, and I didn't want Ryan to leave.

Jasper ran up to me and made a sad face, as though he knew what I had said. I leaned down and petted him with a sigh. "Don't worry, you did a very good job," I reassured him.

"What's this?" Ryan asked, nodding toward something in the living room.

I stood up straight. "What's what? Oh." I saw what he was looking at. I hurried over to the whiteboard and tried to cover it up by throwing a blanket over it but the blanket missed and ended up on the floor, leaving my sketches of Amanda and Julia right there for everyone to see. Along with the details of their deaths scrawled underneath.

"Just some drawings I was doing. I do that in my spare time." I let out a loud laugh. "I'm not very good," I said, trying again to cover the board with the blanket. "I'm a little embarrassed for you to see them actually."

Ryan moved up behind me and pulled the blanket back a little. "Hmmm, because it looks to me like you are doing detective work."

I let out a little laugh. "Not detective work. Just an art project. A craft project!"

"George." His voice was full of concern. "What's going on? I don't think it's healthy for you to obsess about this."

I stopped fussing with the blanket and turned to him, raising an eyebrow. "I'm not obsessing," I said. "I'm simply concerned that these two crimes have gone unsolved. And that the Pottsville Police," I said pointedly, nodding at him, "have ignored important details."

I almost immediately regretted what I had said. I didn't have many friends in Pottsville, and I couldn't afford to lose the one I did have. I quickly checked Ryan's face to try and see just how much offense I had actually caused.

He pulled the blanket back and looked at the board. "You really think the two are related?" he asked gently.

"I, um," I said, a little taken aback. I'd been expecting a lecture, but he was being kind. I cleared my throat and stood up straight. "Yes, I do," I said. "I believe these women fit the same profile. They were both in their early to mid-forties, they both lived alone, and they both died as the result of a fall down a flight of stairs."

Ryan raised his eyebrows. I couldn't tell if he was impressed or skeptical. There was definitely a flash of amusement in his eyes. "Those are coincidences, though," he said gently.

"Yes, well, that might be. But do you know another thing they have in common?" I pulled the blanket back completely so that the board was fully exposed and tapped my finger against my most recent discovery. "See here," I said, staring at Ryan. "They were both crafters."

Ryan stared at the board for a long while. *Is he taking this seriously? Does he think I'm mad? Is he...worried about me?* He finally switched his attention back to me. "A lot of women your age are into crafting though, aren't they? It's not that unusual."

I stood up even straighter and folded my arms across my chest. "Women my age?" I arched my eyebrow.

He looked away. "You know what I mean."

"Yes, crafting is a popular hobby amongst us ancient old crows."

"George..."

"But it is also a popular hobby amongst younger women as well. And men for that matter. We have a man in my crafting circle as a matter of fact."

He looked at me in surprise. "You do?"

I nodded. "A very nice man. A dog lover. A very nice dog lover who has asked me to attend the funeral with him tomorrow."

Never mind the fact that he had retracted the offer. That was a small detail that I could clear up later. The point was he had asked me. That was the important bit.

I saw a flash of something on Ryan's face. Was it jealousy? I leaned forward a little. *Come on, please be jealousy.*

"And are you going to attend the funeral with him then?" Ryan asked.

I shrugged casually. "I'll probably just go on my own. That's more my style."

Ryan's face dropped a little. "Oh," he said. He turned back to the board. *Darn it.* I'd overplayed it and turned him off as well. I wasn't having a great 'people day,' was I? He looked over the drawings of Amanda and Julia again. "George, we don't need you doing our job for us, you know."

His tone was gentle enough but I knew there was a little bit of a sting hiding underneath.

"Someone has to do it," I said. Again, instant regret.

He turned to me. "I just think that maybe you're being a little...now, don't take this the wrong way..."

I braced myself to take it exactly the wrong way. "Yes?"

"A bit paranoid." He held his hands up. "Not that I blame you."

I wondered if I could, at that moment, very politely

85

kick him out of my house and ask him never to return. *Friends, remember, George. You want to make friends in this town, not enemies.*

"No, I don't think I'm being paranoid," I answered calmly. "I think I'm seeing a connection that other people might have missed, that's all."

Ryan nodded and placed his hat back on. "I'm not saying you're wrong," he said with a sigh, flinging one last glance toward the whiteboard. "I'm just saying, for your own sake, don't dwell on it."

I followed him back to the door. "Are you worried about me?" I asked a little flirtatiously.

He turned around and stared at me just before he exited. "I'm worried about every resident in this town. It's my job."

"Oh."

He shot me a little smile. "But yes, George, I am worried about you especially."

I smiled back and leaned against the doorframe, being mindful not to walk through the smashed glass. I'd have to clean that up. It seemed like the sort of thing that could wait until morning, though. Or until the next week. Knowing me, the next month. Actually, knowing me, that glass would still be sitting there a year from now.

"I guess I'll see you tomorrow," Ryan said. "Seeing as you're so independent and love going to things on your own, I won't offer you a lift." There was just the teeniest hint of a wink as he turned and walked down the path to his waiting police car.

Darn it. Should have played up 'damsel in distress,' not 'independent woman.' But I'm not great at pretending to be something I'm not, at least, not long term. I stayed there, leaning against the doorframe, until Ryan climbed into his car and drove away.

Even if he wasn't far too young for me, there was the other small matter of him being a cop. And being involved in the case I was currently 'investigating.' Going out with him, even attending a funeral with him, would be a conflict of interest. *No,* I decided. *It was a good thing we were going separately.* Besides, I didn't need a ride. I was getting used to walking everywhere. It suited me.

"Come on, Jasper, let's go in," I groaned, noticing too late that he already had his paws in the mud outside the front door. He was desperately digging at something. "Oh, Jasper, this is really the last thing I want to deal with tonight," I said, trying to pull him away from the dirt without stepping in the broken glass. I tugged on his collar, gently but firmly, trying to pull him back to the house and once again wondering just what kind of owners raised him before I did. I loved Jasper, but they hadn't exactly raised him to be obedient. Or maybe he was just partly deaf.

"Jasper! No!" But no matter how hard I pulled on his collar, he wouldn't budge. There was something he was desperately trying to get to.

"Fine!" I exclaimed, giving up and letting go as I threw my hands in the air. "You win!"

Jasper ran straight back to the dirt and pushed his nose right into it, digging for something. "Great," I said, sitting down on the stoop with a heavy sigh.

After a few seconds, Jasper came running over to me and I saw something white in his mouth. "What is that?" I asked, sitting up straight. "Have you found a bone?"

He dropped it at my feet. "Good boy," I said brightly, surprised, as I gave him a pat. I leaned forward and picked it up gingerly, being mindful of the dog drool and looking it over curiously. It did look rather bone-like, but it wasn't a bone.

Or was it? I turned it over and tapped it. In that light, I wasn't quite sure what it was made of.

It was white and thin and smooth, about half an inch wide and six inches long with a tapered point. I turned it over again and looked at it carefully. Huh. What was it doing in my front yard? What was it doing buried in my front yard? I placed it in the pocket of my robe for the moment.

Jasper sat down proudly, his tongue wagging. I laughed at him. "Yes, Jasper, you've been a very good boy." I ruffled the top of his head and looked at the mud around his mouth. "You've made a very good mess for me to clean up. Thank you very much." I stood up and this time, he followed me inside. We went up the stairs and each to our beds, side by side.

There might have been rustlings outside again that night, but I was too tired to hear them.

Chapter 7

"There are no dogs allowed at the funeral," I said firmly to Jasper, who was already sniffing at his leash, jumping up to try and grab it off the bench. I sighed. It was my fault. I'd been taking him everywhere with me, so as soon as I put my shoes on, for any reason at all, he took that as a sign that he was about to leave the house as well.

But it would be entirely inappropriate to bring him to Amanda's funeral. I glanced at Casper, asleep in her bed. Maybe it would be less inappropriate to bring her along. I half-considered it for a moment, before deciding that the whole thing would be too distressing for her. She'd just gotten settled in her new home, and I didn't want to upset her.

"You two be good," I said, before pulling the door shut. As I walked away, I caught Jasper's face, glum and unforgiving, pressed up against the glass.

* * *

About halfway to the cemetery, dark clouds began to gather and I stopped dead in my tracks as I stared up at the sky. Walking may have suited me—I may have even been getting used to it, enjoying it for the most part—but the weather didn't. I hadn't even brought an umbrella with me. I wasn't even sure if I owned an umbrella. If I did, it was that old bright, polka dot number with yellow material and bright pink spots. Not exactly appropriate for a funeral. I glanced down at my black clothes, not my usual color but at least black would be forgiving if I got soaking wet on the walk. My hair was another matter entirely.

Maybe I'd get lucky. Maybe the rain would hold off for another fifteen minutes while I walked the rest of the way to the cemetery.

I stopped again. "Oh, rats!" The heavens had opened and wasted no time in pouring down thick, heavy drops of rain. I glanced around. Nowhere to run, nowhere to hide. Well, there were the woods to the right of me—but I was going to look a bit mad, fleeing into the woods, wasn't I?

A car pulled up beside me. "Need a lift?"

I jumped at the noise and placed a hand over my heart. Ryan. "Sorry, you scared me for a moment there." I grinned at him. "You always seem to be around exactly when I need you."

I climbed into the car, shaking myself off first, just as the rain hit even harder. I sighed a little. "It really is a day for a funeral, isn't it?" I became somber. "I think I've been so caught up in...well, everything. You saw the whiteboard. It hadn't quite sunk in that Amanda was gone before now. She was a nice woman," I said quietly as we drove along. "And I would have liked to have gotten to know her better."

The rain had eased a little by the time we reached Pottsville Cemetery. It was still drizzling, but the heavy, fat drops had eased and I thanked Ryan before walking down the aisle of chairs lined up in front of the grave to pay my respects to Amanda's family.

They didn't know me, of course, but I grasped first her sister's hand and then her mother's and told them how sorry I was for their loss, before glancing over my shoulder to try and see where Ryan had gone. Not that I really cared too much, of course. I was just curious.

Ryan was on one side of the aisle, Billy at the other, both in the back rows. Two dates, one funeral. Or was that zero dates, one funeral? I raised an eyebrow. It was more likely the latter.

But as I walked back down the aisle, both of them smiling at me, both of them with empty chairs beside them, I knew I had to make a decision. And I didn't have much time! I had to choose which side of the aisle to turn to. The left, where Ryan was, or the right, where Billy was?

Suddenly, someone stepped out in front of me. "Georgina. It's nice of you to come."

"Oh, hello, Brenda."

She looked quite different, dressed in a sharp black suit rather than her usual dowdy clothes, and she was wearing makeup. I'd barely recognized her.

I was surprised that she seemed genuinely happy to see me. "Would you like to sit with me? I've got a spare seat beside me," she said, gesturing to the side. I was only about halfway down the aisle at that point.

"Erm," I said, glancing first at Ryan and then at Billy. At least this would solve my dilemma for me. "Sure, why not. Thank you, Brenda." I squeezed past her and the rest of the seated guests as I made my way to my chair. Brenda sat down beside me and shot me a firm smile. "My husband couldn't make it, you see," she said, explaining the spare seat. "He's feeling a little under the weather."

"Oh no!" I said sympathetically. "I am sorry to hear that." Maybe Brenda wasn't so bad after all. Maybe she was just a little tightly wound. That wasn't the worst crime in the world, was it?

Brenda nodded. "Thank you," she said. "I really am glad that you came today, Georgina. Amanda was a nice woman and a good neighbor."

I had to bite my tongue at that one. *A good neighbor that you spied o*n. Or maybe she hadn't spied on the house while Amanda was still alive. Maybe that just came after. I wasn't sure I believed that, though. I was pretty sure if she was snooping around when Amanda was dead, she was snooping around when she was alive. She was a busybody.

I looked at Brenda. Busybodies knew things, didn't they? Maybe she'd be able to help me with something. I reached into my coat pocket and pulled out the small bone-like tool I'd found in my yard. Well, the tool that Jasper had found. Credit where credit is due, right?

I'd cleaned it off and brought it with me, just in case. A bit of a strange item to carry around, sure, but I was used to carrying around strange items on my person.

"Brenda," I said quietly, extending my palm toward her with the tool sitting on top of it. "You don't happen

94

to know what this is, do you? I found it last night in my front yard. Jasper found it, I mean."

She stared at it for a moment before raising her eyes to me, giving me a look that seemed to say, *you've got to be kidding me, right?* There were no words from her. Just a glare.

"Brenda? Do you know what this is?"

"Is this some kind of a joke?" Brenda asked.

I shook my head slowly, confused. "No. It's no joke, Brenda. What is this?"

She let out the loudest scoff and shook her head, like she was totally disgusted with me. "I knew it," she said with a bitter little laugh. "I knew that you were not a serious crafter."

I pulled my hand back. "And what makes you say that?" I asked, shaking my head. Just when we'd been getting on so well.

Brenda stopped shaking her head and rolling her eyes long enough to answer me. "That is a crafting tool," she said. "One of your little friends in your craft circle must have dropped it last night."

Hmm, so she knew all about the craft circle meeting at my house then. She just decided not to come.

I shook my head. "No, it wasn't just laying on the front path or anything. It was buried deep," I said.

She frowned a little. "Well, I suppose it belonged to the woman who lived there before you then."

"Oh." I turned it over in my hand and nodded slowly. "You're right," I said softly. "It must have been hers." I felt a little sad now. Appropriate for a funeral, I guess.

"So what is it then, this tool?" I asked quietly.

Brenda shook her head again in disbelief. "You really have no right running a crafting store, do you?"

I shrugged. "I didn't know one had to earn the right to open a craft store."

"Why did you even open that shop in the first place?" she asked, her mouth back to looking like she'd just sucked a lemon while she crossed her arms.

"I thought it would be a good way to meet people and make friends." I stared at her, keeping a straight face.

Brenda let out a heavy sigh. "It's a bone folder," she said.

"Oh," I replied. "So it is bone then!" I turned it over in my hand. "No wonder Jasper loved it so much."

Brenda shook her head and glanced down at it. "No," she said. "That's the name of it because traditionally they are made of bone, but that one looks like it's synthetic."

"So what is it used for?" I asked, frowning. "Folding bones?"

Brenda's mouth dropped open. "No. It's used for paper crafts. Scrapbooking. For folding paper sharply. Scoring paper as well, sometimes."

"Huh." I looked at the thing again.

Brenda shook her head and leaned back in her seat. "You sure have a lot to learn."

I popped the bone folder back in my pocket. "Lucky I have you here to teach me, Brenda."

The ceremony was short and sweet—well, bitter-sweet—as one by one, Amanda's family and friends got up and spoke about what a wonderful person she was. I started to feel a bit like a fraud, calling myself her friend when I barely knew her at all.

Once the official ceremony was done, I took my chance to escape from Brenda and rushed down the aisle to the back rows.

I still had that choice: left or right?

I ducked left, while Billy was preoccupied in conversation with someone I didn't recognize. Ryan was just standing up and together we followed the rest of the congregation out; everyone spilling from the confines of the aisles to approach the grave and throw dirt and rose petals on top.

Ryan extended his arm for me. I was a little unsure if I should take it. *Remember, George. Too young. And a cop.* But I figured he was just being friendly, and if people were going to stare, I should just let them.

"It's nice that you're here," I said as we exited the aisle. A little strange, as well, I had to admit, though I didn't say that part out loud. "Did you know Amanda well?"

Ryan shook his head. "Not well, no. I saw her around town and talked to her a few times. It's just, well, I thought I should be here seeing as I was the one who..." He lowered his voice. "Found her body."

Billy shot a look at us and I gave him a little smile. Did he look jealous? Hard to tell from that distance, especially with the rain and fog drizzling down, but yes, he definitely looked jealous that I was walking along with a man almost two decades his junior. With my arm linked through his, no less.

"I notice no one else from the station is here today," I said. "You're a good police officer, Ryan."

And he was. Ryan had been the one to find Amanda's body; he'd been first at my house within minutes when I'd phoned him.

I started to get a funny feeling in my stomach. What was that feeling? I tried to swallow it down. Indigestion? I hadn't actually eaten any breakfast, so it couldn't have been that.

No, it was...it was suspicion.

Why had Ryan been first on the scene, and so quickly, at both those incidents?

I suddenly got an icy cold feeling down my spine when I remembered something else he had told me.

He'd told me he'd been first at the house—my house, now—the day Julia had died.

Was that all really just a coincidence?

"Hang on," I told Ryan, stopping suddenly. The rain started to fall a little heavier. The grass underneath my feet was soggy and I could feel the sharp heel of my shoe sinking into it. "How did you get to my house so quickly last night?" I tilted my head. It was an innocent enough question, wasn't it?

Well, it may have been an innocent enough question, but it clearly wasn't an easy one to answer; it seemed to have Ryan positively stumped. He opened and shut his mouth a few times like he was a goldfish and I could see his eyes darting around a little.

He mumbled the answer when it finally came. "I was already nearby."

How nearby?

Like, right in front of my house nearby?

Ryan cleared his throat. "I should go pay my respects to Amanda's family." He backed away a little, not meeting my eyes. "I'll catch up with you later, George."

I stared after him as he walked away.

What was all that about?

I shivered; the rain was starting to pour down more heavily again. I frowned, trying to remember if I'd double-checked (or even single-checked) that the glass sliding doors at home were shut. If they weren't, my pair of fluffy little monsters were going to drag mud from the garden all through the house.

"Hey," Billy said, offering me his coat. "You look cold."

I was a little startled to feel him standing right next to me. I was still staring after Ryan. He hadn't gone to speak to Amanda's family at all. Instead, he'd returned to his police car and climbed into it. "Thanks," I said, nodding as I took the coat off Billy. "Suddenly I am rather cold."

Ryan started his car and drove off while I just stood there, shaking my head. I guessed I was supposed to find my own way home then. I mean, not that I wasn't capable of such a thing. But not even an offer? Not even a goodbye?

I pursed my lips and stared as the car swung out of the cemetery and down the road back to town.

I had something else to add to my whiteboard as soon as I got home.

A list of suspects.

"You know what, Billy," I said, giving him my widest grin as I pulled his coat on tightly over my shoulders. "I would love to go on that date with you after all. What time would you like to pick me up?"

Chapter 8

I stood back and admired my work. "What do you think, Jasper?"

He was too busy running around, chasing after a ball, while Casper was incessantly scratching at the glass again, this time wanting to go outside, not come in. I sighed and let her out just in case she needed the bathroom, though I knew it was far more likely she just wanted to roll in the mud.

Yep. Suspicions confirmed.

"Come on, Jasper," I said, calling him back to the whiteboard. "I need to know what you think." I was interrupted by my phone beeping.

"Be there in ten," the text message from Billy said.

I almost let out a little groan. I needed more time to prepare. I quickly sent him one back. "Make it twenty? A girl's got to put her face on, you know!"

But I was already perfectly ready for the date—that was the least of my concerns. I was dressed in a simple black cocktail dress with bright red accessories, and my makeup, subtle as it was, was long done.

But I still needed time at home. My suspect list wasn't completed, and I didn't want to walk out the door with it half-finished; it would be at the back of my mind all evening. And I was supposed to enjoy my date, wasn't I?

I commanded Jasper to sit and he did as he was told, looking eagerly at the whiteboard.

"Good," I said grinning. "So now that I have your complete, undivided attention." I tapped my pen against the board. "We've got two suspects," I said, pacing back and forth just a little as I explained the whole thing to Jasper.

"First on the list, we've got Ryan," I said, pointing the pen to the sketch of Ryan's face I had drawn.

Jasper cocked his head to the side.

"I know, I know," I said. "I don't want to suspect him either, Jasper. But look at these facts I've got written here. He was on the scene when both Amanda and Julia's bodies were found *AND* he got here within minutes the other night after the alleged break-in." I shook my head while Jasper pouted. "Don't look at me like that. I'm only going where the evidence takes me."

Jasper didn't look convinced. Or, he might have just been hungry. I looked at my watch. "Don't worry. I'll feed you before I leave." Rats, I didn't have much time. Returning to the whiteboard, I continued.

"Then we've got suspect two." I slammed the pen against the face I had drawn of a severe looking woman. "Brenda."

This time, Jasper looked a little more convinced.

"That's right," I said. "She was Amanda's neighbor, and she has it out for anyone who's not a serious crafter. Perhaps she thought that Amanda and Julia were stinking up Pottsville with their sub-standard crafting efforts." I swung around and stared at Jasper. "Perhaps I'm next on her list."

Jasper started to whimper so I walked over and kneeled in front of him to ruffle his ears. "Don't worry, Jas, nothing is going to happen to your mommy! I won't let it." I winked at him and stood back up, taking the cap off my marker. "Now, I've just got to fill in a few blanks." I wrote "Motive" under Ryan's name with a question mark. That was still something I hadn't been able to figure out. I needed some time to think on it.

There was a knock on the door.

"Hello?" Billy's voice called out. "Are you there, George?"

I looked at my watch. It had only been ten minutes.

"Hello there," I tried to say as breezily as I could, pulling the door back. Billy was standing there with a bunch of flowers, his arm outstretched. "Didn't you receive my text message?"

"Oh," Billy said, frowning. "No, sorry."

"I asked for an extra ten minutes. Never mind," I said with a tight grin, taking the flowers from him. "We'll just have to make the best of it, won't we! Now, tell me where we're off to!"

* * *

"I really like you, George."

I put down my fork with the bit of crab on it still left uneaten and gave Billy the brightest smile I could manage before taking an extra long gulp of wine. He'd chosen a quiet little boutique restaurant called Neilson's, with roaring fires and oak everywhere, the kind of restaurant where the wait staff sits your napkin on your lap. The kind of restaurant that makes me feel uncomfortable. I'd rather sit my own napkin on my lap, thank you very much. Or not use one at all, for that matter! I'd have been happy with a diner. Or fast food.

"Thank you," I finally managed to say once I'd swallowed my wine. We had just started to eat our salads, with the crab salad being my choice. I still had a medium-rare steak coming. I picked up my fork again and tried to eat as quickly as possible.

"And how about you, George?" Billy asked.

"How about me, what?" I asked, wiping my mouth with my cloth napkin. I was a little confused.

"Do you like me?"

I almost spat my crab right out. Talk about forthright. I mean, I'm a pretty forthright lady myself, but I don't believe in putting people on the spot like that. Especially when it came to personal matters and there was no escaping. The restaurant was so cozy it was starting to feel claustrophobic.

"I, um, think you're a very lovely man, Billy." And that was true. I wouldn't be spending my time with a man I didn't find lovely.

He looked a little hurt and set his own fork down.

"But you don't have romantic feelings for me," he said a little sadly.

Awkward. I started wondering if I could make a

quick dash out the back door without him knowing. Well, obviously, he would know eventually when I didn't return to the table and my crab went uneaten, and the steak arrived and I was not there to eat it, but by that stage, it would be too late for him to stop me.

A waiter came to clear the salad plates and asked if we were ready for main course. "How about you, George?" Billy asked. "Do you still want to stay?" he asked gently. "Or would you rather we just call it a night?"

I shook my head. "Of course not. We're here now and we ought to enjoy ourselves." I winked at the water. "Bring on the steaks!"

The steak was cooked to perfection, still pink in the middle, just how I like it, but not dripping blood onto the potatoes. "Mmm," I said. "I'll have to come here more often. Pottsville seems to have more to offer than I first thought."

Billy smiled at me and cut into his own steak. "You're a breath of fresh air in this town, George. I'm not sure how you ever ended up here, though. Are you a very long way from home?"

I leaned back in my chair a little and thought about that. "Not so far," I finally said. "Still having a few issues with some folks in this town, though."

Billy laughed. "Brenda?"

I nodded. "Brenda."

He told me about his interest in crafting and how he got into it. "It was a few years ago, after a difficult time in my life. I suppose it was a distraction at the time, a way to relax. Now, it's just something I enjoy." He smiled at me. "And I get to meet very interesting people?"

I raised an eyebrow cheekily. "Brenda?"

He let out a loud laugh. "She's definitely interesting!" He sat down his wine glass. "But I was talking about the woman in front of me."

I returned his smile. I was glad now that I hadn't run out the back door. It had been worth giving the date a chance. We were getting along far better than I would have imagined a few hours earlier. In fact, I was a little surprised to check the time and realize almost four hours had passed and a little disappointed when the restaurant informed us it was time for them to close up for the night.

"I think it's time for me to drive you home," Billy said, walking me out of the restaurant. I noticed that he left a hefty tip for the wait staff, which always put a person in my good books. A good tipper and nice to dogs, those are my two things, and Billy had both of them.

"Oh! I left my purse inside. I would honestly forget my own head if it weren't screwed on," I said to Billy, turning to head back inside.

"It looks like they are locking up. You wait here and I'll see if they will open the doors back up."

"Thanks, Billy," I said gratefully.

I waited by the car for a few minutes while Billy went to try and retrieve my purse. The restaurant was on the same street as every other shop, café, and restaurant in Pottsville. The same street as my craft shop, which I could see across the street and down a few yards.

I frowned. There was movement across the street. It was very late for someone to be exiting a store—or to be working this late, close to midnight. I leaned forward to try and get a better look.

"Oh my goodness," I said out loud. I suppose that is one of the problems with constantly talking to animals—you get into the habit of talking out loud when there are no other humans around, even if the animals aren't there either. "Is that..."

It was Prue. The woman who came to my craft circle—and house—and verbally assaulted my two dogs. The biggest no-no I had. She was wearing that same expensive pink suit. And she was coming out of the local newspaper office.

I stopped and stared at the building. Prue had keys in her hand—she was locking the door. So she wasn't just visiting, and she wasn't breaking in. "She works for the newspaper," I whispered. Why had a news reporter been to my house?

"Hey," I said, calling out to her. "Prue!"

She started to walk quickly and then when I called her name again, her walk turned into a run. I could have sworn she saw me when she glanced back over her shoulder, but she kept on running anyway. I shook my head.

Billy returned to the car and extended his arm proudly, my purse on the end of it. "Took a bit of persuasion, but they opened the doors again. And I gave them another tip!"

"Thanks, Billy, you're a life-saver." I climbed into the car but the drive home was a little sober. I couldn't stop thinking about what I'd seen. Billy tried to make idle chatter and I felt guilty that my mind was elsewhere. Something was definitely not right about Prue.

I couldn't wait to get home. I needed to make an addition to my suspect list.

Billy walked me to the door and there was an awkward moment where he seemed to not know whether he should lean in for a kiss or not. I placed my hand on the door handle, thinking that I would make things easy for us and just unlock it before wishing him a goodnight. To my surprise, the door opened with no need for a key. "Oh, geez!" I said in alarm, realizing I hadn't locked it.

"Is everything all right?"

I nodded. "Just my usual absentmindedness. I really need to get inside," I said, quickly wishing him goodnight. "Thanks for everything, Billy!"

"Oh, I thought..."

I raced down the hall to make sure that Jasper and Casper were all right. "Thank goodness," I said when they both ran to me. I was a few hours late in feeding them, though. I gave them some extra food when I filled their dishes and they gulped it down happily. I collapsed on my sofa and shook my head, glancing at the whiteboard. This was taking up too much of my time. I'd been so distracted by my suspect list that I hadn't even locked my door or fed my pets before I'd left the house!

I stared at the whiteboard and stood up. Maybe I should just drop the whole thing. Did I have the time— and mental capacity—to try and solve this mystery, and run a craft store, and a craft circle, and to date? "Something has to give," I said to Jasper, who had finished his meal and was now curled up sleepily. "Maybe it's the dating that should go, though," I said with a heavy sigh as I added Prue's name to the suspect list. I didn't know anything much about her, just that her name was Prue. Or was it? And that she worked at the paper. And was a fake-crafter. Geez, Brenda would probably hate her.

"Then again," I mused as I tried to do a rough sketch of Prue. "Maybe it's not dating all together that I need to give up. Maybe it's just the particular person I'm dating."

I stared at the whiteboard, at one particular sketch. And it wasn't of Brenda or Prue. Why couldn't I stop thinking about Ryan? I shook my head as Jasper barked. "I know. He's a cop, and a suspect on top of that. I need to stay away from him." But what I didn't say out loud was that I really didn't want to stay away from him.

I pulled a blanket over the top of the whiteboard and turned in for bed. Maybe sleep would clear up some mental space and keep these thoughts from becoming overcrowded, chattering against each other.

Chapter 9

"Come on, Jasper!" I called from the door, jogging in place. I was almost out of breath already and we hadn't even left the house. I hadn't even moved an inch yet!

Jasper came to the front door with about as much energy as I was feeling. "Come on!" I said, jumping up and down in my sweats. "We've got to get active, don't you know!"

I took Jasper's leash and we went outside, both breaking into a run. Well, I was jogging. Jasper had to run to keep up with me. And I suppose dogs don't really 'jog,' do they?

Still, it didn't take long until I was out of breath. We were about halfway up the hill and about to enter the woods, where I'd be able to take Jasper's leash off and let him run free. If we ever got there.

It was a new week, and a new start. That was what I'd told myself anyway. I was hoping a run would clear my head. I was also hoping I'd be able to make it a regular thing: I'd always fancied myself as being the sort of person who was really into running. Of course,

I'd never actually done it before. I figured that Jasper needed the exercise as well; it might stop him from going stir crazy in the house and ruining all my rugs and furniture.

He seemed to be faring better than I was, tugging on the leash when I stopped, doubled over with a pain in my side. He was barking.

"Just give me a..." I glanced up and saw that Billy was standing there, also dressed in his jogging wear. It had been a few days since our date and I hadn't replied to any of his messages in the meantime. I felt my face redden and it wasn't just due to the physical exertion.

"Billy," I said, trying to straighten up even though another pain had formed in my side, making me wince. "I've been super busy the last few days. I think I meant to reply, and then just forgot." I tried to let out a light laugh but it came out far too forced. "You know how I am."

Billy nodded a little. "It's okay, George," he said gently. "I can take a hint. I suppose I was just surprised because we had such a nice time at dinner."

"We did," I said quickly, cutting him off in a hurry to reassure him that he was right. "We had a great time."

"So what happened?"

I looked at the ground, unsure of what to say and knowing that I might be making a very bad decision.

"It's okay," Billy said finally. "You don't owe me an explanation."

I looked up at him. "I'm sorry."

He shook his head and smiled. "I hope I'm still welcome at these craft circles of yours."

I let out a deep breath. "Of course you are. Don't be silly."

"So there are no hard feelings?"

I shook my head. "Not on my end."

He jogged away with a promise that he would see me the following day at our craft circle meeting. I wondered if anyone else was even going to show up. It was going to be super awkward if it was just Billy and I there.

I looked around and tried to catch my breath. I realized that we were across the road from Amanda's house. Uh-oh, that meant... I turned to my right and realized I was standing right in front of Brenda's house.

The curtain quickly shut, but it was too late—I'd already seen her peering out at me. I closed my eyes and cringed. That meant she'd seen the whole conversation with Billy. Great.

"Jasper, sit," I said. He was still trying to run forward and I was not ready to move again.

Brenda was Amanda's neighbor. Or had been. I wished I had my whiteboard with me right there and then. There were still some blanks I had to fill in with her. "She had access," I said to Jasper, who was finally sitting. "And motive. She seems to hate every crafter in this town that isn't her." But she'd seemed to like Amanda. And she was so tiny. I couldn't imagine her even having the strength to push any of the victims down a flight of stairs.

Maybe there was something I was missing. I knew what I needed to do: I needed to speak to Ryan. I looked down at my old sweats and knew that my face and hair must look a fright as well. This was not the way I wanted to look when I saw him.

"Come on, Jasper," I said. "Let's jog home so I can get a shower and make myself more presentable."

As we were jogging away, I saw the curtain pull back again and Brenda's beady eyes following us.

Was I going to be the next victim on Brenda's list?

* * *

As luck would have it, Ryan was exiting the station right as Jasper and I arrived. Or rather, as luck wouldn't have it, because I had to race over to him before he hopped into his car. I'd already done enough running that day to last all week. And it was far harder to run in heels than it had been in tennis shoes, and that had been hard enough, let me tell you that.

"Ryan!" I said, racing over to him. "I haven't seen you for the longest time—or at least, it certainly feels that way." It was only a few days, but it felt like forever.

I was not met by his trademark smile. In fact, he was downright cold to me. "What is it, Georgina?" he asked, not even meeting my eyes as he opened the car door.

"I, um, I just wanted to catch up." I was a little startled by his reaction. I'd been intending to flirt and charm my way into getting some new information about the case, but that seemed like a lost dream now.

Was he still mad about what I'd said at the funeral? He'd left in such a hurry we'd never had a chance to address it. I took his rudeness toward me with a little bit of offense, though. After all, it had been him that left abruptly, not me.

"You know what," I said, stopping him before he could climb into the driver's seat. "I'm not sure why you're the one giving me the cold shoulder! You left the funeral in a sulk, without even saying goodbye to me!"

He glared at me. "I wasn't in a sulk. I got called away to a disturbance. I figured that was a little more important."

"Oh." I shifted from one foot to the other. "Well, you are in a sulk with me now. Don't try and deny that!"

Ryan was silent and stony-faced for a few seconds.

"I saw it," he said.

I blinked a few times. "Saw what? There are quite a few things to see in this world, Ryan."

"I saw that thing in your house."

I stopped. "Well now, what were you doing in my home?"

"I came by the other night to check that you were okay, seeing as I hadn't gotten a chance to say goodbye to you at the funeral," he said pointedly, giving me a look. "I wanted to apologize for that and make sure everything was all right between us."

I gulped.

Ryan kept talking. "When I got there and your front door was wide open." Uh-oh, no thanks to my scatterbrain, that date night just kept dredging up more and more trouble, didn't it? "I called out and there was no answer," Ryan said. "With your door wide open and no sight of you, I thought you might be in trouble or something," Ryan said, shaking his head. "So I thought I'd better check."

So he'd entered the house. My stomach suddenly dropped. The whiteboard. That was what he had seen. That was what he was talking about. I might not have had time to 'finish' it before I'd left, but I'd had plenty of time to sketch Ryan's face and write out in detail the reasons why he might be a serial killer.

"Ryan, please, let me explain. That's just a little project I was working on! A craft project."

He finally climbed into the car and put his keys in the ignition. "Do you think I am completely stupid, George?"

I thought about that. A little naive...yes, maybe. A little blind to the obvious, definitely. But not completely stupid. "No," I said. "I don't think you're stupid."

He shook his head and cut me off by starting the

engine. I wondered if he had another disturbance he needed to get to or whether he just wanted to get away from me. Probably the latter.

He switched the ignition off for a brief second. "You suspected me, George? You honestly think I could do such a thing?"

I wasn't quite sure what to say.

"Ryan, you have to admit, a few things didn't quite add up."

His face was full of offense and betrayal.

"Why were you the first cop on the scene in both the deaths?"

"Because I am the one who's always on duty," Ryan snapped back. "Because I'm always on call. Because I'm a good cop. Being the first on the scene doesn't mean I did it, George! By that logic, all crimes would be committed by cops."

I was lost for words again, which was rare for me. I was really starting to think that I was out of my depth with the whole detective thing. Now I was truly losing the one good friend I had in Pottsville.

"I'm sorry, Ryan. If you could just let me explain. Maybe we could go get some coffee and I could tell you a few things."

"You need to leave, George. I can't help you with anything from this point on. I've already told you far too much." He glared at me as he started the car again and started to pull away. "All of which I now thoroughly regret."

Chapter 10

Jasper came bouncing into the living room with something in his mouth, but I was too tired from a late night trying to untangle the notes on my whiteboard— and half a bottle of wine—to really acknowledge him, even though he was jumping up and down with excitement, clearly proud of whatever it was he had done.

"What is it?" I groaned, sitting up. "You haven't dug something else up from the yard, have you?"

He dropped something onto the carpet and proudly sat down before it.

"Oh!" I said, leaning forward to pick it up. "I didn't know you knew how to fetch the paper, Jasper!" And here I was thinking he hadn't been taught any tricks or good behavior.

I frowned at the paper. I also wasn't aware that we got the local paper delivered. I looked at it and saw that it was only a monthly affair. That explained it. I'd only been in the neighborhood a little under a month.

Still tired and glassy-eyed from the night before, I

absentmindedly flipped through the paper while some coffee brewed nearby.

The front page was about an up-coming local election so I just flipped past it.

It was page four that really caught my attention.

It was a profile. On me.

Or rather, it was more of an expose on the "crazy dog lady" who'd moved to Pottsville and taken up residence in the town's spookiest house. Basically, it painted me as a few sandwiches short of a picnic.

I gritted my teeth. *News really must be hard to come by in this town.*

There were details about everything, about the so-called 'haunted house' I lived in, to the contents of the whiteboard in my living room. I felt my cheeks reddening. Ryan was going to read this.

"She fancies herself as an amateur sleuth, but could it be that the house's spooky energy is going to her head?" There were further implications that I was paranoid and delusional and that the "few friends I actually had" were "extremely worried" about me.

"What kind of crazy woman lives in a house like that?" one quote said from a source that was apparently 'close' to me. "That woman does not belong in this town."

"Brenda," I muttered, shaking my head. She must have sent Prue into my home to get all of this stuff. She was such a busybody!

And I bet she was reveling in my now very public humiliation.

"I can't believe this!" I said, my mouth dropping open as I threw the paper back down onto the kitchen counter. "That woman really has some nerve, coming into my house and then writing an article like this!"

I was starting to wish that no one had ever taught Jasper the trick of how to fetch a paper. Then again, wasn't it better to know what was being said about me behind my back?

I'm not sure. I think I would have rather lived in ignorant bliss.

* * *

The shop was swarming with people. Unusual even for during the day, but even more so for a Tuesday night.

"Are you Georgina Holt?" a woman with a large red bouffant and blue eye shadow asked me.

"Unfortunately, I am."

After the disaster that had been holding the craft circle at my house, I'd decided to give myself—and my carpets—a break by holding the next one in the shop. Okay, the real reason I'd decided to have it away from my house was because I was afraid that only Billy would show up and it would be too date-like.

I needn't have worried.

It seemed like my new reputation had made me the talk of the town, and people in Pottsville wanted to see me up close. I wasn't sure I liked it. I don't mind being the center of attention, but I like it to be over things I've actually done, or achieved, or made. Not for some ridiculous news article. A ridiculous news article that painted me as nothing more than a circus attraction. And had given away my real age.

I took a swig of wine and looked out at the group who had already devoured half the cheese platters I'd set out, and who looked only marginally interested in crafting.

Billy saw that I was looking a bit weary.

"Don't worry, George, I'll take the reins," he offered. "I'll guide the group discussion tonight so that you can just sit quietly."

"Thank you, Billy."

The others made small talk about their day, then the conversation moved to various crafting pursuits— crocheting and quilting and stained glass—but my mind drifted. I wanted to be anywhere else.

I wondered if I could escape out my own back door.

No, that wouldn't work. I had to lock up.

Maybe I could lock them all inside. I tilted my head as I considered it.

Maybe it wasn't just the shop I didn't want to be in right now. Perhaps the problem was larger in scope.

Maybe I wanted to be in any other town. Had coming to Pottsville been one gigantic mistake? I looked at Jasper. He wouldn't mind a change of scenery, would he? Maybe we'd move to an even smaller community, or better yet, a place with no community at all. A farm in the middle of nowhere. Maybe we could live by the beach, miles away from any other human being. Casper would like that as well.

I knew one thing, though. I had to give up this whole

detective thing. It had only caused trouble and made me enemies. And now it had made me the laughing stock of the town.

I had to just let it go.

The woman with the large red hair laughed loudly at something and looked over at me. She'd been casting me furtive looks all night, just like the rest of them. When the meeting finally came to an end, she came up to me and not so quietly asked, "Do you really live there?"

I could tell she'd wanted to ask that all night.

"I sure do," I said, finding myself answering with a very short tone. "But maybe not for much longer!"

I'd startled myself a little bit. Did I really mean that?

Perhaps the two deaths were complete accidents. Maybe Amanda really did just fall down the stairs. Maybe Julia did as well. It happens. Coincidences happen.

Perhaps life in Pottsville had been so dull and dreary that I'd just had to invent a drama, invent a mystery. Once I'd become suspicious, it was hard to break the habit.

Maybe I'd just been seeing things that weren't

128

there.

Even if it wasn't a coincidence, I didn't like to be the sort of person who ran away from problems. I'd rather face them head on. Or at least try to. But I had tried in Pottsville—the town and I just weren't a good fit. It was better to cut my losses.

"This has been great, George," the red-haired woman said. "We should do this every week."

Yes. Every week. Finally, a successful crafting circle with people who actually wanted to attend.

Be careful what you wish for.

Chapter 11

From upstairs, I heard the sound of Jasper's booming bark and Casper's little squeaky one. "What is it?" I called out. I could hear two sets of claws at the front door.

I threw another shirt into my packing box and walked out onto the landing of the staircase to peer over. Through the cloudy glass I could make out a silhouette of a woman in a suit with blonde hair piled high on her head and stiletto heels on her feet.

She was back.

"I'm so sorry," the real estate agent said as she followed me down the hallway. "I'm not even from this area. I had no idea about the history of this house. I really hope you don't think I was trying to scam you."

She was having trouble catching me in her high heels and I had little patience with her at that moment. I had packing to do. And I wasn't sure I wanted to hear her excuses.

She began to cough a little. "I don't suppose I could trouble you for a glass of water, could I?"

I spun around in the kitchen and nodded. "Of course," I said, filling a glass with tap water and handing it to her while she gulped it down.

"Sorry," she said. "I've come down with this terrible cold. I've been so rundown lately." She put the glass down and looked at me. "And I've been feeling so stressed about this house." She reached into her briefcase and started searching around for some papers. "Please believe me when I tell you that I didn't know." She stopped and threw a furtive glance toward the bottom of the staircase. "I didn't know that anyone had been killed here."

I sighed heavily. I supposed it wasn't her fault, if she really didn't know. "What's been done is done," I said. "But I need out of this house now after everything that has happened."

"I understand." She looked anxious though as she flipped through her notes. "But it might be a little difficult."

Well, I knew that it would be almost impossible to sell the house again, unless they managed to find another new-to-town sucker like I had been. But I didn't want to hear that from her. I wanted to hear that she would do everything in her power to offload the house and get me my money back.

"List it right away," I said.

"I will. It just might take a while to sell."

I crossed my arms. "I should never have been sold this house in the first place. I need it sold, quickly."

She nodded. "Of course. I will do everything I can to sell it. Do you mind taking...considerably less than you paid for it?"

I let out a far heavier sigh than I'd meant to and shook my head a little. I supposed it was all my fault. I'd snapped up the house too quickly without doing any research. Without even doing a quick Google search. I'd been so impressed by the cheap price tag that I'd greedily snapped it up, thinking I'd grabbed myself the bargain of the century. Well, I had gotten more than I'd bargained for.

Moving to Pottsville was more of the same—a knee-jerk reaction to when things had gone south in Paris. Perhaps I should have just stayed there. At least that was a big city. There had been places to hide there. There was no hiding in Pottsville.

Jasper came running up to me, begging to be petted. I smiled down at him and laughed. Okay, it was lucky I came to Pottsville after all. There had been no room in my tiny Paris apartment for a dog his size. Even if there had been, that dog wouldn't have been Jasper. He was one of a kind.

My nervous looking real estate agent stepped back a little, clearly wary of Jasper leaping up onto her pristine suit.

"Don't worry," I said. "He's a little more house trained than he was a few weeks ago."

She nodded but didn't look too sure as she walked to the sink and rinsed her glass. "What's this?" she asked, nodding to something in the window as she placed the glass in the dish rack. She reached out and started fondling a piece of paper still blowing in the wind outside, flapping around.

I frowned. "Oh, it's a note from a friend," I said. "I'd better get rid of that before I leave. It's been so rainy and cloudy, today is really the first day I've had the window open like that." I glanced over at the note from Amanda. I'd forgotten all about it.

"So you've really made a decision?" she asked, looking hopeful, as though I might still back out of it. I knew it would make her life a whole lot easier.

I nodded down at the outfit I was wearing: blue

jeans and a button-down shirt with a scarf around my head. My packing outfit. "I've already got the boxes out," I said.

She nodded and sighed heavily, leaving with a promise that she would try but could give me no guarantees. I felt like promising her a lawsuit if the house didn't sell, but I'm not that sort of gal. Instead, I just watched her scurry away. Great, even my own real estate agent didn't want to be inside the haunted house with the crazy dog lady.

I checked my phone, not sure what I was hoping for. No new messages from anyone in town begging me to stay. Of course, Billy had texted me earlier and tried to talk me out of it, but he was the only one.

I knew the person I really wanted to be texting and asking me to stay. But I hadn't heard from him since he'd driven away from me in front of the police station the week before.

There was nothing to stay in town for. Time to cut my losses and leave. I already had my sights set on a house way upstate, six hours away, next to a lake. The weather was a lot better up there as well. I wouldn't be met by cloud and drizzle every day, nor judgmental stares. And the dogs would love it.

"Looks like we're moving, Jasper," I said, patting his head while he made a sad little growling noise. "Don't worry, you and your sister are coming with me," I said, picking up Casper and giving her a cuddle. "I would never leave you two. You're going to like living by the lake."

The dogs liked living here as well though, with the big backyard and the house that I let them have free reign inside.

There was another knock on the door. My heart leapt a little thinking that it might be Ryan. I glanced in the mirror and made sure the scarf around my head didn't look too ridiculous before I answered.

"Oh, hello, Billy." I pulled the scarf off my head completely. "You've caught me in the middle of packing, I'm afraid."

His face fell a little.

"So is it really true?" Billy asked. "When I didn't receive any texts back from you I wasn't sure. I'm really sorry to hear that you're leaving, George."

"Yeah, well, I think it might be for the best," I said. "I'm not sure this town and I are a good mix." I invited him inside for one last coffee. I hadn't even gotten around to unpacking the kitchen in the first place, so there wasn't a lot of work to be done there, but I did have to rummage around in a few boxes before I found the coffee cups.

The coffee smelled amazing when it was brewed and just for a moment, with my hands wrapped around the warm mug, I felt peaceful, like maybe I should stay. Maybe things weren't that bad after all. I mean, I had a friend, right? And I had coffee. Things in Pottsville weren't exactly torturous.

Billy suddenly turned serious. "You're not leaving because you feel unsafe in your home though, are you?"

I shook my head slightly, but I wasn't sure that was entirely true. I thought it was definitely a factor in my decision to flee, actually. Every time I climbed the stairs, it was all I could think about. I'd even considered moving my mattress downstairs or just sleeping on the couch. I could maybe put up with being an unwelcome laughing stock if I didn't also fear for my life in my house.

Billy didn't seem too convinced. "Because you know what happened to those two women was just a coincidence, right? Two terrible accidents."

"I know that," I said, trying to sound convincing. I finished my coffee and rinsed out my cup, the note blowing in the wind catching my eye again. I really had to bring that inside. It was under cover of the porch, so it hadn't been rain-damaged, but sooner or later, it was going to blow away.

I heard movement behind me. Billy was standing and pulling his jacket on. "Let me know if you need help with moving anything, George. Even though I hate to contribute to anything that might lead to you leaving." He walked over to the whiteboard in the middle of the room and gave it a strange look. "This might be a bit of a pain to pack up."

I let out a short scoff. "I don't think I'll bother," I said. "I think I might just burn the darn thing."

But once Billy had gone, I walked back to the whiteboard. Why hadn't I packed it up yet? Or at the very least, erased all of its the contents? It was half-covered by a blanket but Ryan's face was still visible. I pulled the blanket back and looked at the whole thing, holding the eraser in my hand.

"Come on, George, just do it," I said, my hand still hovering.

Jasper barked at me and I spun around, unable to tell if the bark was meant to be encouragement or a deterrent. I gave him a questioning look as I slowly moved my hand back toward the whiteboard. He barked even louder this time.

"Well, that's helpful. I can't tell if you want me to erase the whole thing or keep it." I placed the eraser down and Jasper started wiggling his tail happily.

"Huh."

I kept a skeptical eye on him as I climbed the stairs again and went back to packing up my wardrobe. My clothes were some of the few items I'd actually unpacked properly, so packing them again was going to take the most time. I looked at the row of coats hanging up and wondered if I ought to get them dry cleaned before I put them into boxes.

"That's probably the smart move, hey, Jasper?" I asked. He'd come and plopped himself down on my bedroom floor. I hadn't exactly stuck to my promise that him sleeping in my room would be a one-time thing. It had become a fairly regular thing and he made himself more than at home there on the floor next to my bed.

I pulled out my coats one by one and made sure to check the pockets for anything left behind before I took them to the cleaners. "Ooh!" I exclaimed, pulling out a ten dollar bill from one. "Nice."

There weren't any more pleasant surprises, but when I got to the last one, my thickest, blackest coat, I felt something hard and rubbery inside. "Oh," I said, pulling out the bone folder and sighing as I threw it on my bed, while Jasper yapped at it wildly. "Maybe I should give that to Brenda as a parting gift before I leave," I said wryly. "Something to remember me by."

I collected all my coats and placed them by the front door. Just a few hours of packing to go, a few loose ends to tie up, and I'd be done with this town.

* * *

"Business For Sale. Inquire Within."

Brenda came bustling into the shop, her mouth hanging open. "Are you really selling?" she asked, practically breathless.

I turned away from her a little. Childish? Yes, a little. But did she really expect a warm greeting after the way she had sold me out in the newspaper article?

"Yes, I am," I said flatly. I was perched up high on a stool behind my front counter, flipping through a gossip magazine, even though I felt a bit guilty about reading it now that I knew what it was like to be written about.

Brenda stood on her tiptoes, clutching her purse. "How much are you asking for it?"

I put my magazine down and raised my eyes at her over the top of my reading glasses. "Are you seriously interested, Brenda?"

She stood up straight. "Yes. I think I would be a far better owner than you are. I would streamline the shop and get rid of all the junk that is littering the aisles."

"As well as my jewelry?" I asked.

"Well, I said I'd be getting rid of all the junk, didn't I?" Brenda asked.

I opened my mouth then shut it again before I returned to my magazine. "The shop is more than you can afford," I said casually. "After all, I don't suppose local newspapers pay very much for tell-all stories, do they?"

I stopped reading and snuck a glance at her. Her face turned red. "That's right, Brenda. I know you spoke to the paper about me. And I know that you sent Prue to my house. Well, I suppose you're happy now that you've chased me out of town on your broomstick."

Now it was Brenda's turn for her mouth to fall right open. "I never..."

"Save it Brenda," I said, interrupting her as I removed my reading glasses. "Those quotes from the paper could only have come from you." I hopped off my stool and stared straight at her. "Not such a nice thing to do to a new gal in town, was it, Brenda? I thought you were supposed to be a good, Christian woman. I haven't seen much of that from you since I moved to town."

Her face had turned completely beet red. She was still stammering, trying to defend herself, but it was clear I had her cornered.

"Just tell me, Brenda. Why do you have it out for me, anyway? What did I ever do to offend you so badly?"

She gulped, looking for a way out of the shop. Almost teary. For a moment, I felt bad, but then I remembered that a) she had sold me down the river, and b) she was still my main suspect in the murders of Julia and Amanda.

"Tell me, Brenda." I folded my arms across my chest. "Where were you on the night that Amanda

141

died?"

Her face may have been beet red a few minutes earlier, but now all the color was draining from her face. "How dare you?" she whispered. "What exactly are you implying, Georgina?"

I kept a steady face. "I think you know perfectly well what I am implying, Brenda. You still haven't answered my question."

She took a step back. "I don't have to answer any such ghastly, offensive questions!" she cried. "I liked Amanda very much! She was a good lady. She was kind, she was sweet, and she was a real, proper crafter, unlike some people!"

I shook my head. "Where were you that night?" I came out from behind my counter. "And better yet, where were you a year ago, the night that Julia was killed in my house?"

"How dare you!"

"I notice you haven't answered any of my questions."

"I don't have to!" Brenda clutched her purse to her chest and started to rush toward the door, her voice almost choked up now. "How dare you accuse me of doing anything to hurt Amanda. She...she...she was going to be my business partner!"

I frowned. "Business partner?"

Brenda had one hand on the door, ready to push it open. "Yes" she said, almost shaking. "We were going to go into business together. We were going to buy this very store."

The words hung in the air for a moment. I took a step toward her. "But Amanda pulled out, didn't she?" I asked in a low voice.

Brenda inched closer to the door.

I kept talking. "She backed out of the arrangement you had, ruined your chance to get your mitts on this shop and to control it, and you never forgave her for it, did you?"

Brenda shook her head. "No, that's not what happened at all! I did forgive Amanda."

I scoffed. "Yeah, right. You were so mad at Amanda that you killed her for it. What happened with Julia? She was a crafter too, right? Did you also strike a business deal with her that she flaked out on? Did she receive the same punishment?"

Brenda's eyes were gleaming. "This store should

have been mine!" she cried. "They did both back out of our agreements, they weren't women who stuck to their word, but I didn't kill either of them!"

I narrowed my eyes. "So am I next on your list, Brenda?" I asked evenly

She swallowed. "You're leaving, anyway, aren't you? That newspaper article saw to that! And after the horrible accusations you have thrown at me today, I have no regrets about what I said to that reporter!"

"Great," I said. "So you did want to run me out of town. That was your great plan all along. Well, congratulations, Brenda, you got your big wish. But you are never getting your hands on this store. You'll be in jail before you have a chance to purchase it."

* * *

"One last hurrah," I said, raising my glass in a toast to the last ever crafting circle I was going to hold in Pottsville.

Billy was there, and the red-haired woman, and a few other familiar faces. No Brenda or Prue, though. "Surprise, surprise."

I set down my wine glass. "So, we should actually get down to business, seeing as this is my last meeting. Let's talk crafting! How has everyone been trucking along this week?"

"I've been having some trouble this week actually," Billy said.

"Oh?" I asked.

"I've been getting back into scrapbooking, which I haven't done in over a year, but I'm having some trouble with some of the paperwork." He let out a little laugh. "I don't mean balancing the books or anything. I mean I'm having trouble because I couldn't find my good tools."

I leaned forward a little and waved my hand around. "Well, you're in the right place. We're having a closing down sale as well, so you'd better get in quick." I smiled at him. "What is it that you're looking for?"

"I lost my bone folder. Probably just over a year ago now. I can't find it anywhere."

Chapter 12

It was freezing cold by the time I returned home and Jasper greeted me at the door, almost knocking me over by leaping on me. "Jasper!" I cried out, chastising him. "Naughty boy!" The jumping up onto people was really starting to become a problem. Usually, I wouldn't have had it in my heart to get upset with him. But that night, I was shaking, and it wasn't just from the cold. I was full of nervous energy as I ran toward the open window and reached for the piece of paper just outside it.

I unpegged the note, thanking whoever was listening that it was still there and hadn't blown away.

I read over it. The same three words were visible.

"Don't. Careful. Watch." I reached into my pocket for my reading glasses and pulled them out, squinting, trying to make anything else out. There was something that looked like the word "out" after the word "Watch."

"Watch out."

This was a note addressed to me. What was she telling me to watch out for? I pulled my phone out of my pocket and dialed Brenda's number. I knew she was far too much of a gossip not to answer the call, even once she saw it was from me.

"You've got some nerve, young lady!" Her words were loud and shrill.

"Brenda. This is important. This is an emergency. I need to ask you something."

She was silent, but I could practically hear her fuming from the other end of the line.

"Brenda?" I asked frantically. "Are you still there? Look, I know you're mad at me, but I need to know something. I know that you kept a close eye on Amanda's house. You have a perfect view of it. Tell me, was she dating anyone before she died?"

Brenda remained silent.

"Brenda!" I was losing patience.

"Yes," she finally said. "But it was quiet, no one knew, and I wasn't supposed to say anything. I don't think it was anything serious."

"Who, Brenda?"

"That same man I saw you talking to the other morning in the front of my house. Billy."

I hung up without even saying goodbye or thanking her and stared at the note again.

Amanda had been trying to warn me to stay away from Billy.

But it had been too late for her.

Well, it wouldn't be too late for me.

Jasper ran up to me and curled himself around my ankles.

"Jasper, he was here...that night that Julia was killed in this house. That's when he dropped the bone folder. It must have gotten buried underneath all that dirt. He lied to me about never being in my house before."

Jasper whimpered.

I stared down at Jasper. "Maybe he came back that night to try and find it." A shiver ran down my spine. "Maybe he realized he had lost it, and just where and when."

The whiteboard caught my attention out of the corner of my eye. All this time, I had failed to add the real suspect to my list. I stomped over to it and wrote "BILLY" in thick, block letters.

I paced back and forth in front of the board, unloading everything onto Jasper's eager ears. "He only joins the craft circle to meet vulnerable women...his victims," I said, stopping. I stared straight at Jasper, who had sat up, ears alert.

I nodded. "That's right, boy. He thinks I'm the next victim. The next on his list. Well, I'm not like the rest of them, Jasper. I'm not that weak and vulnerable. If Billy wants to kill me, he's going to have to kill me first! Hmm, that doesn't really work, does it?"

Jasper looked nervous.

"Come on, Jasper, we're going out."

He whimpered. He seemed to know exactly where we were going. How do dogs manage to do that?

"We need proof," I explained slowly and clearly to him. "Don't worry, Jasper, we won't be in any danger. I've got you to protect me, don't I?"

* * *

Billy's house was dark. I'd been pretty sure he wouldn't be home, because the others at the craft circle had made plans to get drinks, which I had declined to be a part of.

"We've probably got about half an hour," I said to Jasper, placing my hand on Billy's front door. I let out a little laugh when it opened right away. Small towns, hey? The kind where everyone keeps their front door unlocked. Looked like it wasn't just something that absentminded folk like myself fall prey to.

It was dark inside the house but I didn't switch on any lights. There were two floors, and I eyed the staircase uneasily. I wasn't even sure what I was looking for, but there had to be something at Billy's house that would identify him as the killer. Not just killer. Serial killer.

Once my eyes had adjusted, I noticed that there was a small dog flap at the back door. "Uh-oh," I said, tugging on Jasper's collar. Too late, he was already running toward it and had managed to push his way through and into the back yard. Oh no!

I heard footsteps coming up the path out the front door. "Cripes!" I ran to the back door and tried to wave Jasper over to me through the window without speaking. "Jasper!" I hissed, trying to get him to come back. I could just make him out, rolling on his back in the yard.

"Jasper, no! Come back!"

It was no use. I was about to be caught.

Chapter 13

I looked down at the tiny little flap. It was too small for me to attempt to fit through. I kept imaging how I would look if Billy came in and saw me stuck half way through the door.

Never mind how it would look—I'd be trapped.

I saw it out of the corner of my eye. The staircase. With the key turning in the door, I had no choice. I flew up it as fast as I could.

But not fast enough.

"Georgina?"

I was halfway up the staircase. I stared at Billy and bolted the rest of the way with him chasing after me. I looked around frantically. There was nowhere to hide. I edged into the doorway of a bedroom while Billy walked slowly toward me.

I gulped. I just needed to stick clear of the landing, and everything would be okay.

Where is Jasper? Where is he when I need him?

"What are you doing here, George?"

I swallowed. "I just... I wanted to see you again." I tried to swallow, wondering if the terror was shining in my eyes. "I regretted not coming for a drink. Your front door was open."

He shook his head. "You didn't want to see me again," he said slowly. "You've been avoiding me ever since our date. And you didn't even want to go on that."

"Of course I did," I said, backing away from him. "I had a wonderful time, Billy."

He shook his head again.

"You're all the same. All you women. Julia, Amanda, you. You say you want a 'nice man' and then one comes along, and you'd rather be with someone else. Someone younger and better looking," he said pointedly, in a low voice. "Like that cop you've been hanging around with."

I shook my head. "No, Billy, it's not like that at all." I gulped.

"I thought that meeting women through crafts would make it easier. I thought you were supposed to be nice, quiet types. Women who might actually give men like me a chance."

I tried to smile at him. "Billy, this has all been a misunderstanding. Of course I will give a man like you a chance."

Until I am safely out of this house and you are behind bars.

"But you crafters are not nice!" he hissed. "You're just the same as all the rest. Only worse, because you pretend to be so nice."

"Crafters pretend to be nice?" I asked. "Have you ever met Brenda?"

His mouth curled up into a snarl. Probably not the right time for me to make light of the situation.

He came around behind me and I had no choice but to move backward until I got closer and closer to the top of the staircase. The closer he got to me, the closer I got to the edge.

I looked down and gulped. It would be quite the tumble. Even if my neck survived the fall without snapping, my head would hit the hard tiles below.

I was getting closer and closer to the edge.

With Billy right in front of me with his arms outstretched, I was about to topple backward.

Would these be my last few moments on this earth?

All of a sudden, I heard the door of the dog flap

apologizing." He shook his head. "I wish I could apologize on behalf of the whole Pottsville police force. We should have seen all this before."

"It's not your fault," I said. "You did your own job well, Ryan. And you just might have saved my life."

I couldn't help but feel, though, that Pottsville might actually need me. Maybe they needed me around to solve the cases that the police were just too scared to touch. I could make a little side career out of this— crafter by day and detective by night.

My neck twisted awkwardly and I had to stop myself from letting out a little cry of pain. Maybe my neck wouldn't thank me for taking on this extra job. Maybe I'd have to take it easy for a little while.

But as I looked out the window of the living room and onto the street in front of my house, I just had this creeping feeling that Pottsville wasn't as quiet as it had seemed at first sight. That this town wasn't going to let me get much rest.

"It's good to have you back to your old self, George. And it's good to have you in this town." Ryan offered me a wink as he walked out. "I'll see ya around."

Arts, Crafts and Murder

Chapter 1

"Hey!" I called out, flying across my office to try to prevent the crime from taking place. "Those aren't for you!"

But Jasper had his eyes trained on the tray, on the rows of freshly cut ham sandwiches. I'd been foolish enough to turn my back for one second, and with a border collie like Jasper on the loose, one second was a second too long.

"Phew!" I said, almost falling to the ground as I grabbed the silver tray and held it high enough so that the jumping dog pawing at my waist couldn't get to them. "If there's any leftovers, they're all yours," I told him. "But these women are a hungry bunch."

My weekly craft circle—and the women who attended—were waiting for me on the other side of the door. I'd made special arrangements to close the shop a couple of hours early so we could all meet to gossip, eat, and swap crafting secrets. I'd only lived in Pottsville for two months and, sad as it is to say, even though I am a rather effervescent woman, this craft circle was still my only real social activity. It wasn't that the women in Pottsville were standoffish, per se. They were more...tight-knit. And I still had to prove myself, apparently.

I braced myself, ready to swing through the doors of the shop with my best, brightest, 'here to make new friends' smile.

"Welcome, everyone..." I stopped in my tracks, the tray of salvaged sandwiches in my hand. Where was everyone?

"Hello?" My store was totally empty. I looked down at Jasper. "Did I get the date wrong?"

No. It was definitely Friday. I can be a bit scatterbrained at times, and like most people, I have a habit of wishing it was Friday when it actually wasn't, but it was absolutely, one hundred percent Friday afternoon.

Jasper ran over to the counter and knocked a pile of loose buttons to the ground as he put his paws up and started to sniff at something.

"Hmm," I said, spotting the item he was sniffing at. A note.

Moved the meeting to the town hall. Meet us there if you like,

Brenda.

I crumpled up the note. Brenda. Trust my newest casual employee and full-time frenemy to pull a stunt like this. She wanted to be in charge of the craft circle, and my store for that matter. It was probably some kind of power play. I decided not to let it bother me, shrugged it off, and picked up the sandwiches. "Come on, Jasper, looks like we're taking a walk to the town hall."

By the time we got to the town hall, it was obvious that the meeting had been in full swing for a while. I frowned but quickly straightened my face as Brenda approached me while I tied Jasper up outside.

Despite only being a year older than me, Brenda could almost pass for a decade my senior, with her matronly clothes and manner. She made a show of looking all apologetic, like it had all been a very innocent misunderstanding. "So terribly sorry for the mix-up, Georgina." She always called me by my full name, though most people called me George. "I hope it didn't put you out too much."

"No," I said. "I'm just the new girl. Ignore me." I flashed a wide grin to show that I was joking. Kind of joking. Sort of.

Yes, just ignore the person who formed the group in the first place. Why should I need to know where the meeting was being held or at what time?

Brenda shot me a sickly sweet smile.

"I just thought we'd start a little bit earlier. It's better for the other women in the group. They are a little bit older, you know," Brenda said knowingly. "They like to get home early, have their dinner early, watch their shows."

Yeah, I knew it. Even though I was in my early forties myself, I sometimes felt like a spring chicken in Pottsville. It was the sort of town people moved to when they retired, and even though there were children, of course, there were very few people in their twenties or thirties. Besides Ryan, that is. But he was a police officer, and he had to live in town. My mind briefly started to wander and I found a smile coming to my lips, thinking about him. Then I remembered I was standing in a musty town hall with a tray of sad looking sandwiches in my hand. I glanced at the circle of women to my left and saw all of their empty plates full of crumbs. They had already eaten.

"And the change of location?" I asked.

"Oh, that was more convenient for everyone as well."

"It wasn't convenient for me."

Brenda shrugged. Less apologetically this time. "I made an executive decision."

Great. So now I'd been superseded as leader of the group I created. Brenda had become the de facto leader, just as she'd wanted all along, while I'd been too busy making sandwiches and minding my own business.

Seemed like you couldn't escape the politics of stuff like this, of friendships and social circles, no matter where you ended up. Even in a teeny tiny town, just trying to run an innocent little craft circle. I'd lived in Paris before Pottsville and in a way, life in a big city had been far more peaceful than this.

"Don't worry, Georgina, it's still your group," Brenda said with a condescending little tap on the arm.

Mmm-hmm.

My group. Sure.

I didn't even have a chance to say hello to my new "friends" before Brenda called a close to the meeting, clapping her hands together and announcing that they'd all meet again next week. I just stood there open-mouthed while the rest of the women stood up and thanked Brenda for being such a gracious host.

They giggled and chattered like a pack of hens while I stood on the outside of the group, close enough to hear them laughing but not close enough to actually hear what they were saying.

I was a forty-four year old woman, for crying out loud. Far too old for any of this junior high-level ridiculousness.

I cleared my throat. "Well then, Brenda, I'm sure that you won't mind my leaving now. Jasper needs to be fed. Please take care of 'my group' for me, won't you?"

She grinned. "Oh, I will, Georgina."

It was still light when Jasper and I returned to my large, glass house by the lake, so we retreated to the backyard so that Jasper could get some exercise. At first, distracted by the events of the meeting, I didn't realize anything was amiss. I threw a ball for Jasper to fetch, which he happily and proudly returned to my feet. I have a sizeable yard and Jasper appreciates all the space. I'd rescued him two months earlier, when I first moved to Pottsville, and even though he could occasionally be a lot to handle, he was my best friend and hardly ever left my side. I had another dog as well, another rescue, a tiny white fluffy terrier called Casper who was a bit shyer and quieter, more independent.

"I wonder if I'm ever going to fit into this town, Jasper. Oh well, at least I have you and Casper. You guys always keep me company." I tossed the ball for Jasper to fetch again so that he could get some more exercise after being cooped up for much of the day. "And on my toes."

My own legs were aching so I stretched them. Maybe I was 'young' compared to the women Brenda had gathered for her new group—sorry, 'my' group— but I still wasn't as young as I used to be and day after day spent on my feet took its toll. I leaned back against the back porch and let the sun hit my face, basking in the last few dying rays of the day.

Jasper put his paws on my knees and started licking my face, which brought me back to life. "Okay, okay," I said, laughing as I tried to push him away. "You don't need to eat my face off."

I could tell he was getting hungry. "Okay!" I said, slapping my thighs before I climbed to my feet. "You've made your point. Let's get you some dinner."

I pulled the dry dog food out of the pantry and opened up a can of wet food while Jasper bounced up and down trying to get to it. "Wait! Sit down!" I commanded him in vain. I had to push the food out of his reach while I went and fetched the two dog bowls. "It's not just you that needs food," I called out to Jasper. "Your little sister needs some too!"

"Casper!" I called, banging the metal spoon against her dog bowl. "Time for dinner!"

Where was she? I'd assumed she'd just been sleeping somewhere when I'd got home. Unlike Jasper, who never left my side, Casper was a little more independent and could keep herself occupied for hours. She'd definitely make herself known when it was dinner time though!

"Casper!" I called again, louder this time. "Dinner is ready!"

Strange. She never failed to come when she heard the magic D word. Jasper was bouncing up and down at my feet, whimpering for me to dish the food out. "Yes, boy, just hold on a minute," I said as I opened the door to the yard and went back out.

Now I was getting worried.

Jasper obediently followed me, even though his food was on the other side of the door. "Jasper? Where is Casper?" I asked as I slowly walked out into the yard. Of course, he couldn't answer me. And he'd been with me all afternoon so he wouldn't know even if he could speak. I was just hoping he had some kind of doggie instinct that would allow him to magically know where Casper was, which would allow him to find her for me.

But he just looked up at me with big wide eyes as if to say, *don't ask me.* "Thanks, you're a big help," I said, my heart pounding a little faster as I did a survey of the yard. I could tell Jasper was getting worried as well; his tail dipped as he followed me around and he'd lost his trademark bounciness.

I held my breath a little as I approached the gate, fearing that I was going to find it swinging in the wind.

I never left the gate open. But it only takes one time, doesn't it? I almost didn't want to look. What if Casper had escaped, and I was responsible?

"Come on, Jasper, let's go check," I said, calling my trusty companion back from the other end of the yard where he was sniffing at something. I needed moral support.

I started to breathe again when I saw that the gate was still fastened tight. Thank goodness.

But if Casper hadn't escaped out the gate, where was she?

Jasper took off again and ran back to the other side of the yard, sniffing in the same spot again near the fence.

"What is it, Jasper?"

As I grew closer, I spotted I something right underneath the fence. "What are you sniffing at?"

Perhaps it was stupid of me, but I'd never checked the fence before. I'd bought the house 'as is' for a bargain (might have had something to do with the murder that had taken place there a year before I moved in) and hadn't yet bothered with any changes or renovations. On one side of the yard there was a forest, and a lake, and on the other two sides of the fence, grassland. The next closest neighbor was a hundred feet away. I'd thought the yard was secure enough to leave dogs in. Had I made a terrible, tragic mistake?

Underneath the fence was a small hole. It wasn't big enough for a big dog like Jasper to get through, but was enough for a tiny dog like Casper.

Oh no.

* * *

"Come on, Jasper, she couldn't have gone too far!" I said, grabbing his leash and my hat as we raced out the door. I wasn't entirely confident on that point, though. Casper might have had small legs but she was capable of trotting along at a great speed. And we were rapidly losing sunlight.

"Casper! Casper!" I called her name as loudly as I could, getting the occasional stare from passersby and even some people cooking dinner in their homes as we raced down the winding roads of Pottsville.

Jasper was full of energy the whole time and kept stopping, pulling on his leash, to sniff at the ground. Every time he did, I thought he must have gotten the scent of Casper. But every time I was bitterly disappointed.

And so was Jasper.

"I'm sorry, Jasper, you must think I am the most irresponsible pet owner of all time." I couldn't believe I had been so careless. I'd never considered that meek and mild, little, well-behaved Casper would even be capable of digging a hole and plotting her escape. Jasper? Yes. I could believe him doing it. That was one of the reasons I never let him out of my sight.

We'd just about lost all the daylight when we came upon a small clearing right near the woods. I let Jasper off his leash so that he could have a run and do his business, knowing with a heavy heart that we would have to turn back soon.

"Come on, Jasper, time to go," I said, calling him back. He had found something though, and was in no hurry to listen to me.

"What is it, Jasper? Have you found her?"

My heart actually stopped beating as I realized that Jasper was standing over something lying very still and limp. He let out a loud bark and then a howl that made me jump, but at least brought my heart back to life.

Oh, please don't be Casper, I begged, running over to see what he was barking and howling at.

"Jasper, is it..." I stopped and gasped.

But the thing he was standing in front of was long— over five feet long. Casper was less than a foot in length.

It wasn't a dog at all. It was a human being.

A dead human being.

Chapter 2

"Looks like we're going through a bit of a heat wave," Ryan Mathews said as he put on his sunglasses and grinned at me. "It's about time it warms up. It always brings the tourists down to the lake."

I wondered why Ryan cared about tourists, given his line of work as a police officer. It wasn't like he was in retail, or any industry that benefited from an increased population. Quite the opposite, actually. More people meant more trouble, didn't it?

"I hate to tell you this," Ryan said, surveying the fence and the hole where Casper had made her escape. "But you really should have walked around your fence to see if your dogs could escape."

"You don't hate having to tell me this," I said to him with my eyebrow raised. "Something tells me you like showing off when you're right." I looked at the fence and sighed. Jasper sat down by my feet and pouted. He had been all out of sorts ever since Casper had disappeared. So had I. But I was trying to keep it together on the outside and I was better at hiding my feelings than a border collie was.

"Well, maybe," Ryan had to concede. "But I am truly sorry that your dog is missing."

There was still a pit in my stomach from when I had found the body two days earlier. "So am I."

"Let's take another walk around the neighborhood," Ryan said, sounding hopeful. "I'll help you look for her." I wasn't about to turn down that offer, and not just because I needed help trying to find Casper. Ryan might be a bit younger than me—twelve years, give or take— but we were on a similar wavelength, and I had more in common with him than I did with the people my own age in Pottsville.

"So have you always lived in this town?" I asked as we took off across the neighborhood. The area of Pottsville I live in is out of the way of the main drag, surrounded by the lake and the forest, and the roads are long and windy and stretched out. I still hadn't gotten around to getting a car, so I went everywhere on foot. I have a tall, slim figure naturally—I was a dancer, once upon a time—and all this walking was doing my figure a lot of good.

Ryan shrugged noncommittally. "Kind of a long story," he said. "But long story short, yes, for most of my life, I have lived here." Huh. Sounded like an interesting story for another time. He let out a long sigh and a light laugh. "I suppose Pottsville feels like home to me. What about you, George? Does it feel like home to you yet?"

I frowned as I thought about the answer to his question while Jasper tugged at his leash. We weren't going fast enough for his liking. "Hmm, does this town feel like home?" I mused, looking at the lake on our right. If I could block out everything else and just concentrate on the idyllic scenes and fresh air of Pottsville, then yeah, it could feel like home to me.

But there were a few other issues stopping me from feeling warm and cozy toward the town just then. There was the small matter of my being on the outs of my own craft circle.

And the big issue of the dead body near the forest.

"Not fitting in?" Ryan asked sympathetically.

"I suppose it's just going to take a little bit of time."

I reached up and wiped a line of sweat from my forehead. Ryan was right; Pottsville was going through a sudden heat wave. Good news for the upcoming festival, I supposed, as we took a lazy walk around the block. But the Pottsville Arts and Crafts festival was something I was trying to put to the back of my mind.

That was next week's problem. I still had this week's problem to deal with. Well, make that multiple problems.

"Casper!" I called, but I felt as though I was just going through the motions at that point. Two days had passed and there hadn't been any word or sightings. There had been nothing.

Ryan was trying his best to be cheerful and positive, though. That was one of the things I liked about him. That and the fact that he was really cute. I also liked that he was a member of the local police force. I'd had an ulterior motive for asking him to come and look at my fence that morning. I was just choosing the right moment to broach a very delicate subject. "I'm sure she couldn't have gotten far. Someone probably spotted her and took her home," Ryan said, trying to reassure me.

"Yes. They probably want her for themselves, she is a very cute little dog," I said. I supposed that was the best eventuality, actually, given the other things that could have happened to her after her escape. "There aren't any coyotes around here, are there?" I asked, glancing toward the forest.

Ryan shot me a look of slight horror, like he couldn't figure out whether I was genuinely worried or just making a sick joke. It was the former, for the record. Sometimes I have a habit of jumping to the worst-case scenario, as a sort of defense mechanism. "George, don't go thinking like that," he scolded me, before adding, "And no, there aren't."

I let out a deep breath and kept walking, trying to make some casual conversation to lighten the mood.

A half-hour or so had passed. We weren't having much luck finding Casper, but it did give me the opportunity to try and build up the courage to ask my questions and to think of a way to make them sound as casual and off-the-cuff as possible. When we passed the forest, and that familiar clearing, the opportunity finally presented itself.

"It's shocking what happened here the other evening, isn't it?" I asked Ryan, acting like it was the first time I'd even thought about the dead body that I'd found there two nights earlier. I let out a strong shiver as if to emphasize my point.

Ryan stopped and glanced over at the clearing. "I'm surprised you're not more shaken up by that," Ryan commented. He frowned. "And I'm surprised this is the first time you are bringing this up."

"Takes more than a dead body to unsettle me," I

replied quickly. "Besides, I am getting used to them by now." I turned to walk away, pulling on Jasper's leash. He was happy to go back to the spot where he had made his gruesome discovery, but I was in no hurry to get up close again.

"I suppose you are," Ryan commented. For once, it had not been Ryan who was the first on the scene of the crime. He hadn't even been at the scene at all, as far as I could tell. Still, he had to know something, didn't he? "We should keep walking," he said quickly, trying to change the subject. I'd been anticipating that. I needed to tread carefully if I wanted to get any details out of him.

"I'm just wondering who the poor girl was," I said, my voice a careful mix of casualness and concern.

"George," he cautioned me gently. "I'm really not supposed to talk about this. Not even with you," he said before glancing around covertly. "I do take my job seriously. I can't discuss it."

"I know, I know," I replied. "But I was the one who found the body, wasn't I? Doesn't that earn me some kind of special privilege?"

"Hmm, not sure about that." He laughed lightly. "I know you think it does, though."

I let out a heavy sigh. "Come on, Ryan. I know I give off the image of a well adjusted, 'nothing fazes me' woman, but it has been keeping me up the last couple of nights." I stopped walking and looked into his eyes. A little difficult given the aviators he was wearing. All I could see was my reflection staring back at me. And I really did look worried. Boy, the town sure had done a number on the carefree, laissez faire George I had once been, hadn't it? I frowned and leaned in a little further, using the sunglasses as a mirror. Had I aged the last few weeks or what? Was that even possible? Was that a gray hair I could see looking back at me?

Ryan finally decided to take pity on me by letting a little tidbit slip, but not before he checked around us first to make sure that no one was listening to our conversation. "Look, so far we don't have an I.D on her."

Now that surprised me. I thought everyone in this town knew everyone else. I was surprised no one down at the station had recognized her. "So she had no identification on her? Nothing?"

Ryan shook his head and took Jasper's leash from me. I hadn't even realized it was slipping from my hands. "How will you figure out who she is? Ryan, you can't just leave her a nameless, faceless woman." I was a little horrified to learn that no one knew who the poor girl was. I was shivering for real now, even though it was almost ninety degrees outside.

"We're working on that," Ryan said as he tugged on Jasper's leash and kept walking, but he sounded a little uncomfortable as he said it. I wondered if that was because it wasn't really him who was working on anything. He wasn't a detective, he was just a uniformed officer, and I sometimes got the feeling he was a little sensitive about the subject. I wondered if maybe he just couldn't tell me anything because he wasn't high enough up the rankings to know, and he was a little embarrassed to admit to it.

We arrived back at my house without me even realizing it. Ryan passed me the leash and pet Jasper goodbye.

The search for Casper had remained fruitless. "Can you call me when you know something?" I asked Ryan as he left.

He sighed and opened his mouth, like he was about to say 'no,' but then closed it and nodded, waving goodbye.

* * *

I piled Jasper's bowl high with dog food and placed it on the ground for him to gobble up. He'd been getting almost a double share since Casper had gone missing, but I knew I couldn't keep indulging him like that for more than a day or two. I'd have to give him some extra exercise to make up for it. Not that he hadn't been getting plenty of walks. We'd basically done nothing but walk the neighborhood for days, putting up signs and calling Casper's name.

I jumped up on a stool at the kitchen counter while I watched Jasper engulf all his food in practically one mouthful. I wondered if he was missing having his little friend in the house. I'd gotten Casper only a few weeks after I'd rescued Jasper. Casper had originally belonged to a woman in Pottsville named Amanda, who had met a tragic end six weeks earlier, much like the poor woman near the woods. There had been no one else to take her dog in, and I hadn't minded adopting her. I'm a dog person, and I tend to like them more than I like humans. Well, that's not totally true. I just have an easier time bonding with them, I suppose. Especially in a new town.

Meanwhile, I hadn't heard another peep out of Ryan, and I could have sworn he was avoiding me. I started to suspect that he knew more than he was letting on and just didn't want to have to tell me, hence his conspicuous absence from my life.

But I soon found out that Ryan hadn't just been bluffing, or trying to blow me off. It seemed like the woman's identity truly was a mystery. "Hello, Brenda," I said breezily as I walked through the door of my craft shop, the smell of craft glue immediately hitting my nostrils.

Brenda glanced down at Jasper from behind the counter and shook her head. I don't know why she was acting so surprised—Jasper was practically a permanent fixture of the shop. And anyway, there was no way I was going to leave him alone until the fence situation was sorted out.

"Terrible thing, isn't it?" Brenda whispered while she curled the ribbon on a gift she was wrapping. I placed a water bowl down for Jasper in the back of the shop and stood up.

"You're talking about the body that was found down by the woods?" I frowned a little, approaching the subject cautiously. I knew that the discovery I'd made wasn't officially public knowledge, but in a small town, people talk. A lot.

And from the whispers I'd heard, no one seemed to know who the woman was. I narrowed my eyes and looked at Brenda. As the resident town gossip, she might just be the exception to the rule.

"You must have the dirt, though," I said, walking back toward the front of the shop. "Nothing escapes you, does it?"

Brenda shrugged. "On this one, I am in the dark as much as everyone else." She put the ribbon down and raised her eyebrows at me. "And I'm not sure I even want to get involved. Or talk about it."

Oh come on, she had brought the subject up! Who did she think she was fooling?

"Come on, Brenda, you usually know everything that goes on in Pottsville. You're really telling me you've got no idea who this woman was?"

I was really hoping that she did have some kind of scoop for me. That way I could stop bugging Ryan for information. That well had been pretty dry lately anyway.

Brenda picked her curling scissors back up and shook her head. "All I can say is that it's a tragic situation. And it's sullied the upcoming festival, hasn't it?"

I rolled my eyes. Trust Brenda to think of that. She curled a long row of ribbon and it bounced back in perfect little ringlets. "I think it's better not to gossip about these things."

Yeah, right.

I glanced down at Jasper, who'd come back to join us and seemed very interested in our conversation. "I think it's time we did some digging," I said to him, quietly. I saw his ears prick up. "Whoops. Not that type of digging. That type only gets all of us into trouble."

I glanced out the window. Actually, this type of digging would probably get us into trouble as well. But I was going to do it anyway, wasn't I?

* * *

Back in the safety—if not the privacy—of my large house with the tall glass windows, I got out my old trusty whiteboard and looked at the large white expanse before me. I was glad I hadn't gotten rid of it after Amanda's death and my subsequent investigation. An investigation that had almost gotten me killed.

Jasper sat in front of the board with a troubled look.

It was as though he knew that the reappearance of the whiteboard in our lives could only cause trouble.

"Don't worry," I said, pulling out my marker and taking off the cap. "That's not going to happen this time." Last time, the victim, Amanda, had been a crafter. And fellow crafters like myself were in the target line. "This crime has nothing to do with crafting," I said, frowning with my pen hovering over the blank board. "Hmm, I'm not quite sure what it has to do with." I looked down at Jasper. "Would be helpful if I at least had something to go off of, wouldn't it?"

Jasper gave me a look that pretty much said, *maybe it would be better if you just quit, then.*

And if that was the message he was trying to convey, then maybe he was right. If I went looking for trouble, I was probably going to find it.

But I'd found something already. The poor woman's body. I was already involved, whether I liked it or not. I looked down at Jasper. "Actually, you're the one who found her body. You dragged me into this, Jasper," I said playfully. "So you're involved as well. Now, don't go giving me any more of those pleading looks!"

I hadn't gotten a good look at the body lying on the ground; it had been dark out and I'd been so shocked.

I'd hardly wanted to linger and stare at the woman's face. But I knew that she was youngish, probably late twenties or early thirties, and she'd had long, medium brown hair. I made a brief sketch of her on the whiteboard. It was something to go off, at least. Better than nothing.

I tilted my head to the side and stared at the crude sketch. Was she a tourist? Or maybe she was just new to the area like me. Maybe I was no longer the new girl in town.

Well, she was dead now. So I supposed I still was the new girl in town. And I still felt like I was.

Besides, she had been fairly young. That didn't fit the profile of a Pottsville resident, most of whom were over fifty-five.

So what had she been doing in town?

I got the sudden feeling that I was being watched and put the cap back on the marker. I glanced around. I was starting to feel like Ryan now; always suspicious that someone was spying on me. In a glass house like mine, it would be very easy for people to see in, but I still hadn't bothered trying to find curtains or blinds that would fit all the windows (and cost a fortune). But I was far enough away from the road and my neighbors that people looking in wasn't really an issue. Unless someone was purposely spying on me.

I walked over to the slider and opened it, peering out into the yard. Maybe it had been an animal. Maybe Casper had returned! I suddenly felt a little hopeful and sprinted outside.

No such luck.

I let out a heavy sigh and closed the sliding glass doors again. It was a beautiful view outside, and a gorgeous day, but I had no enthusiasm to enjoy it.

I walked back to the almost blank whiteboard. I needed more. And standing around staring at a board in my house wasn't the way to get it. I picked up Jasper's leash. "I know you're not going to like this, Jasper, but we're returning to the scene of the crime."

* * *

Jasper whimpered and refused to budge from his spot on the pavement. "Jasper," I said, pulling on his leash. "Come on." It wasn't that Jasper was a badly behaved dog per se. He just hadn't been very well trained to follow commands. Lord knows who his previous owners had been or what they'd let him get away with. One of these days, I was going to have to take him to doggy training school. One of these days.

He was a smart dog, though, and there was no denying that. Border Collies usually were. He seemed to know exactly where we were headed and he wanted no part in any of it. I couldn't blame him. But it was starting to get dark and we needed to get to the crime scene before I was stumbling around, using a flashlight to look for clues.

Eventually he budged and started to follow me. Flustered from the exhaustion of trying to get him to walk with me, I flung my messy hair back and straightened up to see Brenda smirking at me across the street. "Thank you, Jasper. Now you've made me look even sillier in front of Brenda." Like I couldn't even control my own dog. And I knew that she wouldn't let me forget it the next time she saw me, either. She'd use it as further evidence that I couldn't be trusted to be in charge of anything.

Thankfully, Jasper behaved himself for the rest of the journey. I glanced over my shoulder before I entered the clearing again, just in case Brenda had decided to follow me. Honestly, I would not have put a stunt like that past her.

Actually, anyone could be watching us. Maybe even the killer. After all, don't killers often return to the scene of the crime?

I shivered, glad that I had Jasper with me for protection as well as moral support. He was already sniffing the ground while I tiptoed carefully through the clearing. I was wearing heels, as I always did, which maybe wasn't the best choice of footwear for most people. But to me, they are the most comfortable type.

It was getting too dark to see properly, so I had to pull my phone out to use it as a flashlight. The ground, usually slightly swampy for being so close to the lake, was considerably dryer after the heat wave we'd been going through, so my heels didn't sink into the earth.

I let Jasper off his leash and gave him free roam of the clearing. A little hesitant at first, he quickly caught the scent of something and went racing. Soon, he was yapping at something on the ground and I hurried, almost tripping in the dark, to catch up with him.

Jasper had his nose firmly buried in the ground and I used my flashlight to illuminate his muddy nose before I turned the light toward the ground.

"No way," I murmured as my flashlight picked up the glint of silver. I reached down and picked up the thin piece of jewelry.

A bracelet with the letter E on it.

I turned it over and admired it in my hands. It looked hand-crafted, even though it was clearly made of fine silver. Whoever had made it had considerable skill. It made me feel a little embarrassed about my own handmade bracelets.

Did it belong to the victim? I couldn't shake the feeling that it did. But, if that was the case, how had the cops missed it? I knew they weren't the most cutting edge police force in existence, but this did seem like a glaring oversight.

"I wonder if she made this herself," I murmured to Jasper, who was already off again, scratching and sniffing in another spot of earth. I slipped the bracelet into my pocket, knowing I should call the police but wondering, at the same time, if that was really the wisest thing to do.

I heard a snapping sound like footsteps on a twig and jumped up, calling Jasper to come quick. If there was someone there, I didn't want to find out who it was.

Jasper was the perfect dog on the walk home. He seemed to sense, like an instinct, that I was not in the mood to be held up and he needed to behave himself.

Now I had something else to add to the white board. I taped the bracelet to it and stood back.

A bracelet. An E. And a dead woman.

And where was Casper? It had been three nights and she still hadn't returned.

I couldn't shake the feeling that the two things were linked, tied up with each other. Don't ask me how, it was just a hunch. Instinct.

Chapter 3

The Pottsville heat wave had hit its fourth consecutive day without the weather breaking and it had lent a calm, relaxed feeling to the town. The summery weather seemed to have cast a spell and people were traipsing around town in long flowing skirts and sunglasses like they were in a Vogue shoot, laughing and ordering iced coffees.

Of course, there was one resident in Pottsville you could always rely on to not have a good time.

Brenda greeted me at the door of the craft shop with her arms folded. *Great,* I thought. *I wonder what I have done now.* It was funny, given that I was the owner of the shop and ostensibly the boss, that I always felt like Brenda was in charge of me. But just try telling her that. Just try telling Brenda anything she didn't want to hear, and good luck getting her to listen to it.

"I had to go down to the town hall and register us this morning," Brenda said, before placing her mouth in a firm line.

"Register us for what?" I asked. "Improv classes?" She could do with some lightening up. I took a sip of my iced latte and waited for her unamused response.

"Haha. Very funny."

"I try my best."

"We have to register the store—and ourselves—if we are to have a stall at the Pottsville Arts and Crafts Festival this weekend," she said.

I wanted to groan. Not the Arts and Crafts Festival again. Or, as one could call it, 'Brenda's sole reason to live.'

"I thought we just turned up on the day with a fold-out table and started selling stuff," I said with a shrug.

"No," Brenda returned angrily. "Georgina, do you have any idea how anything works?" she asked, appalled. "You can't just turn up!" She shook her head. "If it wasn't for me, we might have missed out on participating at all."

Heaven forbid. I swallowed my pride, though. "Thank you, Brenda." That was what she wanted from me, wasn't it? A thank you? From the look on her face, maybe she wanted me to grovel at her feet.

"And you've sorted out what you are bringing to the festival, haven't you?" Brenda asked as I tried to push past her to get to the back of the shop. My escape. "I don't want you embarrassing us!" Brenda called.

* * *

I hid in the back of the shop when one of my least favorite customers—and Brenda's apparent best friend, a woman named Lisa Riemer with short cropped brown hair—came in for their daily gossip sessions. She never, or rarely, ever purchased anything so it was better if I just stayed out of the way. Lisa was actually one of the 'younger' women in the town—she was probably only 38 or so—but like most of the woman in Brenda's gang, she acted like she was already heading toward old age. Even though she was interested in a lot of arts and crafts, her main passion was knitting. When she did actually spend money in the store, it was on yarn. But on this day, she had come in just to gab.

I could overhear fragments of their conversation. "I intend to take no prisoners," Lisa stated firmly. "I will do whatever it takes this year, don't you worry about that."

I had no idea what she was talking about but it sounded slightly scary. I busied myself by hanging my bracelets—large, bold, and colorful with heavy beads—onto a display case. Some of them had price tags on them, as I'd intended to sell them at the festival, but now I wasn't so sure that was the brightest idea. Maybe Brenda was right. Maybe they'd only embarrass us. Maybe I needed to come up with something better before the weekend.

I heard the front door open thanks to the bell over the top of it that always jingled when we had a new customer. Assuming that Brenda would take care of greeting our new patron, I stayed focused on my bracelets. Maybe the display stand wasn't the right place for them. Maybe the trash was.

The heavy footsteps of our new customer approached me and I lifted my head, surprised, but ready to ask them if I could be of any help.

"No, thanks, just browsing," Ryan said with an easy grin as he took his police cap off and cradled it in his hands.

I was pleasantly surprised to see him and couldn't hide my smile as I stood in front of the display stand, trying to hide it.

"Long time no see," I said as I raised my eyebrows.

He grinned back at me. "I've been busy," he said,

sounding genuinely apologetic. "I came by to tell you something, actually. As long as you keep it between the two of us," he said, lowering his voice.

"You'd better keep your voice low unless you want Brenda to overhear you," I pointed out. "I can keep a secret. She can't."

Plus, Lisa was still buzzing around. She was in second place, only behind Brenda, for the title of town gossip.

Ryan turned around and noticed both women staring at him with silent expressions and their mouths wide open. "Erm, actually," Ryan said. "Maybe it's better if we go outside."

"Agreed."

Outside may have been slightly more private, but the sun was beating down, almost causing me to break out in a sweat. Not exactly the way I wanted Ryan to see me.

"The bracelet was actually helpful," Ryan commented.

"I can't believe your detectives missed it."

After much deliberation, I had delivered the bracelet to the Pottsville police station and told them where I'd found it. I hadn't actually expected to be kept in the loop, however, so Ryan's presence, and his being forthcoming with details, caught me a little off guard.

Ryan nodded. "That was strange, actually." He shrugged. "I suppose that sometimes, these things just happen though. Things get missed."

I wondered if things would get missed if they had better detectives on the force. Detectives, for example, like Ryan. Maybe he should use this as an opportunity for promotion. I thought that I might bring that up with him later. He had clearly come to see me for more serious business than that.

I kept my voice quiet and turned my head away from the front of the shop in case Brenda could read lips. I wouldn't have been surprised, actually. "So, you know who she is now?"

Ryan nodded. "The detectives did some digging. Her name was Erika. Erika Joyce. She was thirty-three years old." He stopped when the door to the shop swung open and Lisa came swanning out, raising her eyebrows at the two of us. Was anywhere safe? We both waited until she was out of earshot before we continued our conversation.

"How did she die?" I asked. "She was killed, wasn't

she?"

Ryan nodded, but barely perceptively.

"The only reason I'm delivering this information to you rather than the detectives on the case is because of my personal connection to you."

Personal connection.

"Well, I'm glad," I said. "The whole thing has been weighing heavily on me. I only hope we...I mean, your detectives, can find out what happened to her now."

"Actually, I was hoping that you might be able to help me," Ryan commented.

"More than I already have?" I raised an eyebrow. "You'll have to put me on the payroll soon."

Ryan let out a soft laugh. "Well, it's more due to your area of expertise."

I had to wonder what that might be, exactly. "Well, I'm an expert in a lot of things..."

"Arts and crafts," Ryan said, cutting in. Oh. That area of expertise. "Apparently, Erika was in town for the Pottsville Arts and Crafts Festival."

"The arts and crafts festival?" I asked, confused. "But that's not until next weekend." Believe me, I was very aware of the dates, no thanks to Brenda and the constant pressure to perform. She had us officially registered, and there was no way that she had the dates wrong. "No one has arrived for that yet. I doubt people will really start pouring in until Friday afternoon."

Ryan frowned. "She got the dates mixed up, I suppose. That, or she was just desperate to spend the extra time in Pottsville."

Huh. I wondered which was the more likely. Probably that she got the dates wrong.

"Well, now I feel extra bad," I murmured. "I didn't know that she was a crafter..." Well, I hadn't known anything about her, had I? But now it was really hitting too close to home.

"It's not like you had anything to do with it, George." Ryan looked around carefully again. "Just keep an eye out, I suppose. Be careful. And if you hear anything, let me know." He placed his police hat back on. "And I mean it. Be careful."

* * *

I did my very best to keep my focus on work for the

rest of the day, even managing to let Brenda's not-very-carefully disguised barbs get to me as I tidied store, ordered new stock, and tried to figure out what I was going to try and sell at the Arts and Crafts Festival.

As I walked home, Ryan's words kept echoing in my head, even more than when I was dealing with customers or trying to drown Brenda out. I kept thinking that he knew more than he was letting on. His words didn't just seem like a caution. They seemed like a warning.

But a warning of what?

What was I supposed to do? Act suspicious of everyone I interacted with? Well, actually, that probably wasn't such a bad idea. I stroked Jasper's head while he lay happily at my feet. After all, I didn't know anyone in this town. Not really. Not well enough to really trust them. There was only one person in town I could trust, and that person wasn't even a person. He was a dog.

And Jasper, clever as he was, seemed to pick up that something was wrong. I'd promised him that this time was different, that this time, crafting had nothing to do with the murder.

But it did. It might have everything to do with

crafting. Maybe Ryan's warning just meant, *back off. You remember what happened last time. You almost ended up with a broken neck and a smashed head. You almost ended up six feet under.*

I glanced over at the whiteboard. The bracelet with the E that I'd taped up had been replaced by a careful sketching of the very same thing.

She was a talented crafter, that was for sure. No wonder she'd been drawn to the arts and crafts festival. Her carefully crafted bracelet put mine to shame. I wasn't glad that she was dead, but I was glad that I wouldn't have to go up against her.

Still, none of it made any sense to me. All I had next to the drawing of her body and her bracelet was a giant question mark.

"Why did she arrive in town so early, Jasper?" I asked, petting his head while he gobbled up his food later that night. "And who in this town could possibly have a motive for killing her?"

Chapter 4

I'd gotten flack for my handmade posters before, but this one served a noble purpose and I was hoping no one would actually be rude enough to run their mouth.

Wishful thinking.

"Much loved pet. Reward offered."

Underneath the dark font, printed on the bright yellow paper, was a picture of Casper. This was the second lot of posters I'd put up. The first had been on plain white paper so I was hoping the new, bright ones might attract more attention and that my beloved and much missed pet might finally be returned to me. She wasn't at the shelter, so I could only assume that someone was holding on to her because they wanted her for themselves. I couldn't blame them, really. She was a cute, sweet dog, and anyone would be lucky to have her. I hadn't been her adopted mom for long and part of me wondered if I had any right to even ask for her back.

More than anything I just wanted to know that she was okay. Even if she was in a new home. Of course, I wanted her home as well. But the most important thing was to know that she was safe and in a good home.

"These look terrible," Brenda commented with her mouth pursed as she hung another sign on a street post. "And you should be specifying exactly what the reward is."

I let out a heavy sigh. At least she was helping me hang up the signs. I couldn't really complain, could I?

Could I?

"I want to attract genuine callers, not people who are only interested in the reward money."

"You mean you don't have much money to offer them," Brenda said sharply as she reached another street sign and taped up another bright yellow flyer.

She was kind of right but I wasn't about to admit it. I didn't have much to offer, but what little I did have, I was going to give to whoever returned Casper to me. I'd only had her for a little while but she was already part of the family, and I wasn't about to go cheap on the reward. It's just that other people might think the amount was cheap. Those who actually had money. And there were plenty of wealthy people in Pottsville. I just wasn't one of them.

"Have you ever thought of looking at Amanda's?" Brenda asked quietly.

I looked at her in surprise and lifted up my sunglasses so I could get a better look at her. "No, actually. Should I do that?" The thought of going back to Amanda's house seemed a little sick to me. I hadn't been there since she'd died. And I didn't much like the thought of turning up there.

Brenda shrugged a little and put up another flyer. "Well, Casper was Amanda's dog. Maybe she went home."

The thought made me a little sad. Maybe Casper really had been missing her old home so much that as soon as she'd escaped, that was the first place she'd ran to. Maybe she still considered that her 'home.' As much as that saddened me, it also filled me with a little hope. "Thanks, Brenda," I said, patting her on the shoulder. "You've actually proved helpful for once."

"Hey," she said, offended. But I had already taken off. I had a clue, a lead, as to the whereabouts of Casper, and I wasn't about to waste any time following it up.

* * *

Amanda's house was just like I remembered it. Well, more or less. It was still a cute little cottage and it still had a rose garden in front, but now the lawn was overgrown and the rose garden was littered with weeds. A 'for sale' sign hung out front. Brenda lived right across the street and hadn't been shy about gossiping over the fact that the real estate agent was having one heck of a time selling the place. I suppose not many people wanted to live in a house where a woman had been murdered. I am one of the special ones. Or, is that one of the stupid ones?

I steeled myself and entered the gate and walked around the property, calling Casper's name. I searched all through the garden, the backyard, and even stuck my face up against the window to peer in. But it was all in vain.

No sign of Casper. I sat down on the stoop, defeated. I'd really thought that Brenda might have been onto something. It did make sense that Casper would come back to Amanda's cottage. But there wasn't any sign that a dog had been there recently. No fresh holes in the earth, no doggie droppings on the lawn. She hadn't been there.

I leaned forward, my head resting in my hands, and sighed loudly. I felt as though I'd let Casper down so badly. Every day that passed made it seem less and less likely that she was ever going to come back to us. I was running out of leads and I felt so sad that I was almost on the verge of tears. I was glad for the setting sun, just in case anyone spotted me. I didn't want people to see me cry.

I saw Brenda's front door open and a figure step outside and head toward me. *Oh great,* I thought. *The last person I want to see me in this condition is Brenda.*

But after a few seconds, I realized that it wasn't her at all. It was her husband, Tom. He was a pleasant looking man in his mid-fifties with a thick head of hair and a fit figure. I'd only met him the one time when he'd dropped by the shop to bring Brenda's lunch to her. She always brought a packed lunch as she said that paying for a lunch was the same as being robbed.

Well, it looked like Tom had stayed true to character and brought me something to eat.

"I saw you sitting out here," he said, placing a tray of cookies and some iced tea down. "Well, Brenda did, but her shows are on now and she didn't want to miss them."

"Thank you," I said, hoping that the last sign of my tears were gone.

"You're sad about your dog, 'ey?" Tom asked in a warm, kind voice. "Don't worry, George. I'm sure she'll turn up soon."

I was surprised that Brenda was married to such a nice man. But, I supposed opposites did attract.

"I'm sure you're right," I said decisively, before I took a long gulp of iced tea. I hadn't realized how parched I was. The heat wave had really sapped my strength. "I've just got to keep positive about this whole thing. Thank you, Tom." I grinned at him and noticed that in spite of his warm smile, he also looked like he'd had a rough day. And I could tell from the look of his tired, weathered hands that he was a hard worker.

"Long day?" I asked.

Tom nodded. "Been battling some particularly strong killer weeds down at the old Parson's place today." He shook his head and grinned. "Thrills of being a freelance gardener, I suppose."

I was a little surprised to hear that was Tom's profession. "You're a gardener?"

"Yep, I have been for nearly thirty years." He took a

cookie off the tray and took a bite. "I was actually working at the Pink Flamingo Lodge where that young woman was staying. Or, trying to stay." He shook his head. "I could never quite tell what was going on. All I knew was I heard an awful argument."

I frowned, trying to figure out what he was saying. Young woman? I let out a little gasp as I realized who he might be talking about. "You mean Erika?" I whispered, though I wasn't quite sure why I was keeping my voice so slow. It just didn't feel right to speak about it in loud tones. "The woman who was killed four nights ago?"

Tom nodded. "That's the one. Terrible thing, wasn't it?" He stopped eating his cookie and stared off into the distance. "I was pruning their hedges that very day. I saw her."

Now I was beginning to catch up. I couldn't believe that Brenda hadn't told me anything about this.

"Wait, hang on," I said, confused. "You heard Erika having a fight with the manager of the Pink Flamingo Lodge?"

Tom nodded again, but he stood up and collected the tray. "It's probably not good manners to discuss these sorts of things though, is it?" It seemed like he couldn't get away quick enough as he collected the cup and tray and started to back away. "Good night, George. I really should be getting back to Brenda."

I wondered if he'd gone to the police with this info. I glanced over at their house. I could make out Brenda in the front room on her sofa, presumably watching some TV show. Surely he must have shared it with Brenda at the very least. What reason did she have to keep it all so quiet and close to her chest when she usually couldn't stop herself from spewing gossip all over town?

Just how much did Brenda actually know?

And why was she so intent on keeping it to herself? Just who was she protecting?

I didn't want to let Tom get away so quickly, even though there seemed to be a magnet attached to his back pulling him toward the house.

"So she was arguing with the manager the day that she died?" I again asked Tom, who was still trying to escape. I could see Brenda keeping a careful eye on us through he window.

Tom made a face like he really didn't want to say anymore but reluctantly continued. "They said they were double-booked and she'd have to find accommodations elsewhere. And she wasn't too happy about it either."

"Huh. No room at the inn, hey?"

Tom shrugged and looked back over his shoulder.

So once she'd been turned away, where did Erika go?

I had to find out. I stood and dusted off the crumbs that had collected on my lap. "Thanks for the refreshments, Tom," I said with a bright smile. But I had far more to thank him for than just cookies and iced tea.

"No problem," he said, but his teeth seemed a little gritted. "And good luck finding your dog, George."

* * *

"Brandi!" I said, getting up to my feet. I threw the celeb mag I'd been reading to the side and took off my reading glasses. "Well. You are a breath of fresh air around here, aren't you? I thought you were at college?"

She grinned back at me, her long blonde curls

cascading over her shoulders. "I'm on summer break," she said, glancing around the store. "Is my aunt in by any chance?"

You would never guess that this bright, young woman was related to Brenda.

I glanced up at the clock. "She'll be starting at ten o'clock," I said. "Feel free to wait for her, though. I could use some young company around here."

Brandi giggled. "I know what you mean," she said with a little sigh. "I can't believe I'm choosing to spend my vacation in Pottsville. Before I went to college, all I wanted was to get away from this place. I've always sworn I wouldn't come back once I'd escaped. Yet here I am." She grabbed an apple from her tote bag and started to munch on it. "This place is cool though," she said, glancing around. "Can't believe my aunt works here."

I still couldn't believe Brenda was her aunt. I had to assume she was related to Tom by blood, not Brenda herself, but it seemed impolite to ask. I'd only met Brandi once before when she'd been in town for a visit, but we'd hit it off right away. I don't have any children of my own, but I always imagined that if I had a daughter, she would be like Brandi. She certainly looked more like me than she did Brenda, with her fair skin and tall, slim figure.

Speak of the devil.

Brenda pushed through the doors and looked startled for a moment when she saw Brandi standing there.

"Hello, Auntie!" Brandi said brightly, reaching out to give her aunt a hug. She towered over Brenda, who looked like a tiny mouse in her arms.

"I thought you were spending your break in the city?" Brenda seemed confused.

"What, you're not pleased to see me?" Brandi asked in mock offense. I could tell she was like me in that she found Brenda incredibly easy to wind up and sometimes couldn't help herself by teasing her. But Brandi was sweet and never meant any real harm.

"Of course I am," Brenda said quickly, any hint of sarcasm going right over her head, as usual. "I'm surprised, that's all. Are you in town for the festival?"

Brandi shot me a look. "Ah, yes," she said to me with a knowing little grin. "The famous Pottsville Arts and Crafts festival. Your first one, right, George? I hope you know what you're in for!"

I gulped a little, catching sight of my jewelry out of the corner of my eye. Did I know what I was in for?

Brenda cleared her throat. "Why don't you go and make yourself at home at my house?" she said to Brandi. "Tom will be happy to see you."

Brandi raised her eyebrow at me again. "Okay, okay. I can see when I'm not wanted," she said with another laugh. "I'll get out of your hair!"

With Brandi gone, it was just Brenda and I. Wonderful. You could feel the tension between us—most of it coming from my direction.

I wasn't trusting her much in that moment. Well, I never entirely trusted her, but right then my defenses were really up. I still couldn't figure out why she'd been playing so innocent about the knowledge of Erika's murder when she practically had firsthand knowledge. Something was up.

"Brandi was right, I hope you know what you're in for," Brenda said, following me to the back of the store where my display of bracelets still stood.

Brenda looked at my bracelets with disdain. "Surely you're going to showcase something a bit more skilled than those ratty pieces of jewelry, Georgina. I thought I had warned you already. They are garbage."

Boy. Tell me how you really feel, why don't you?

"I don't consider them ratty," I said, holding one particularly bright pink-beaded one—flamingo pink, really—up to the light. "I think they are some of my best work."

Brenda shook her head. "We are supposed to be representing the shop, not embarrassing it," she grumbled. She pursed her lips together and looked thoughtful for a moment before she spoke like she'd just come up with the grandest idea of all time. "Maybe I should set up my own separate stall."

Oh, why don't you do just that then, I thought. Maybe I could take off for the weekend. Take a vacation and get away from the chaos and hundreds of tourists that were about to descend on the town. Avoid the festival all together.

But what about Erika? I still felt responsible for finding out what happened to her. I couldn't take off, not now. I let out a heavy sigh while Brenda swayed back to the front of the shop. I still didn't know if I was off the hook. Was she going to set up her own separate stall or not? Don't leave me in suspense!

The doorbell jingled and I saw that it was Ryan. Usually I was thrilled to see him but in this instance I ducked, hoping he wouldn't see me.

No luck there. With my height, ducking doesn't work so well.

"Have you heard anything about Casper yet?" Ryan asked me.

I shook my head sadly. "Nothing. I've been leaving a bowl of food out for her every night, just in case she comes back." I tried to hide the bracelets while Ryan was distracted. "But she never does. And Jasper just ends up eating it in the morning."

Ryan looked down at Jasper. "He does look like he's put on a few pounds," he teased.

I batted at him. "Don't! He's a little sensitive about his weight."

Ryan laughed and then looked back up just as I was trying to push the bracelets out of the way behind the curtain. I'd been caught.

"What are those? Did you make them?" Ryan nosily tried to take a look.

"Oh, don't look at these," I said, pushing the bracelets out of the way. "They aren't quite ready for public eyes yet."

Ryan still tried to push past to get a look at them.

"When will they be ready for these so-called public eyes?" he asked with a grin. "I can't see anything wrong with them."

"I'm not sure they will ever be ready, actually," I said, shoving them behind a curtain. "And certainly not by Saturday."

I shook my head. What was I doing letting Brenda get into my head like that? She was hardly the go-to woman for style and fashion anyway, with her long beige tunics. She probably just hated my jewelry because they contained actual colors, not just grays and beiges.

Ryan smiled. "Well, I think they're great. And I think they are going to make a killing this weekend."

I grinned back at him. "Thank you, Ryan. That was just the sort of confidence boost I needed right now."

Pottsville Arts and Crafts Festival, here we come...

Whether I liked it or not.

Chapter 5

"Ow!" I said, rubbing my shoulder after a particularly hard bump. I wanted to add, 'watch where you're going,' but then I remembered that we were in a small town, not a big city, and I was supposed to be welcoming these newcomers, not causing them to run away.

You could hardly walk down the street without bumping shoulders with someone, or getting knocked down. On a normal day in Pottsville, I could let Jasper off his leash and he would happily walk down the relatively empty main street of Pottsville without any trouble. If I let him free now, he would get lost. Or trampled.

Jasper whined and looked up at me as if to ask, *make all these people go away.*

"I know, Jasper, there are suddenly too many people in this town." I shrugged. There was little I could do about it, unfortunately. I wished I could make them all disappear with a snap of my fingers, but there was no way to explain to Jasper that it just wasn't possible.

I ducked into a cafe and asked the waitress if it was all right for Jasper and I to sit outside, and if we could have a bowl of water for him. She replied that it was fine and Jasper and I grabbed the last available table in the outside setting.

I'd moved to Pottsville for the peace and quiet and the idyllic lifestyle. Ha. It was as busy and as bustling as a city on that particular day. And on any other day... Well, it might have been a bit emptier, but so far, life in Pottsville had been anything but idyllic. Or peaceful.

Now the town was overflowing with tourists. "This is going to make our investigation a little more difficult, Jasper." So many people, so many suspects.

Once I'd finished my latte and Jasper had lapped up every drop of his water, it was time for us to leave, refreshed and ready to return to the fray.

And our first port of call?

The last place that Erika Joyce had been spotted alive.

* * *

"Here we are, Jasper, the Pink Flamingo Lodge."

The place that Erika had apparently been staying at, before her exile from the place, and her death soon after.

The Pink Flamingo Lodge was sort of a cross between a motel and a B&B. And it lived up to its name—it was painted bright flamingo pink, the same color as my best bracelet. It had fake potted palm trees out front and a weird fake 'tropical' vibe to it, which made it look kind of tacky in Pottsville, the home of forests and lakes. Far from tropical, despite the strange heat wave we were experiencing. The lodge, from the looks of it, had about twenty rooms or so, and during the quiet seasons, probably only used about a quarter of them at any one time. But this wasn't one of the quiet seasons. It was always full during the summer, even if there wasn't an arts and crafts festival.

I tied Jasper out of sight of the reception area. He wasn't going to help the ruse I was about to put on. With a dog in tow, I wouldn't be able to put on the act of someone who had just arrived in town, and I doubted they allowed dogs.

I could see the receptionist through the window as I approached. She looked like a no-nonsense type with her glasses and stern look, and my heart sunk a little as I realized this might not be as easy as I'd thought.

"Hi there," I said, putting my best innocent, tourist voice on. "I was wondering if you had any rooms available."

"Ha, fat chance." This lady did not beat around the bush. "We're double-booked, triple-booked. We've got a hundred names and numbers in the queue to call up if there are any cancellations before we even get to you. You still want to put your name down?"

I shrugged a little and decided to play along. "Sure, why not," I said, reaching for the pen the woman handed me, while she shook her head in disbelief.

She took the piece of paper with my name on ir and placed it carelessly on top of a large pile.

"Hey," I said, lowering my voice. "This probably isn't true, and I'm sure that you don't know anything about it, but..." I let out a forced laugh of disbelief. "Some people were saying that this is where that girl was staying before she was killed." I whispered the last bit and gave her an exaggerated look of shock.

She raised her eyebrows and leaned closer to me. "That's right," she said with a proud grin. Aha, so she was willing to talk about it then; she seemed like she was practically salivating at the prospect of discussing it.

I took her lead. "Wow," I said, impressed. "This place should gain some notoriety then."

It looked like the thought pleased her. "She only stayed one night though, before we had to kick her out."

"Why did you have to kick her out?" I asked. "Did the two of you have a fight?"

Suddenly her face changed. She got the same look Tom had when I'd started asking too many questions. "Of course not," she replied, closing up.

I decided to change track. "Erika was a crafter, wasn't she?"

The receptionist nodded a little uncertainly. "That's right. She was in town for the festival, only she'd mixed up her dates."

I frowned. "How could she have gotten it wrong by a week?"

The woman shrugged. "Said she'd gotten an email— a fake one, I suppose—with the dates wrong. She was very upset by it."

So that's why Erika had been in town so early. Interesting.

But who had sent her the email?

I wanted to ask more questions but the woman had lost her patience with me. "You'll have to move along," she said. "I've got a full house here and guests to tend to."

* * *

"Someone had to have sent that email to her," I said to Jasper as we made our way quickly from the Pink Flamingo. He had to break into a bit of a run to keep up with me. "Someone who wanted Erika to miss the craft festival."

I slowed down while we rounded a bend. It had to have been someone I knew, right? After all, I knew all the crafters in town. They might not have wanted to know me, but they did. They came to my shop. They sat in my craft circle. The thought that one of them could set Erika up like that—and maybe even kill her—made my blood run cold.

But could it really be one of the local crafters? Was it someone in my craft circle?

I had to stop and take a deep breath. It was too hot to be out and about, running in heels. Jasper was also panting. "Sorry, boy," I said. "We're a little far from home." I stopped as I saw a front door open across the street and watched as Brenda spilled out of it. "Uh oh," I said, gently pulling Jasper behind a bush. "Stay low and quiet."

It wasn't her house so it had to belong to one of her dear friends. Just as she was leaving, I caught sight of Lisa Riemer waving good-bye through the window.

"Aha!" I whispered to Jasper. "A local crafter who would do whatever it takes," I murmured, recalling the fragments of her conversation I had overheard the other day. But whatever it took to do what, exactly?

I needed to find out.

"Come on, it's your time to shine, Jasper," I said, straightening up. "I'm going to need all your help with this one!"

I knocked on the door and grinned when Lisa opened it. "Hi, Lisa! I don't suppose I can trouble you for a bowl of water for this little guy, can I?" I said, pulling an apologetic face. "He's been racing around and gotten too thirsty. You know this heat we've been having really takes a toll on our animals."

People had a hard time saying no to a dog. She was hardly going to let Jasper suffer from dehydration, was she?

"Sure," she said, "Come on in."

She led Jasper and I to the kitchen and ran the tap to fill an old plastic bowl. But when it came to Jasper's time to shine, he suddenly got stage fright and refused to take even a sip. He sat down on his hind legs and just stared at the bowl.

"Come on, Jasper," I whispered. "Drink!" Great. This was not the time to embarrass me. Or break my cover.

But he just pouted at me and shook his head a little bit.

I straightened up and looked at Lisa, forcing a little laugh. "Not sure what's wrong with him. He was panting a few minutes ago. Maybe he just needs a little time to feel comfortable in a new place."

Lisa told me not to worry about it, that he could stay there for a minute. But still, he just sat and stared at the water, turning his nose up at it like it was poisonous.

"You're free to stay for some tea or coffee," Lisa said. "Maybe Jasper will feel more like drinking in a little while," she said knowingly. Like she suspected that my asking for the water bowl was just a ruse to get into her house. What reason did she have to be suspicious of me, though? Unless she had something to hide.

I nodded. "That sounds nice. Thank you. Do you have any peppermint tea? It will be refreshing on a hot day like this."

I offered to put the kettle on in the kitchen, saying that I could keep an eye on Jasper that way and that Lisa should relax in the living room. She seemed happy to agree, happy to put her feet up, and I breathed a sigh of relief once she had retreated from the kitchen.

"What is wrong with you, Jasper?" I asked quietly. "You've got some lovely fresh water there." I shook my head and looked at him in mock disappointment. "I thought you would make a better undercover detective than this, to be honest."

He just pouted at me in return. "Okay, suit yourself," I said, turning back to the cabinets. I noticed, as I pulled them out, that most of Lisa's mugs and cups were handmade. Hmm, she had quite a skill about her as well. I was starting to wonder if I really was the least skilled crafter in town. Even though I had a passion for crafting, for making things, I'd always considered it more of a fun hobby than anything else. It was clear that some of the people in the town—some of those people being Brenda and Lisa—took it very seriously.

I returned to the living room, awkwardly carrying a tray with a hot teapot and two mugs on top, clattering on the top of two saucers.

Lisa cast me a sharp look up over the top of her knitting needles. "Are you all right with that?" she asked, skeptical.

It always struck me as strange to find her knitting because she looked too young to be so passionate about something you usually associate with retirees. Especially with the cat-eyed glasses she was wearing. The whole thing aged her about thirty years.

I sat the tray down and did a little bow. "Made it!" I said over-enthusiastically, wondering if she was buying any of this. Lisa and I weren't exactly friends. She had to have found it strange that I would just drop by, even if under the pretense of asking for water for my dog.

I poured Lisa a cup of tea. Over-poured it actually, and it spilled over the top of the mug. "Shoot," I said, trying to clean it up using a box of Kleenex sitting on her coffee table.

"Don't worry about it," Lisa said with a heavy sigh. Which meant "do worry about it, just stop making it worse." The tea sank into her white tablecloth, making it look kind of aged. I wondered if she liked antiques.

We sat there in awkward silence for a few minutes. I had run out of small talk—if I'd ever had any in the first place. Lisa always made me feel uneasy, in the same way Brenda did. They were both lacking the humor gene and it made any casual conversation with them hard work, unless I was purposefully trying to wind them up. Which in this case, I wasn't.

Well, I might as well cut straight to the chase.

"Lisa," I said. "Where were you on Friday evening?"

She lowered her knitting needles. "Why do you ask?" She glared at me with her tiny black eyes. Were they actually black? I leaned forward to get a closer look. Surely not. They must simply be dark brown. But they sure looked black in that moment.

I took a sip of peppermint tea, bracing myself. "Just wondering," I replied casually. Or at least I tried to say it casually. My actual tone betrayed me, and Lisa was having none of it. She might not have much of a sense of humor but she was sharp. She hadn't been buying my act since the second I knocked on her door.

"You're talking about the night that body was found?" Lisa slammed the needles onto the table beside her. "How dare you?"

Wow. I hadn't meant to illicit such a strong reaction from her. What did she have to hide? I placed my mug back down on the table a little too hard and it spilled over the top again. She glared down at the puddle. I sure as heck wasn't making a new friend on this day, was I?

But her anger told me something.

I was starting to form a little theory in my mind. If Tom had witnessed the fight, or whatever it had been, and Brenda had kept whatever she knew to herself, could it be because she was trying to protect her good friend? Her best friend, Lisa Riemer. She had her guard up now, but I wasn't about to back off. I was like a dog with a bone.

I decided to try a little bluff to see if I could get her to slip up and admit to something. She was sharp, sure, but just how sharp was she?

I kept my voice steady as I stared into her eyes. I tried to keep my tone light though, like this was a causal thought I'd just had. "It's just that someone told me that they saw you at the Pink Flamingo Lodge that night."

"Oh, someone told you something?" Lisa said

mockingly, before she crossed her arms, furious. "What a perfectly fine excuse to come into someone's home and accuse them of something!"

I kept my cool. "I haven't accused you of anything," I pointed out. "I was simply asking where you were on Friday night."

Lisa stood up and started picking up the still full tea mugs and the teapot. She almost spilled the tea herself, which I would have found a little funny. She saw the look of amusement on my face and glared at me. I straightened my face quickly.

She looked seriously offended. "I thought you came here because you were feeling a bit lonely and wanted to visit me. That you just used your dog being thirsty as an excuse to knock on my door. Because you have no friends in this town and you wanted to make one."

Now it was my turn to be grossly offended. I wasn't that pathetic that I'd need to use my dog as an excuse to make friends. I just used him as an excuse to snoop on people. That was far better.

I stood up and called Jasper's name. "I'm sorry to have bothered you," I said, grabbing Jasper's leash and heading for the door.

"You certainly did that," Lisa replied, practically

pushing us out the front door. "And don't think that you are welcome here again."

She stood in the doorway, her hands on her hips, as Jasper and I spilled down the steps. "If you're trying to make new friends in this town, Georgina Holt, you are going about it the wrong way."

She was probably right.

* * *

I was glad to see the happy, smiling blonde waiting for me at the picnic table.

The park was fuller than it usually was, but it was still one of the emptier parts of Pottsville. Most of the tourists were pooling in the town center, flooding the cafes and restaurants.

A picnic with Brandi was a welcome distraction from everything.

Brandi opened up the plastic containers she'd brought, filled with salads and coleslaw, and started to dish it out onto paper plates while I filled her in on what had happened at Lisa's. Not all the details, but the main points—her outrage, her practically kicking us

231

out on the street.

Brandi laughed as I told the story. I really liked her so far. She wasn't like the other people in town. She was laid back and had a sense of humor. Too bad she was only there for the summer. "Don't worry too much about Lisa. She has a bit of a pointed tongue." She made a face. "She's close with Auntie Brenda, so I have to see her quite a bit, unfortunately. Those two are joined at the hip. Sort of like sisters."

"So that would make Lisa your aunt as well?" I joked, shoving a large forkful of salad in my mouth.

Brandi laughed a little. "That's a scary thought. One of them is bad enough."

I glanced over my shoulder to see that two people on ladders were hanging a very large sign that stretched right across the main street. "Welcome to the Pottsville Arts and Crafts Festival."

I turned back to Brandi. "Looking forward to the festival?" I asked her.

Brandi shrugged. "Eh, the competition aspect isn't really my thing," she said, making a face. "I prefer a more chilled out atmosphere."

I was confused. What was she talking about?

"Competition aspect? What competition?"

Brandi looked at me for a few seconds like she was trying to figure out whether I was ignorant or just a bit dim. "At the festival this weekend, there's the competition for best arts and crafter. That's why there's such a large turnout. That's the main reason that people flock to it. It's a big deal." She tilted her head. "You have noticed that our population has practically doubled the last day, haven't you?"

I nodded slowly. "Yeah, I knew about the festival," I said. "I just didn't know it was a competition." I'd thought the festival was more of a fun thing. A casual day out. Now Brenda's attitude toward it suddenly made a lot more sense. As did us having to register for it. Just what had I signed up for? I slowly realized that my jewelry wouldn't just be up for sale, it would be up for judgment. I got a sinking feeling in my stomach.

Get me out of this town, now.

I stared at the sign hanging in the air and the flocks of people filling Main Street. Were they all there to compete?

I turned back to Brandi. "What is the prize for first place?" I asked her.

Brandi raised an eyebrow and dug her fork back

into her salad. "It's a cash prize."

"How much is it worth?"

Brandi stopped chewing. "This year? Twenty thousand dollars."

"No way," I whispered. "You're kidding me, right?"

Brandi shook her head and crossed her arms. "Nope. I'm telling ya, George, this is the biggest crafting competition in the state. Maybe the country. It's serious business."

I was starting to realize that myself.

I thought about Erika's bracelet, how skilled the silver-work had been. She was talented. Really talented. She could have taken home top prize.

It suddenly made sense why someone would lure her out here early by sending that fake email and switching the dates on her. It was just a shame she wasn't smart enough not to fall for it. It had been a tragic mistake that had cost the poor lady her life.

But just how many people knew about Erika's talent? Why was someone so threatened by her that they wanted her out of the competition?

Maybe one of the locals had seen her in town early, recognized her, and taken her out. One of the more competitive women could have been willing to kill for the title.

And I knew a couple of them.

Chapter 6

I could barely open my eyes. They seemed glued together. Panicking for a moment, thinking maybe someone actually had taken to my face with a hot glue gun, I tried to call out and realized that my throat was swollen. I groaned and threw off the covers, finally prying my puffy eyes open.

The big day had finally arrived, with much fanfare, and I was sick. Figured. My body must have been subconsciously trying to keep me away from the festival. "Maybe I should take this as a sign not to participate," I said to Jasper, who gave me a knowing look in return. "I know, I know," I said, "I need to pull myself together." It was not the day to call in sick. I was just going to have to suck it up and do my best.

I fluffed my hair in the mirror and applied about twice the makeup I usually do, hoping that it would help to cover up my puffy eyes and slightly green pallor.

Still, as I headed out the door, I considered turning back and burrowing under the covers.

But the excitement of the day seemed to pull me

down to the center of town, and before I knew it, I was in the center of the festivities. I realized I'd made the right decision to leave Jasper at home because walking through the center of town was like trying to wade through thick mud; it was so full of people hustling and positioning their stalls and their finest creations. There were even news cameras. Quite a few of them, actually. I grinned at one of them and shot the anchor a wink, suddenly feeling not so ill.

I started to think that maybe, just maybe, this thing might turn out to be quite enjoyable after all. I did like a celebration, and a camera.

Now, focus. Time to find Brenda. I can't go having too much fun.

It wasn't just the arts and crafts that were on display that weekend, though of course that was the main attraction. There were live bands and music flooded the street. There were also rows and rows of stalls with street food, and local produce such as cheeses and fruits and vegetables, and fancy jams and jellies. There was even a stall of gourmet dog treats. I stopped for a second and pulled out my purse, buying a couple of pig's ears for Jasper. I also bought a small one for Casper, for when she returned. I still knew she would.

Even though there was a nervous energy in the air, there was a sense of joyfulness and for a moment I forgot everything—my sore throat, Erika, and my apprehension about the festival. I purchased a corndog and a funnel cake and sat at a picnic table to eat them. When was the last time I ate like this? I couldn't remember. Had I even eaten a corndog since I became an adult? I was really missing out.

And then, of course, the heat wave chose that moment to break. Thankfully, I had just stuffed the last bite of funnel cake into my mouth.

People started to shriek as heavy, sharp rain suddenly poured down. Anyone who had a cover over their stall quickly pitched it and others scrambled to hide their prized possessions from the rain. The band quickly pulled their amplifiers clear and unplugged their guitars, and suddenly there was silence, apart from the sound of the rain splashing on the ground and people wailing.

Hmm. Almost seemed like a higher power didn't want this festival to take place. The rain temporarily took the wind out of my sails and I started to wish I'd stayed home.

But the festival couldn't be killed off. It had a life of

its own and nothing was going to stop it from forging ahead and sucking all of us in with it. Soon the storm had passed and everyone rallied, mopping up the puddles on their stall tables and shaking themselves off.

The band started up again and folk guitars once again filled the air.

There was no getting out of it. I was going to have to find Brenda and face the music.

* * *

"Don't touch that!" Brenda said, swatting my hand away from her vases. "I want the judges to see them just as they are."

"All right, all right," I said, staring down at the green, glossy clay creations. This was what she was entering into the big competition? Oh well. I supposed that was her choice. "I won't touch them again," I said, holding my hands up in the air before I handed some passersby our business card. "If you're still in town on Monday, please come by and see us! We're having a half-price sale!"

"We are?" Brenda asked.

"We might as well capitalize on the tourism."

Lisa shoved past Brenda and I with her nose up in the air. Not even a hello. I, personally, wasn't expecting a hello after I'd accused her of murder, but I was shocked to see her snub her honorary sister, Brenda.

"What's up with you and Lisa?" I asked, surprised that the besties were on the outs with each other. "I thought you two were as thick as thieves."

"We have to put friendships aside for this weekend," Brenda said through gritted teeth. "This isn't about friendship. It's about competition. It's every woman for herself."

"Surely you can say a polite hello to each other."

"You have a lot to learn about this competition, Georgina."

Apparently. But Brenda always thought I had a lot to learn about everything: business, manners, festivals, life. I'd been hoping that Lisa's stall was going to be near us so that I could keep an eye on her, but she disappeared into the crowd and I lost sight of her. I was going to have to track her down later.

"Does Lisa stand any chance of actually winning the

top prize?" I asked Brenda casually.

"Ha, she wishes," Brenda replied, surprising me to hear her throw her friend under the bus like that. "Maybe if she took out the rest of the competition first."

The competition was serious business and after the early joviality, nervous tension broke out everywhere. It seemed it wasn't just Brenda and Lisa keeping each other at arm's length; the competition seemed to have turned all friends into foes on that day. None of the ladies in the gaggle at Brenda's—sorry, my—craft circle even acknowledged her on that day. They didn't acknowledge me either, but that was nothing unusual. It was sort of funny to see Brenda be on the outs. But she ignored them just as hard back.

I couldn't help but think about what Brandi had said, and I agreed with her. The competitive aspect wasn't really my vibe. Couldn't we all just get along? The tension in the air was getting to me and that, combined with the throngs of people, was making me feel a little claustrophobic.

I was just about to excuse myself for a minute when Lisa came wandering back over to our table. This time, she managed to give Brenda a curt hello, but I got nothing but the evil eye.

"Are these what you plan to enter into the competition?"

Lisa scowled at my bracelets. I wondered why she was giving them such a dirty look if they were so terrible. It's not like they were competition for her, were they? If they were as tacky as Brenda claimed, surely she would be happy to see them

"Yes, they are, actually," I said proudly. I gave Lisa my widest grin. She may have hated me at that moment, but I planned on killing her with kindness. "And I think they actually stand a chance."

A look of worry suddenly crossed Lisa's face. "Well, good luck," she said, scurrying away.

A man with glasses carrying a clipboard started to walk toward us and Brenda straightened up. "Oh my goodness. He is one of the judges," she whispered nervously.

"What, is it already judging time?"

Brenda shot me a *you are so stupid* look. "No, Georgina. The actual competition is tomorrow."

"Tomorrow?" Oh, great. I had to get through another full day of this. "Then why am I even here?"

"Because it is the preliminary judging," Brenda

whispered, nodding toward the man who was drawing closer. "He decides on the finalists, those who actually get to compete tomorrow, based on what he likes." She was so nervous that she could barely speak.

The man was wearing a paper nametag that said Ken on it. By the time he reached our stall, Brenda had practically keeled over. He inspected her vases first, picking one up and turning it over before placing it back on the table with an "oh."

I saw Brenda's face turn bright red. I had to wonder what 'oh' meant in this situation. Maybe it meant nothing. He was probably like one of those judges on TV, staying neutral and unimpressed by everything. There was probably no reason for those veins on Brenda's neck to look like they were about to pop.

But then he got to my bracelets. "Wow. These are very, very good," he said, scribbling something down on his clipboard. He looked up and shot me an impressed look. "I can't say too much, but don't make any plans for tomorrow."

I straightened up proudly. "Well, thank you very much, Ken. And enjoy the rest of the festival, and your time here in Pottsville," I said with a wide grin, which he returned.

I suddenly turned and glared at Brenda. Had she just been trying to get into my head all this time, not because I was in danger of embarrassing her but because I was in danger of actually beating her for the crown?

Now I was on to her, though. "Are you going to congratulate me?" I asked, but she turned away and stuck her nose up in the air.

Shoot. Maybe I really had a shot at this thing.

* * *

"Don't go getting too ahead of yourself."

These were the first words Brenda had managed to speak to me in an hour.

"I'm not," I said. "I don't think it's getting ahead of myself to assume that I'll be in the finals tomorrow. The judge wasn't exactly ambiguous with his comments."

"Erika probably would have won if she was still alive," Brenda commented. "So count yourself lucky."

I turned and stared at her. Had she really just said

that? Did she realize she'd actually said that?

"And what do you know about Erika?" I asked Brenda, looking her up and down carefully. "I thought you didn't know anything about her."

She took a moment to collect her thoughts before she answered. Probably smart. "I know that she was a skilled crafter. She almost won the competition last year. She was runner-up."

"Hmm," I said. "Maybe someone killed her to take her out of the running."

"You're not really suggesting that are you, Georgina?" Brenda held her hand up to her cheek like she was shocked by the very suggestion.

I shrugged and glanced down at my bracelets. "Maybe I'm lucky that I escaped with my life intact," I said. "Considering how well received my jewelry has been."

Brenda turned red. "I think you'd better be careful what you are saying, Georgina. And what you are accusing people of."

Ha! So she had spoken to Lisa, hadn't she! Brenda sure was a crafty one. And I wasn't talking about the lime green vases sitting in front of us.

In fact, I'd never seen so many crafty people in one place.

Was one of them the killer?

* * *

I never would have guessed that Brenda would be the one to leave early on that day, leaving me there all alone. My success had clearly left a sour taste in her mouth and she excused herself before the day was done, asking if I wouldn't mind packing up. She took her vases with her.

The place was finally beginning to clear out a little. Which was lucky for me, considering what was about to happen. I just didn't realize it yet. For just a moment, I was starting to miss the crowds, and the excitement of the day, as Ryan Mathews approached me.

"Hey there," I said, grinning at him as I waved my hand over my display. "Come to check out the talk of the festival, have you?" I asked. "You're never going believe this—I mean, really not going to believe it—but it looks like I might actually..."

I stopped talking when I caught the look on his face.

He did not look amused. Or happy. Or impressed. He looked dark and stormy.

"What is it?" I asked, my stomach dropping. For a moment I thought he might have some bad news about Casper. Did they send police officers to give bad news about pets? Maybe in a small town they did.

"George, I'm going to have to ask you to come down to the station with me to answer a few questions."

Escorted by the law to the back of a police car, yeah...I was relieved that the crowd was thinner. But there was Lisa Riemer, watching me get driven away, wearing the smuggest smirk I had ever seen in my life.

* * *

"This is outrageous," I said. "I've never been this insulted in my whole life." Well, I had been, many times. But this was one of the worst. "Am I a suspect?"

We were in a room with a plain table and a couple chairs. I wouldn't necessarily call it an interrogation room, but that's what it felt like. And from Ryan's demeanor, I very much felt like he was interrogating me.

Part of me—an itsy bitsy part—was pleased to be away from the festival and getting out of packing up the stall. Brenda wouldn't be pleased about coming back into town to do that, but she'd have to grin and bear it. Even though I had been practically picked as a finalist, the whole competition thing and the festival itself had still been stressing me out. I was even starting to have cold feet about actually competing the next day.

Well, at least I had a change of scenery. "It's very cold in here," I stated. I wondered if that was on purpose. Ryan still didn't answer. He was poring over his notes.

Surely being questioned by the police gave me an excuse to miss the rest of the weekend's festivities, if I really wanted to. Surely it let me off the hook. Maybe even for the whole weekend. With Brenda, you never know though. She'd probably expect me to compete behind bars.

That was if she even wanted me to compete. Sure, she'd been a little bitter that day, but I think deep down she would prefer that one of us represented the store rather than no one at all. I was sure that once she'd cooled off a bit, she wouldn't let me back out of the finals unless I was dead.

Ryan switched on a tape recorder and gave his name for the record. Mine as well. "Miss Georgina Holt."

He could barely make eye contact with me as he began the interview. "I need to ask you a few questions in relation to the death of Erika Joyce."

"How can you possibly think that I had anything to do with this?" I asked Ryan. Why was he the one interviewing me? Surely they had other officers in the station, or detectives for that matter. Ryan wasn't even a detective. Things just weren't adding up.

"It's all hands on deck for this investigation," Ryan mumbled, shuffling the papers in front of him. "So I'm sorry you're stuck with me here today, George...I mean, Miss Holt." He cast a quick glance toward the tape recorder.

Sure, I thought.

"Can you tell me where you were last Friday night?" Ryan asked.

"I was out looking for my dog," I said. "She went missing earlier that day."

"Can anyone verify what you were doing that evening?"

"Only my dog, Jasper," I shot back quickly.

"Not the most reliable of witnesses, I'm afraid," Ryan said. It sounded like a joke. Did he really think any of this was funny? I certainly didn't find it amusing that my only alibi was my dog. Though, to be fair, I think that Jasper would make a VERY reliable witness, if only he could actually speak.

"You did find the body," Ryan said. He shifted the notes in front of him uncomfortably.

My mouth dropped open. "That's why I'm here? I already told you, I was only out there in that clearing because I was looking for my dog. I mean, not the one who is my alibi. My other dog."

"So on any other night you wouldn't be creeping around that clearing?"

I paused for a second. Was this a trap? "No," I said carefully. "I don't believe I would be."

Ryan let out a low "hmm" and searched through his pile of notes for a minute. "Are you sure about that, Miss Holt?"

"Well..."

"Because we have a witness here saying differently. You were spotted snooping around the scene of the crime several days later."

I thought about how killers often return to the scene of the crime. That had been my exact reasoning for going there that night. Now it had turned around to bite me on the backside.

"What witness was this?" I asked indignantly. I would have put money on the name starting with either an L or a B.

"So you were there that evening?" Ryan asked.

"Yes. That's when I found that bracelet!" I exclaimed in disbelief. "You know that. I handed the bracelet over to you." I crossed my arms. This was unbelievable.

"Yes. Er. About that." Ryan shifted uncomfortably in his chair and glanced at the clock on the wall. Did he have somewhere better to be? "Tell us, Miss Holt, where did you really find that bracelet?"

I was speechless. Literally. I didn't even know what to say. I didn't even know what he was accusing me of. I started to wonder if I should say anything else without a lawyer present. Were there any lawyers in Pottsville?

Ryan tried to keep a steady voice. "Our officers and detectives swept the crime scene and they found no trace of it."

"I can't help it if this town's police force is incompetent!"

A blush of red tried to creep up Ryan's neck, but he managed to keep it at bay and held his cool.

"Aren't you a crafter, Miss Holt?"

I hesitated a moment before considering my answer. Could I take the fifth on the grounds that my answer might incriminate me?

I had nothing to hide, though. Might as well speak the truth, with or without a lawyer present. "Yes. It's one of many things I do. One of many things I am good at."

"And you had planned to enter the competition at the Pottsville Arts and Crafts show?"

I frowned. "Well, no, well, yes." I was stumbling over my answers and I didn't like how foolish I was sounding. I reached for the glass of water and quickly took a sip. "I was sort of railroaded into it. I hadn't even decided if I was going to enter my pieces."

"And what pieces would they be, Miss Holt?"

"What do you mean?"

Ryan leaned forward a little. "Is it jewelry that you make?"

I stared back at him. He knew very well that it was. He was treating me like I was a total stranger. But I had to answer for the record, for the tape recorder. "Yes," I replied flatly.

"What kind of jewelry, Miss Holt?"

The question hung there, heavily, for a moment like rain about to fall from the clouds before I finally answered. "Bracelets," I whispered.

"Hmm," Ryan replied, finally leaning back. "The same items Miss Joyce made. Sounds like she was your biggest competition, Miss Holt." He had one last question for me.

"And aren't you a finalist in the competition tomorrow?"

Saved by the bell. There was a knock on the door and Ryan was called away for a moment. I shook my head and tried to calm down, using the opportunity to check my phone.

I sat up straighter when I saw that I had numerous missed calls and texts from the same unknown number. I read one of the texts.

"**I saw your posters up around town. I think I have your dog. Please call me back on this number.**"

My heart started beating faster as I quickly tried to return the call, but Ryan entered the room again just before I was about to dial.

"Can I go now?" I said to Ryan, standing up before he could say anything. "I just got a call about my lost dog. And unless you are going to charge me with something, you've got no right to keep me here."

Chapter 7

Ryan refused to look me in the eyes as I was escorted from the station. I knew he was only doing his job, and I could cut him some slack for that, but, to be honest, I wasn't in much of a mood to meet his eye either. I also wasn't in much of a mood to speak to him any time soon.

I almost dropped my phone on the pavement, I was in such a hurry to return the call.

"Hello?" I said frantically once a woman's voice had answered. "You said you've found my dog?" My words came out so quickly that they sounded blurred together. *Yousaidyou'vefoundmydog?* I took a deep breath and started over again. "This is Georgina Holt," I said, a little more calmly. "I received a call from you in relation to a lost dog?"

The woman on the other end of the line took a second to collect herself. "That's right." I could hear her fumbling with something in the background—It almost sounded like she was crumbling paper. After asking her a few questions, I managed to find out that she lived off Sunday Avenue. I paused for a moment, confused.

255

Sunday Avenue was on the other side of Pottsville. "How did Casper get so far from home?" I asked.

Again, it seemed to take a century for the answer to come. "I guess he is a fast little thing."

"She," I said, correcting the woman. "Casper is a female dog."

There was no answer so I had to push the point. "Let me write down your exact address. How soon can I come by? It will take me about half an hour to walk, but I will leave right away." I couldn't wait to see Casper again.

"Erm, can you come by tomorrow?" the woman asked.

"Tomorrow?" Why couldn't I get Casper right then?

"I'm sorry," a suddenly croaky voice replied. "It's just that I'm feeling a little under the weather and was about to turn in for the night." I glanced at the time. Almost 6:00pm. A little early for bed, but maybe she'd caught the same bug I had, or the same bug that Brenda had pretended to catch.

"Very well," I said with a sigh. "Casper is safe though, right? Is she doing well?"

"Oh yes, very well," the voice replied a little too

chipperly. Not so croaky this time. "I have to go, dear," she quickly said, correcting herself, the croak magically reappearing. "See you tomorrow."

* * *

"Where on earth are you?" Brenda's text message read.

"I'm sorry, I need to do something important," I replied back. **"I'll be there in time for the judging, I promise."**

It took me a long time to reach Sunday Avenue and the address of the lady who I'd spoken to yesterday. It was a half-hour walk from town and if I wanted to get back to the festival in time for judging, I'd pretty much have to grab Casper and run back to town with her in my arms.

Jasper had sulked with me that morning when I'd left him at home. Two days alone for him was almost unheard of. But all would be right again when I returned with Casper later that evening. He'd have his little playmate back and I'd be back in the good books, with all wrongs forgiven.

I frowned when I got to the front of the building and double-checked the address. It was a little sunken wooden cabin that backed off onto the lake with no fences surrounding the property. Not the best place to have kept a dog for over a week. Especially a small one with a habit of running away. Had this woman even let Casper outside at all?

I eyed the lake carefully as I approached the door. I didn't like the thought of Casper being so close to it. I wasn't sure she could swim, and she was such a tiny dog for such a large body of water.

The sooner I get you out of here, Casper, the better.

I knocked on the door and a woman in her mid to late forties with straw-like blonde hair answered. She had weather beaten skin and was smoking a cigarette. I don't usually like to judge, but if Casper was cooped up inside all day, that air couldn't have been good for her. Was she getting any fresh air at all?

"Hello, I'm Georgina Holt. Most people just call me George, though," I said, introducing myself. I extended a hand but she didn't take it.

"I'm Patty," she said, looking me up and down. "Lisa told me you were offering a reward?"

Lisa? What did Lisa have to do with any of this?

"I, um..." I hadn't been prepared for her to ask about the reward. I decided to answer with confidence. "Yes. You may come into my store—George's Crafts—and pick out anything you desire."

Her face dropped into a look of disgust. She shook her head. "Turns out I was mistaken," she said.

"Mistaken? About what?" I tried to peer into her house. Was she really trying to bribe me into giving her more money in return for my dog?

"Mistaken about your dog being here," she said, stepping in front of me so that I could no longer get a look inside.

"Please," I said, trying not to beg, but still letting her know how important this was to me. "Okay, I can give you a better reward other than store credit. I..." I remembered the festival, and the prize pool of twenty thousand dollars. Maybe I really had a shot at placing in the top three. "I can offer you a thousand dollars if you give Casper to me. Possibly even more, depending on how today pans out."

If it took much longer, I was going to completely miss the judging. I glanced down at my watch. "Please," I said. "You'll just have to take my word on it."

Patty's face fell even further. She shook her head

and sounded genuinely full of regret as she spoke. "I'm sorry. I can see how much you want your dog back, but she just ain't here, I'm afraid." She stepped out of the way and let me get a look. I could see all through her cabin. There was a tiny kitchenette combined with a dining room, and a section at the back for a bed. Everything was in view except for the bathroom, and I doubted Patty was hiding Casper in there. She'd be barking to get to me if she was trapped.

"Right," I said, stepping away. "I see."

"I'm sorry," Patty said but I had already turned around, hurrying away from her cabin. I didn't want to hear her weak attempt at an apology.

I must have been lured there under false pretenses. I shook my head, trying to fight back the tears. How cruel to use my beloved missing dog as bait to get me there?

They probably wanted me away from the festival.

A thought occurred to me.

So that I'd be out of the running for the prize.

Maybe the same person who killed Erika, who'd lured her to town early, had lured me away as well.

Lisa.

Lisa told me you were offering a reward.

I glanced down at the four-inch heels I was wearing. They weren't the highest heels I owned—I actually referred to them as my 'walking shoes'—but they were still not the most ideal footwear for a half-hour, uphill sprint back into town. "All right, girls," I said to my shoes. "You are coming off." I took a deep breath and gave thanks that the heat wave had broken before I'd had to run the marathon of a lifetime.

I ran back, heels in hand, panting, sweating, and cursing the day I'd ever met Lisa Riemer as I clawed my way back up the hill. It took me fifteen minutes to reach the top, and after that, the descent back down into town seemed like sweet relief. But the journey wasn't over, and I had to run, skip, and hop back down to the heart of the festival, my feet flying out from underneath me as I finally made it....just not in time.

I was doubled over, panting and nursing a pain in my side, ready to throw my heels to the ground.

I'd made it in time for the ceremony. For the big announcement.

They were just announcing the winner. "Congratulations, Lisa Riemer!"

Chapter 8

I stared at the whiteboard, Jasper lying dutifully at my feet. There was a new face sketched there now, a woman in her mid-forties with short brown hair, who could almost have passed for Brenda's twin except that she did occasionally smile.

I sketched the gold trophy as well, and a check with the prize money on it. It was all starting to fall into place now. And it was all starting to fall into place for Lisa as well: her master plan, I mean. Lure Erika to town a week early, get rid of her, lure away her next biggest competition (me), and then claim the prize for herself. All while trying to frame me for the murder by snooping on me and telling the cops. She was clever, but she wasn't clever enough to get away with it.

"Lisa had to have done it, Jasper. I just have to figure out how." I glanced down at him and saw his ears prick up a little, before they dropped again. He had a sad, rejected look. "Especially if I want to stay out of jail."

I went to the pantry and fetched one of the treats I'd bought for him at the festival in order to try and cheer him up. There was no way for him to humanly know what had taken place at Patty's cabin, but he seemed to feel it somehow. It was like all the hope had gone out of him.

I petted his head while he chewed on the pig's ear. "Don't worry. We're going to get Casper back." I stared at the whiteboard, the fresh sketch of Lisa Riemer staring back at me. "And I am going to get Lisa back for what she has done."

* * *

I could see the silhouette of her sitting, knitting, through the window. It was dark out but I wasn't going to let that stop me.

But something else almost did.

A cop car pulled up beside me and rolled the window down, Ryan sticking his head.

Cripes.

I wouldn't have been in the mood to talk to him even if it had been the best of times, and this was definitely not the best of times.

"You shouldn't be walking around here after dark."

"Is it a crime?" I asked, not quite turning around to meet him. I don't like giving people the cold shoulder, but in this case, it was justified.

"No..."

"I'm just taking my dog for a walk. I'm pretty sure you can't arrest me for that." I kept my voice cheery and chipper, yet cold at the same time.

Ryan cleared his throat. "In front of Lisa Riemer's house?"

I forced a surprised expression to my face while Jasper tugged on his leash. "Well, look at that," I said, nodding towards the house. "So it is. I had no idea where we even were." I shrugged casually while Ryan sighed and started to roll the window back up. "I'm only trying to warn you, George."

"I don't need your warnings. I'm a big girl."

I pretended to walk away from Lisa Riemer's house until his car was out of sight, then quickly scooted back down the road and ran up her driveway, a not very eager Jasper in tow. I thought we'd better make it quick in case Ryan decided to head back down the street.

"Hello, Lisa!" I exclaimed when she answered the

door. "I just thought I'd drop by and congratulate you on your big prize." I widened my grin. "I saw it on the news. You looked really good on screen."

Lisa wasn't able to resist the thrill of being paid a compliment and I saw the smile curl on her lips, even though she probably didn't want to give me the satisfaction.

"Can I see the trophy?" I asked, practically breathless in my adoration now. I let out an exaggerated sigh. "I mean, I know I never have a shot of winning it myself but I would love to hold it in my hands."

Lisa considered my request for a moment, but in the end, my flattery won her over. "Come inside," she said, looking down at Jasper. "He can come in too. I'll give him another bowl of water."

This time, Jasper actually lapped up his water, though I kept a sharp eye on Lisa while she ran the tap and placed the bowl on the ground. Would she really stoop so low as to hurt a dog? Considering what else she was capable of, I wasn't about to take any chances. I watched and waited until Jasper had finished and then made sure he didn't leave my side until we were back in the den. I was actually a little surprised that Lisa let dogs into her house; Brenda always made me tie Jasper up outside whenever I dropped by her house.

"This is it," Lisa said, picking up a heavy gold statue that she just barely managed to lift into the air. She paused a moment before she handed it to me.

"Impressive," I murmured, and I actually meant it. It weighed a ton in my hands and just for a second, I found myself wishing I had actually won it. It would look good inside my glass house. I looked at Lisa. If not for her, it might actually be sitting in my house right then.

"I know what you did, Lisa."

"Excuse me?"

I placed the trophy back on the shelf and stared at it while Lisa went back to her seat and picked up her knitting again like I hadn't said anything. Jasper, much to my shock, walked over to her seat and sat in front of her. Talk about a traitor!

"I'm talking about Erika," I said quietly. "And me. And Casper. And the lengths you went to win that competition. Was it all worth it?"

She turned her head away from me and went back to her knitting. The trophy glistened on the shelf behind her. "I have no idea what you are talking about," she said innocently, frowning at her knitting as though it was the most complicated stitch in the world and required all of her concentration.

She really was stone cold.

A stone cold killer?

I took a step closer to her, wondering if Ryan's police car was still circling the neighborhood. I might actually need him. Much as I didn't want to admit it. Much as I wouldn't admit it, not until the very moment my life was in danger, and maybe not even then.

I looked down at Jasper. *You realize you need to be on my side if anything goes down?* Lisa reached down and petted Jasper's head slowly, while she kept her eyes fixed on me. "I can't figure out what's gotten you so upset, Georgina."

Stop petting my dog.

"I know that you lured me down to Patty's cabin to get me out of the way..."

Lisa let out a shrill laugh and abruptly stopped petting Jasper. "Out of the way of what?"

I flipped my hair over my shoulder. "I was going to be a finalist. You were worried that I was going to beat you. So you had to get rid of me."

Lisa just stared at me in disbelief. "Georgina. You'd better be very careful what you are accusing me of. Last time you came here flinging around accusations, I only threw you out of my house. I might not be so nice this time." Her voice was low and dark. A warning. A threat.

After staring me down for what felt like a full minute, she went back to her knitting.

"You don't even deserve that trophy," I whispered, looking at the giant statue behind her. That thing could land quite an impact if someone wanted to use it as a weapon.

Lisa eyed me over the top of her yarn. "And I suppose you do deserve it?" She let out a laugh. "Don't flatter yourself, Georgina. If I wanted to get someone 'out of the way,' as you put it, there are hundreds of people I would have picked before you. You might have gotten some praise from that judge, but that doesn't mean you had any real chance of actually winning. He was probably only flirting with you. I wouldn't go getting a big head, Georgina."

She looked at me with a satisfied expression, as though that settled the matter. As though that made perfect sense. She had a very good way of making a person feel paranoid even when that person's suspicions were completely founded.

I wasn't going to let her get to me or allow her to make me second-guess myself.

"I don't believe you," I said, my head held high in the air. "It's not the first time someone has tried to knock my confidence in my creations, in my jewelry, when really, they have a lot of merit. I had a chance of winning. A good chance. And you used my lost dog to get me out of the way. How do you sleep at night, Lisa?"

"You had no chance of winning." Her knitting needles clicked against each other. "And I sleep very well, thank you. I have a chiropractic mattress."

"Jasper, come here," I said, bending down to call him to me. He looked up at Lisa for a second, as though asking for permission, and she nodded. Only then did he walk back over to me. This time, I clung to his collar, determined not to let him return to that maniac who inexplicably had some kind of power over him.

"You never told me where you were on that Friday night," I said to Lisa.

A wide, sly grin spread across her face. "Oh, that's right, I never did," she said. She sounded almost gleeful. "I suppose I really should tell you."

She put her knitting down and got up, walking toward a cabinet. Getting just a little close to the heavy gold trophy for my liking. I backed away, taking Jasper with me. She opened a drawer and pulled something out. From a glance, they looked like airline tickets. "This ought to clear a few things up for you," she said, smiling as she handed them to me.

I looked down at the tickets in my hand. No. No. No.

Lisa's self-satisfied expression magnified as she explained, even though I needed no explanation. The evidence was clearly spelled out in my hands. "I flew into Chicago on Wednesday night and didn't return until Saturday evening. As you can clearly see."

I looked up at her, sharply. Yep. Just as smug as I had expected. "Call the airlines, and the hotels too, if you like." She winked at me. "The police already have."

* * *

I wrapped my coat around myself tightly as I escaped Lisa's house. It seemed to have dropped about ten degrees during the half an hour I'd been inside her house.

Jasper was barking at me. "Yes, boy," I said, distracted. "We'll go home and get your dinner now."

He wagged his tail excitedly and started pulling on his leash. I didn't have the strength to try and rein him in so I let him lead me home, even though it is terrible dog ownership to allow your dog to lead the owner like that.

That was it then. She couldn't have done it. A rock solid alibi. The feeling was like a pit in my stomach. Like a rug had been pulled out from underneath me. Not only had Lisa not been in town when Erika had been killed, she hadn't even been here the day before when Erika had arrived. She was in the clear. It wasn't her.

How could I have been so certain of something and been so wrong?

The pit in my stomach grew as we reached the house. If Lisa didn't do it, and had already been cleared by the police, who did that leave as a suspect?

Me. It left me.

I knew I hadn't done it, but the police didn't know that. I felt like the walls were closing in on me and I had no idea how to escape.

I looked up at my whiteboard while Jasper gobbled down his food like he hadn't been fed in a week. I'd put a bowl of food out the front for Casper like I did every night in case she came back. Jasper would eat that later as well.

I shook my head and erased Lisa's face from the board. Then I scrubbed out the trophy and the prize money as well. All I had left was the drawing of Erika. That was it. I felt like I was back at square one.

"Maybe I should draw my own face up on the board," I half-joked. "Maybe I did it and just don't remember." I had been down at the clearing that day. And I did have a habit of being absentminded.

I shook my head vigorously. *Come on, George! That is a crazier theory than anything else.*

But I didn't have any more theories. Nada.

No clues. No leads. No Casper.

No prize at the festival. I hadn't even sold a single piece of jewelry. Not that Brenda would have put much energy into selling it for me while I was away, so it wasn't that surprising that I'd had every piece returned to me. Maybe she hadn't even put it out on display when I hadn't turned up. Any attempt by me to contact her the past day had gone completely ignored. She'd probably gotten news that I was a suspect and decided she no longer wanted anything to do with me.

I was sure that wouldn't stop her from working at the shop, though. Or running my craft circle.

I sighed and let Jasper outside so that he could use the bathroom before it was time for bed. "Maybe I should just give up, hey, Jasper?"

He made a whimpering sound.

"No, I don't mean give up on finding Casper," I said. "We're going to get her back, boy, don't worry about that."

* * *

A police car pulled up in front of my house, causing Jasper to bark wildly. "It's okay," I said, calming him. "It's just Ryan." Even though I was trying to remain calm for Jasper's sake, my heart was beating a little fast, thinking that maybe Ryan was there to arrest me. But I managed to glance at his face and there was a trace of an apologetic smile on it.

Ha. So he wasn't coming to arrest me. He was coming to apologize. That was almost even less welcome.

Luckily, I was doing my gardening, so I had an excuse not to look at him. The sun was out again and I had left Brenda in charge of the shop for the afternoon. "I think that would be for the best at the moment," she'd said, barely looking at me with her nose up in the air. "Considering your reputation in the town at the moment, people will probably feel safer with me in charge."

"Yes, because I might just start killing innocent people when they walk into the store," I'd said, causing Brenda to turn red. Oh well. It hadn't bothered me too much. I needed the afternoon off to recuperate, and my flowers needed watering.

And when I'd received a text from Brenda during the afternoon saying, **"How dare you accuse Lisa! She had nothing to do with any of this!"** I tried not to let that bother me either. Let the terrible twins have each other. I still had my dog.

I didn't even greet Ryan as he strolled up my garden path and stood beside me. I acted like he wasn't even there. I didn't like this side of me coming out, but I was still boiling mad with him, and I figured that the cold shoulder routine was at least a little better than screaming in his face. Or turning the hose on him.

Ryan sighed and took off his hat.

"So we're not friends anymore?" he asked.

"I just need to get these flowers watered," I said. "I'm a little busy right now, sorry. No time for a friendly chat."

He sighed again and moved a little closer to me. "I'm really, really sorry, George. I never wanted to be put in that position."

Just as I had started to soften a *little* with his apology, he had to end it like that. He was sorry 'he' was put in that position. What about *me* being put in that position?

I was acting like Lisa Riemer with her knitting, but for me, it was the hose instead of the yarn that suddenly needed all my intense attention while I did my best to block out the man standing beside me.

"George? Are you listening to me?"

"I can hear the words you are speaking," I said, finally acknowledging him a little. But clearly not in the way he wanted me to.

"You understand why I did what I did, don't you George? I didn't have a choice."

I turned the hose on and started watering the peonies, my back to him fully now. "Oh we're back to George now, are we? I thought it was Miss Holt. Or do you only call me that when you are interrogating me for murder."

"George, did you hear me? I didn't have a choice."

"Aren't there any other police officers in town? Or are there none with our 'close and personal' relationship? Is that it, Ryan?"

I finally turned to look at him, the hose spraying right into his face. He jumped out of the way, wiping the water off his face as he coughed and sputtered a little bit like he was choking on it. He dropped his hat to the ground.

"Sorry, that was an accident," I said without looking up at him. *Kind of. Sort of.*

I had to admit it was a little funny. I had to try hard not to laugh. That would only break the ice. And I wanted the ice to remain very much intact.

"Look," Ryan said with a heavy sigh as he dried his face with his sleeve. "I didn't want to tell you this because I didn't know if it was for certain yet, and I wanted to keep it close to my chest. Sort of like speaking it out loud might jinx it."

I turned the hose off. Okay, he kind of had my attention now. Kind of.

"Didn't want to tell me what?"

He cleared his throat and stood up straighter. "I've been trying to make detective. There's a promotion up for grabs and it looks like I'm in the running."

I just stared at him and swallowed. I couldn't tell if he expected a congratulations from me or not. At any other time, I would have been thrilled for him. I knew how much he wanted to make detective. And he would make a really great one.

But what was he willing to give up to get the promotion? Our friendship? Because it sure as heck looked like he was willing to throw all that away for a chance at a higher salary and the chance to wear a suit to work.

"So that's why you did it, hey?" I asked, turning the hose back on, using all my focus to concentrate on the stream of water coming out of the hose. "Just to impress those that are higher up?"

"George, it's not like that."

"It is like that," I said flatly. "You couldn't turn down the chance to interview a murder suspect. Even if she was your friend. Even if she thought she actually meant something to you."

"George, you do mean something to me," Ryan said gently.

"That is very hard to believe right now," I said. "And for the record, you don't mean very much to me right now."

I knew immediately that was the wrong thing to say. I hadn't meant it, at least, not the harsh way it had come out. And I knew immediately from the way Ryan's voice changed—no longer soft—that he had taken it very wrong indeed.

"Look, the only reason you ever became a suspect at all is because you kept sticking your nose into the case," Ryan said, sounding grumpy for the first time. "If you'd just stayed out of it and minded your own business, none of this would have happened."

I shook my head and turned the hose off. I was in danger of actually drowning the flowers if I continued. There was only so much water they could take.

"Look," Ryan said, sighing again. "I don't think this conversation has gone very well. I came here to apologize and..."

"I'm going to put all my energy into finding Casper from this point forward," I said. "So you don't have to worry about me getting in your way, or screwing with your investigation any further."

"Okay," Ryan said slowly. "Do you want me to help?" he asked hopefully.

I switched the hose on again even though I knew I shouldn't. My poor flowers. "No, thanks," I said. "I'll be fine on my own."

* * *

It was time to double down my efforts. I was going to get Casper back or die trying. It was all that mattered to me anymore.

New posters, new fliers, and a new attitude.

This time when I put up new signs, I offered a cash reward. I decided to offer not only a reward if she was found, but also for any information that would lead to her coming home. Even if they'd only had a sighting. It would all be worth it. I needed any and all leads if I was going to find her.

And that was when the calls starting rolling in.

Chapter 9

I felt like I was operating a full-time switchboard. I practically needed an employee to help me. Actually, I did need an employee to help me take the calls.

Even though she was still being snobby toward me, there was one person in Pottsville who was always there in an emergency when I needed her. Plus, she already worked for me. And she was already in the shop.

"Thank you, Brenda, I really appreciate this," I said to her once she'd answered her twelfth call of the day.

She pushed her glasses back on her nose. "I care about that little dog as well, you know. She was Amanda's dog originally."

Amanda and Brenda had been good friends before Amanda's death. Well, that was what Brenda always said. I saw them together one time and they didn't seem all that close. But they had been neighbors and I guess that counted for something.

"That doesn't mean I don't appreciate the help," I said.

"I would do this to help Amanda, if no one else."

Well, at least she was doing it to help someone. It didn't really matter who, as long as we got Casper back. I finally felt like we had some hope of doing just that. All we had to do was not give up.

Most of the calls were junk, just people looking for a quick buck. "See, I told you this would happen if I offered a cash reward," I said to Brenda, but she had the phone to her ear and held up her other hand for me to be quiet.

"Really? You spotted a small white terrier. Was she wearing a collar?" Brenda waited a moment for the answer while I waited with bated breath.

"Who is it? What did they say?" I whispered. Brenda shushed me and hung up the phone, staring at me. "You're not going to believe this," she said. "Some guy who lives in the house next to the Pink Flamingo Lodge just called up. He says he saw your dog a week ago right before Erika's body was found."

* * *

It was a day after the Pottsville Arts and Crafts

Festival had officially ended, but the Pink Flamingo Lodge still had a "No Vacancies" sign flashing.

Brenda trailed behind me as we walked past the lodge and found the address she had been given over the phone. It was a cabin not that dissimilar to Patty's, only it was on the other side of town, far closer to my house, making it far more likely that Casper had actually ended up here.

"Do you know who lives here?" I whispered to Brenda.

She looked up at the cabin and frowned. "A long time ago a man named Joe lived here, but I would be surprised if he was still alive."

Joe ended up answering the door and Brenda looked very surprised indeed. She blinked a few times. "A man named Martin called us. About a dog?"

Old Joe coughed and nodded. "That was my son. I can't figure out how to make phone calls these days." His voice sounded rough, like it had endured years of smoking. "I was the one that spotted the dog, though." He looked at me sharply. "You got the cash?"

"I've got the cash if you've got the info," I said, raising my eyebrow. "Did you really see my dog last week?"

Old Joe cleared his throat again and nodded. "I did," he whispered, his eyes wide open. "Your little dog was with a girl." There was a frightened look in his eyes.

I looked at Brenda and then back at Joe. "What girl?"

"That dead girl," he whispered.

The hairs on the back of my neck stood up. "Erika Joyce, you mean? The woman who was killed here a week ago?"

He nodded. "I saw her with a small white dog. Looked exactly like the one in your photo. She was acting like it was her own dog though, walking it on a leash and everything."

I shook my head. "No, that can't be right. Erika was only visiting from out of town. She wouldn't have had a dog with her; she was staying at the Pink Flamingo. They don't allow dogs in the lodge."

Unless....

Unless that was the reason she'd been turned away from the Pink Flamingo.

"I have to go," I said abruptly. "Thank you for all your help, Joe."

"Hey!" he called out, spluttering as I ran away.

"What about my reward?"

* * *

I was glad Jasper wasn't with me, knowing what the owners of the lodge did with people who had pets with them—throw them onto the street to fend for themselves by the sounds of it. There was a fresh, handwritten sign on the window that hadn't been there the first time I'd visited. "No pets allowed—no exceptions!" Yikes.

It might have been a fresh note, but it was the same receptionist I'd spoken to the last time who now greeted me from behind the desk, the one who had taken my name and number in case they'd gotten any vacancies. I assumed that piece of paper ended up in the trash.

This time she was wearing a name tag. Leanne. Good to know.

I decided that I would try and catch flies with honey and be as nice to her as possible, even though the last time we'd met we hadn't gotten along too well.

"Good afternoon, Leanne" I said brightly. "I see that you are still overflowing with guests."

"Fancy seeing you here again." She turned her nose up at me and returned to the magazine she had been reading. "We've still got no openings, I'm afraid. Check the sign."

Yes, yes, the lodge was very popular. There was no denying that. But I had far more serious things to discuss than a vacant room. I pretended to be sorely disappointed. "Aww, that's too bad. I was hoping that I might be able to spend a night here before I leave town. I've only heard good things."

She looked at me skeptically. "Well, I've still got your name and number, but I wouldn't go holding your breath. This is our busiest time of year."

I fumbled with some business cards sitting on the desk, glancing around and trying to figure out my next plan of attack. "So no more troublesome guests?" I asked casually.

She glanced up at me from her magazine. "No. We've been very careful to check that." She stopped talking suddenly and blushed a little.

"Careful to check what?" I asked. Check for pets? Why hadn't she finished her sentence?

Leanne didn't answer me. She returned instead to her magazine and tried to pretend like I wasn't there.

"You never told me why Erika got thrown out that day she was killed."

Leanne stood up and gave me a cold stare. "Because that is none of your business." She put the magazine down and looked me up and down. "I don't know why you would care."

"Because my dog went missing that night," I said, hearing an air of desperation creeping into my voice. "And I think that Erika might have had her. Please. I am only trying to find my dog. I don't care about anything else."

Her face softened and she put down the magazine. "I'm sorry to hear that," she said softly. "It's horrible to lose a pet. Was she...was she a little white thing? Fluffy?"

I nodded. "Yes. Did you see her?"

Leanne sighed. "I saw her. But she was with that girl. I assumed it was her dog."

"Erika?" I asked, desperate to know. "Erika Joyce? The woman who was killed."

Leanne still didn't seem sure whether she should answer or not. Like if she said too much it might incriminate her or something.

My blood suddenly ran cold. Maybe Leanne had been the one who'd killed Erika.

I'd always had this strange feeling Erika's death and Casper's disappearance had been linked. Maybe Leanne had been so angry about the unwanted guest in the room that she had lost her temper with Erika.

But surely Leanne wouldn't kill over an unwanted dog in her lodge? Would she? No matter how much it shed? Besides, I brushed Casper every day so she hardly had any loose hair anyway. And I bathed her once a week, so she wouldn't have stunk up the room.

"Is that why Erika got thrown out? Because she had a dog staying in her room with her?"

Leanne finally let the words fly out and they hit me like a storm in the face. "I wasn't having some mangy dog stay in my hotel! Not when I was about to have a hundred tourists flock to the town!"

I took serious offense to her words. "Casper is not mangy. How dare you call her that!"

Leanne took a deep breath and calmed down a little. "I'm sure you take very good care of your dog," she said, a little more gently. "And I'm sure she is a perfectly sweet dog. I wish no harm on her. I just didn't want her staying at my lodge."

I cleared my throat. "And you have every right to decide that. It is your business, after all." I looked at her pleadingly. "But after Erika left and she took Casper with her, what happened?"

Leanne shrugged. "I don't know. I never saw either of them again. I'm sorry."

So Erika had found Casper, had her with her right before she'd died... Maybe even while she'd been killed.

None of this made me feel any better. Not one little bit. It only made me feel worse. Casper might have been found by a kind woman, and she might have even been intending to return her to me.

But Erika was gone. It didn't matter how well she had taken care of Casper, she wasn't around to look after her anymore.

So who had Casper now?

* * *

"Any luck?" Brenda asked as I swung back into the shop.

I shook my head and rested it in the palm of my hand as I leaned against the counter. "Nope. I'm starting to feel more dejected than ever about the whole thing."

Brenda sprayed some cleaning fluid and wiped the counter. "I'm sorry," she said. "I really thought that phone call from Joe was going to lead somewhere."

"It did," I said with a heavy sigh. "It's just that it didn't lead where I wanted it to is all."

Brenda reached out and patted me on the back, much to my surprise. "Don't give up hope just yet, Georgina. There's still hope." It was the kindest she had ever been to me and I felt tears spring to my eyes. I quickly wiped them away before she noticed.

With my tears gone, I had to ask her something. "Why are you being so nice to me all of a sudden?"

It seemed to take an eternity for Brenda to actually answer. "I spoke to Lisa earlier."

Oh great. I couldn't figure how this could have possibly worked out in my favor. If anything, I would have expected any conversation with Lisa to only turn Brenda even further against me.

"I think I owe you an apology," Brenda said. She was having a little trouble meeting my eye, but I could see that there was guilt in hers.

"Lisa admitted that she sent the email to Erika to get her to come to town on the wrong weekend." Brenda shook her head. "I knew Lisa was competitive, but I never knew she was that bad. It's crossing a line, in my opinion. It was wrong of her."

My eyes widened to hear Brenda speak about her bestie in this way. Well, well, well. You could have knocked me over with a feather I was so surprised. This definitely explained her sudden change in demeanor toward me.

Brenda looked at me. "And it was Lisa who tricked you into going to Patty's cabin on the day of the competition. She was behind it all."

"Well, I already knew that," I said, taking a heavy sigh. "But I'm glad you've finally been able to see things my way, Brenda. There really is a first time for everything."

"I've already said sorry. You don't have to heap on the guilt trip," Brenda said.

"I wasn't aware I was."

But Brenda really did seem wracked with guilt. She bit down on her lip and stared into the distance.

"Now I just don't know what to think," Brenda said.

"After you got taken to the station, I thought you must have had something to do with Erika's death, but now I'm starting to think Lisa might have..." She couldn't even say the words.

I shook my head. I felt bad for Brenda. "She couldn't have done it, Brenda," I said gently. "She wasn't in town. She was in Chicago."

"Really?" Brenda looked up hopefully, like she wanted to believe it. Maybe she was on the outs with Lisa, but she still didn't want to believe she could be capable of such a horrific crime.

I nodded reassuringly. "Don't worry, Brenda. Your friend isn't a killer. She's got a rock solid alibi." *Unfortunately.* I didn't say that bit out loud.

"Well, she still did the wrong thing. She shouldn't have the trophy sitting on her bookshelf." Brenda straightened her shoulders. "You should have it, Georgina."

I actually burst out laughing. I'd never expected her to say that. "That's very kind of you to say, Brenda, and the money sure would come in handy right now with all the rewards I'm having to hand out. But I guess Lisa won it kind of fair and square. Hey, it's not like she actually bribed the judges or anything."

Brenda glared at me with her lips drawn in a thin line. "Lisa might not have killed Erika, but if she'd never sent that email, Erika would still be alive. She isn't innocent in Erika's death." Brenda turned away. "And I don't think she deserves to profit from it."

She had a point. A good point. But what did Brenda intend to do? Rat Lisa out to the judges? Actually, Brenda was the kind of woman who would do just that.

"I think I feel a headache coming on," Brenda said wearily. "Do you mind if I head home early?"

I shook my head. It was quiet in the shop after a busy morning. The tourists had started, slowly, to trickle back out of the town. "Go home and get some rest. You've had a rough day."

She shuffled to the door, a troubled expression still on her face.

"Say hello to Brandi for me when you get home," I said breezily as I waved Brenda good-bye. "I haven't seen her for days. Actually, ask her to drop by if she feels like it! And she can bring me a coffee too, if she really feels like it," I said with a big grin.

"When I get home?" Brenda asked, frowning. "I don't think Brandi will be at the house. I haven't seen her for days either."

"Huh? She's been out of the house for days?" I asked.

"Well, she hasn't visited in days," Brenda said, one hand on the door. She seemed in a hurry to leave and didn't quite understand what I was asking her.

And I was having trouble understanding her. Brandi hadn't visited Brenda's house in days? Why would she need to visit if she was staying there? Unless...

"Hang on, Brandi isn't staying with you?" I asked, confused. "Is that what you are saying?"

Brenda shook her head. "No. She's been staying down at the Pink Flamingo Lodge."

"Oh," I said. "That's strange. I just assumed..."

Brenda shook her head and finally managed to get through the door. "She said she doesn't want to stay with her aunt and uncle. I suppose we are not young and hip enough for her."

* * *

"Hello, boy! Sorry to leave you again! Your mommy's home now, though!"

Jasper jumped up on me, his paws on my chest. I

293

laughed as he licked my face. "Woah, that tickles!" I yelled, trying to gently push him off me as my cell phone rang. "Down, boy. Come on, this might be a call about your sister! I have to answer it!"

I finally managed to push him off me and ran to grab the phone from the counter.

"Hello?"

"Hello?" the voice on the other end of the line answered. The voice was familiar, but I couldn't quite place it. "This is Leanne calling from the Pink Flamingo Lodge."

Aha. So that's where I knew the voice from.

"We've had a cancellation, and your name, believe it or not, was next on the list. Are you still in town? Did you still want the room?"

I couldn't believe it. Did she know who she had actually called? I'd never actually said my name out loud to her, and I'd always assumed she'd thrown the piece of paper on the pile without actually looking at it.

I was about to answer that it was fine, I'd left town now, or some other excuse. After all, I'd never actually wanted to book a room. But a thought suddenly occurred to me and before I knew what was happening,

I heard the words coming out of my mouth. "Yes, actually," I said. "I'd love to book a room for the night. Tonight suits me just fine. Should I come down now?"

* * *

Yep, there was no lie about it. The 'no' part of the sign was now gone and for the first time, the sign read "Vacancies."

I smiled and approached the reception area. I had a little bag with me and everything, just so I wouldn't look too suspicious. Leanne was in her usual spot behind the reception desk, nose in a gossip mag as per usual.

"Oh. It's you." Leanne looked a little disappointed as she reached for the keys. "I thought it might be, but I wasn't sure." She frowned at me. "I thought you were a local, seeing as you were looking for your dog."

"I brought my dog with me for the trip," I lied. "But seeing as she's missing, I am free to stay, aren't I?"

Leanne nodded, but she didn't seem too sure.

"I can't wait for my stay here," I said cheerfully. "I'm surprised you had a cancellation, though. Given how wonderful this place is."

Leanne paused with the keys in her hands for a second before she slowly handed them to me. She was still sizing me up, trying to figure out what my game was.

"It wasn't a cancellation so much, more that we had to throw someone out."

"Again?" I asked, in mock shock. I wasn't totally surprised. Leanne did have a habit of throwing her guests out. I was just surprised that she was so forthcoming with sharing that bit of gossip with me. But it was what I had come for, after all. The gossip.

"Yes," Leanne answered, tutting. "Can you believe it? There was another person in here trying to keep a dog in their room in secret. People these days really have no basic respect."

I grabbed the keys from her, wondering why there were so many keys for a single room "How do you know they were keeping a dog in the room?" I asked.

Leanne shook her head in disgust. "Housekeeping saw the room. Covered with small white dog hairs. I can't believe she thought she could get away with that when the evidence was all over the room!"

I gulped. "Was it Casper? Was it my dog?"

Leanne shook her head. "Sorry, I never actually saw the dog itself. Just the evidence of its stay here."

I had to try and stay calm and collect my thoughts. Okay. Someone else had Casper. Someone had taken her from Erika.

Probably after they'd killed her.

"What was her name?" I whispered. "What was the name of the woman you had to kick out? The one with the dog?"

Leanne hesitated for a moment. "Her name was Brandi."

"Thanks," I said, handing the keys back to her. "I won't be needing the room after all."

I can't remember much about my walk from the lodge back to my craft store, only that somehow my feet took me there even when the weight of dread in my stomach was threatening to drag me to the ground. I had to find Brenda. I had to know where her niece was. If she had Casper, then my dog's life was at stake.

I wouldn't trust Casper in the hands of a killer.

I'd known my instincts were right. Erika's death and Casper's disappearance were connected.

But I didn't feel vindicated. I felt terrified.

Chapter 10

"Where have you been?" Brenda asked, thin-lipped as I barged through the door of the craft store. "I've been run off my feet without you here."

I had no time for a scolding. Especially considering that Brenda had held back important information from me. And the police. She tried to lay the blame at Lisa Riemer's feet. Well, as far as I was concerned, she was just as culpable.

"Did Brandi know Erika?" I asked Brenda nonchalantly. Brenda busied herself straightening a stack of already perfectly stacked papers and ignored my question.

"Brenda, it's important. I think your niece has Casper. And I think she is the one who killed Erika."

"She didn't know her! She doesn't know anything about any of this!" Brenda exclaimed, her face as white as a ghost. "You sound like you've gone insane, Georgina. To accuse Lisa was one thing, but Brandi? How dare you."

I shook my head at her. "I know that you know

more than you let on about the night of Erika's death, Brenda. I spoke to Tom."

If it was possible, even more color drained from Brenda's cheeks.

"He told me he was there on the day Erika died, that he witnessed her being thrown out of the Pink Flamingo Lodge. Yet you claimed the next day to know nothing about it. I thought maybe you were protecting Tom, or Lisa, but all this time you've been protecting Brandi, haven't you?"

"I...I..." Brenda's face fell. She shook her head and whispered, "I KNEW that Tom must have said too much to you that night. When he returned to the house, he would barely even look me in the eyes." She sounded seriously ticked off.

"Brenda, that is hardly the point right now!" I had to remind her. "Please, tell me the truth now. What did Tom really see that day when he was at the lodge?"

"I think I need a paper bag to breath into..."

More divergent tactics. "Brenda!"

She really did seem to be having trouble breathing. I wasn't sure if it was for real or just for show. I patiently waited until she finally found her words. "Tom saw...

He saw Erika having an argument with someone."

"Yes. He told me she was having an argument with the manager. Because she was found with a dog in her room. MY dog," I said firmly.

Brenda didn't look so sure. "That might have been true, but that's not what Tom saw. He saw her arguing with Brandi." She looked up at me, tears swimming in her eyes. "He was just trying to protect her. You have to understand, she is family."

I was fuming on the inside but doing my best to push down the fire threatening to erupt. "It's okay, Brenda," I said, lying. It wasn't really okay, but she had to feel like it was safe to tell me the truth without being in danger of me giving her a quick slap to the face. Not that I would ever do that. I just felt like doing it. "Anyone would have done the same thing to protect a family member."

Brenda nodded. "You have to understand, Georgina, that I never, ever truly thought that Brandi had anything to do with Erika's death! I just knew how bad it would look when...when..."

"When what, Brenda?"

Brenda was wringing her hands together. "Tom didn't hear everything. Just an argument they were having. You see, Brandi was only staying at the lodge because she thought she was too cool to stay with a couple of middle-aged fogies while she was in town. But she must have gotten into a fight with Erika. I think they were staying in adjacent rooms."

A customer stepped into the shop. "Sorry! We're closed!" I said to the poor, wide-eyed woman as I gently pushed her back out onto the street and turned the sign around to 'closed.' I was worried that Brenda was going to lose her nerve if we got any more interruptions. "Then what happened, Brenda? What did Tom hear?"

"Erika was accusing Brandi of stealing something from her." Brenda shook her head. "Tom wasn't really sure what it was all about. A bracelet or something. But Brandi would never steal anything."

"A bracelet with the letter E on it?" I whispered.

That was why the police hadn't found the bracelet when they'd found Erika's body. Because Brandi had it. She must have returned to the scene of the crime and purposely dropped it. "It would have looked bad if the police found it in her possession," I murmured.

"What are you talking about?" Brenda asked.

I felt sorry for her as I looked at her. She really didn't know what her niece was capable of, did she?

She really had no idea. "Brenda, I think Brandi did steal that bracelet. And I think she did kill Erika. And now, she has Casper. You have to help me find her."

"Come on," Brenda said, grabbing her purse. "I know where she'll be. She'll be where she always goes when she gets into trouble. My house."

* * *

I could see the white hairs on the carpet as we stepped into Brenda's house. They were obviously new. There was no way Brenda had ever let a dog, willingly, into her house.

"Stay out of the way," Brenda whispered to me. "Here, hide in the den," she said as she crept down the hallway. I did as I was told. In this situation, unlike most, Brenda knew best.

"Brandi?" she called out, raising her voice this time, while I stayed hidden on the other side of the door. "Are you home, sweetheart?"

I heard the sound of a small dog yapping and my heart skipped a beat. Casper. I wanted to run out into the hallway and grab her, but I knew I had to wait.

"Auntie Brenda?" I heard a tearful voice call out.

"Yes, sweetheart, I'm home now." I heard Brenda drop her purse on the kitchen table. I'd never heard Brenda sound so warm and loving. I wondered if she was just putting it on to make Brandi feel better, or if this was how she always spoke to her loved ones when no one was around. From the sound of genuine warmth in her voice I had a feeling it was the latter.

I felt terrible for Brenda. She didn't deserve a family member like this.

I heard Casper yelping again. It sounded like Brandi had her in her arms and wouldn't let her go. "Auntie Brenda, I did a terrible thing," she whispered. It sounded like she was crying.

"It's okay, sweetheart. Why don't you give the dog to me?" Brenda asked.

"No!" Brandi cried out. "The dog stays with me."

So it was Brandi who really killed Erika, and now she was holding Casper hostage. Could this woman get any worse?

Just put Casper down, just put her down, I thought, leaning my head against the wall and closing my eyes.

"Brandi," I heard Brenda explain, a little less

304

patiently this time. "You know how I feel about dogs in the house." This was not part of the act; this was the real Brenda shining through. "She can't stay here."

"But I have nowhere else to go," Brandi cried. "And this dog stays with me!" I heard her yell, "No!" Then Casper started violently barking. I wondered if Brenda had tried to grab her.

I opened my eyes and saw a police car pulling up out the front of the house.

Oh no.

I ran to the window and saw Ryan, still dressed in his uniform, climb out of the car. I guessed he hadn't gotten the promotion yet. I really did feel bad for him. But maybe this could be his shot.

But he had to tread carefully.

I tried to get his attention through the window. I shook my head and made a slashing motion against my throat. I'd meant it more as a 'cease and desist' signal, but Ryan must have taken it as a sign that someone was about to get their throat slit because a look of horror crossed his throat and he started sprinting to the door.

Great. Just great.

Before I could stop him, Ryan was knocking loudly

on the door and calling out, "Who's in there? Open up! This is the police!" I ran to the door and tried to calm him down and stop the yelling, but it was too late.

"Who's here?" I heard Brandi scream. Suddenly, she was in the hallway, a terrified Casper in her arms. She looked like a totally different girl than the usually bright, cheerful Brandi I knew. Even her blonde hair looked darker and limper. I realized I had never really known her at all. Boy, I really had a knack for picking friends, didn't I?

"Casper!" I whispered, moving away from the door and finally allowing Ryan to spill through it.

"What's going on in here?" Ryan asked, taking a moment to catch his breath as he moved his eyes from me, to Brenda, to Brandi, and finally to the trembling dog in her arms.

"It's a hostage situation," I said to him, holding him back. "And she's got my dog. Don't make a move."

Brandi was shaking as she held Casper close to her chest. "Don't move any closer or...or..." She couldn't quite finish her threat, but I knew what she was implying. She was trying to say, "One more move and the dog gets it."

"Brandi," I said carefully. "I don't care what else you

do now, if you run away and escape or..." I caught Ryan glaring at me out of the corner of my eye. Okay, so maybe he cared if she ran away and escaped, but I wasn't working for the law. I only cared about one thing.

"Just put the dog down. Put Casper down. She doesn't deserve to get hurt."

"I don't want to hurt her," Brandi said. "But if you and the cop don't leave me alone, I might have to."

This girl was a sociopath. "Ryan," I pleaded with him. "Please stay back." I stared straight at Brandi. "I know that you saved Casper after you killed Erika. And you've obviously taken good care of her. Please, I know that you don't want to hurt her. You love her."

"I do love her," Brandi said, cuddling Casper.

"Then just put her down. Please."

Casper was whimpering in her arms and I knew that Brandi was torn. She didn't really want to hurt the dog, but she was capable of anything.

"Why did you do it, Brandi?" I asked. "Why did you kill Erika?"

"I didn't mean to," she whispered. "But she was going to turn me into the cops." She stopped and gave

Ryan a death glare. "Just because I stole her stupid bracelet." She looked at Brenda and started sobbing. "But I only did it for you, Auntie Brenda. So that you could win the competition."

Brenda's mouth fell wide open. I was in shock. Brandi really thought her aunt had a chance of winning? She did all this for those lime green vases?

"That's it," Ryan said, moving forward with the cuffs in his hands.

"No!" I screamed, worried about Casper.

But Brandi dropped her before she ran, and Casper, finally free, ran straight to me while Ryan chased Brandi into the back yard.

"Casper!" I fell to my knees as she ran to me and I scooped her up into my arms. "Oh, I've missed you so much, little princess! I bet that Jasper can't wait to see you either!" She licked my face, and I let out a long sigh of relief. "I was really starting to think I might never see you again," I admitted, standing up.

It was all going to be all right now, though. I stood and watched, Casper still licking my face, as Ryan cuffed Brandi. With this to add to his resume, he was no doubt a shoe-in to get the promotion.

Brenda walked back to me, looking like her legs were about to buckle beneath her. She came over and managed to pet Casper with shaking hands. "I'm glad you've got your dog back," she whispered.

I couldn't help feeling bad for Benda. For once, the town gossip was going to be the talk of the town. And I had no idea how she was going to take it. I reached over and placed my hand on top of hers and squeezed it. No matter what anyone in this town said about her, I was going to stand by her side. I knew what it felt like to have no allies here.

Brenda looked up at me in surprise.

"This wasn't your fault," I said. "Don't blame yourself."

Brenda stared out the window. "I always knew the Pottsville Arts and Crafts Festival was going to be the event of the year," she said, as she watched her niece get led to the police car. "I just never knew it was going to end like this."

Epilogue

"I suppose a congratulations is in order," I said, holding up my glass of champagne. My entire kitchen and dining room was full of people. Well, it was half full of people. It was slow going, but with Brenda on my side, I was starting to make friends in Pottsville. And I wasn't letting anyone speak badly of Brenda or her family. I was her little attack dog. At least, I would be until this whole thing died down.

Ryan laughed and spun around in his suit. "Thank you," he said, taking a glass of champagne.

"You did good," I said as we clinked our glasses together. "You deserve this promotion."

Ryan nodded toward the small gold statue sitting on my coffee table. "Do I need to congratulate you as well?"

I shook my head, a little embarrassed. "Brenda got that for me. She still says I should have won. She bought it from the trophy shop and had it engraved and everything."

"That's sweet of her."

I took a swig of champagne. "She has her moments."

Ryan frowned. "You know, you could still go about getting Lisa disqualified. Do you want me to look into it? From everything you've told me, she deserves to get the trophy taken away from her. She might have even broken some laws."

I shook my head. "I'm sure you have far more important things to concentrate on, Detective." I sighed. "Let Lisa keep her trophy. It can't mean that much to her, knowing how she got it." I glanced down at the trophy on my coffee table. It was only a quarter of the size of Lisa's, but it was worth far more.

Ryan cleared his throat. "I still feel like I should address the elephant in the room."

I looked around. "I don't see any elephants." I took a sip of champagne, waiting for him to continue.

"I'm sorry," Ryan said. "I should never have suspected you, George. And I should never have put our friendship in jeopardy like that."

I shrugged a little. "Well, we're even now. I did accuse you of murder once, remember?"

Ryan nodded. "Yeah. I remember that very clearly."

"Let's make a pact to never accuse each other of

murderous crimes ever again."

Ryan laughed. "Sounds like a deal to me." We clinked our glasses together.

"What is that noise?" Ryan asked.

I spun around to see Casper clawing against the glass sliding doors, desperately trying to get in. "I think she wants to join the party," I said, raising an eyebrow. "Don't worry. The yard is secure now. She can't run away again."

"Let her in," Ryan said with a laugh. "Dogs are welcome at any party in my honor."

I walked to the doors and pulled them open, Casper almost getting stuck as she ran in before the gap was wide enough. She jumped into my arms and I laughed while Jasper ran over and licked both of us. It was good to have my little family reunited. I petted them both and looked up at my guests, laughing and drinking champagne. I was finally starting to feel at home in Pottsville.

A Finely Crafted Murder

Chapter 1

I felt as though I had just seen a ghost.

Not a literal ghost, because the person I'd seen was not a figure I thought was dead. But a figure that I thought I had buried long ago in the past. One that was dead to me. And it had made my heart stop, as well as my feet, in the middle of the street.

The wild winds which had been tormenting Pottsville for days whipped my short, curly—still blonde but greying just a little on the eve of my forty-first birthday—hair into my eyes, while my rowdy dog yapped at the wind as though it was something he could chase.

By the time I pushed my hair of out my face and tried to focus, the figure had disappeared into a shop. I am inquisitive by nature, but I didn't want to chase after the strange figure. It would only be tempting fate. If it really was him, then it was better to put my head down and pretend I had never seen him. And if it wasn't him, then there was no sense in chasing after ghosts.

The wind blew suddenly and widely, scattering fallen leaves all over the pavement. Jasper pulled on his leash, trying to chase after them.

Perhaps it is just a coincidence. Maybe it's just someone who looks like him.

Because it wasn't possible for my ex-husband to have tracked me down. Right?

But there were only 1,500 full time residents in the town, and it was very unlikely that he knew someone else in Pottsville. And I'd never known him to be into arts and crafts. Then again, once upon a time, neither had I.

And it was a craft shop—one that I own—that I was attempting in vain to get back to, but the wind was blowing with so much force that it pushed me in the opposite direction.

"What are you barking at, Jasper?" He was refusing to behave or to respond to my directions. Just like the wind, he wanted me to go back in the direction I'd just been, wanting me to chase after that mysterious figure.

Jasper seemed overly excited, almost like he had picked on a familiar scent, but that wasn't possible.

Jasper had never met Adam.

I'd only adopted Jasper from Pottsville Pet Rescue a few months earlier. And Adam and I had been married...geez....it was so long ago I could barely remember.

Finally we reached the door and shelter from the wind. I turned the sign I'd put up—"back in ten"—over, now that I was, indeed, back. Even though it had actually taken me twenty minutes to go to the bank and get lunch.

Jasper was still barking at the door, trying to get back out, as though he wanted to chase that man—that ghost—down the street.

"You don't even know Adam. And it wasn't him anyway," I added quickly, wanting to correct myself, even if it was only to my dog. Jasper was a border collie and highly intelligent. If he thought something was up, then it made me uneasy.

"Just...go take a nap in your bed," I said, pointing toward his cushioned dog bed in the corner. I brought Jasper into the store with me most days. He wasn't the most independent dog and if I left him at home, I tended to come home to chewed up sofa cushions or a ripped up back lawn, depending on where I left him.

Jasper did as he was told, which was unusual, but he didn't sleep. Instead he remained guarded, his eyes fixed on the front window.

It just wasn't possible. How could Adam have even found me, hidden away out here in Pottsville? We didn't even have high internet speeds, thanks to the fact that we were hours from the nearest city; I had absolutely no online presence anyway. None of my other ex-husbands had found me out here and they were all a lot savvier than Adam.

"And more to the point," I murmured out loud, even though it was only Jasper there to listen to me. "WHY would he have tracked me down?"

"Who has tracked you down?" a voice called out.

I jumped, thinking that Jasper had suddenly learned how to answer back. And suddenly acquired a middle aged female voice. But it was only my assistant manager, Brenda. I hadn't even expected her to come in that day; it would have been more helpful if she'd been there to cover my ten—sorry, twenty—minute break.

"No one," I said quickly, arranging a display of ribbons that sat on the front counter. "I just thought I saw an old, familiar face."

"Those look terrible," Brenda said, then she scolded

me. "You're doing it all wrong! You're tangling all the different colors together! Here, let me do it." She tutted loudly as she pushed me out of the way. I heard her muttering, "I have to do everything myself around here."

"Have fun," I said, picking up my purse and grabbing Jasper's leash. I was as restless as he was and needed to find out if it was Adam, once and for all. That required action. Standing around staring out the window wasn't going to cut it.

It was time to face the storm.

I'd only just stepped onto the curb when I immediately regretted my decision. There were flashing lights and a loud siren, and I jumped out of the way as a police car swerved around the corner, nearly knocking Jasper and I clean over. I was less concerned about myself than I was about Jasper—I quickly leapt in front of him and pushed him out of the way. Luckily the car missed both of us, if just barely, and sped away. As my heart rate was returning to normal I strained my neck to try and see who had been driving.

Ryan.

I shook my head and tutted a little. I was going to have to give him a stern talking to when we next went out for a drink.

Jasper pulled on his leash and barked loudly. He was yanking me along the pavement in the wrong direction again. This time he wanted to follow Ryan. This dog really needed to make up his mind.

"We're not going to chase the police car, Jasper," I said to him, feeling a little embarrassed that I had so little control of him on a busy street while I tried to ignore the judgmental looks. Jasper wasn't a bad dog at all, but whoever his humans were before me, they hadn't trained him very well and he could be boisterous. He certainly had a mind of his own.

I glanced over my shoulder to the shop where the stranger, which I was absolutely, completely, one hundred percent sure couldn't have been Adam, had disappeared into. "Jasper, come on," I said, trying to lead him the right way, but he was darn insistent on following the police car.

"Fine!" I said, giving in and letting him have his way. "It wasn't as though it was Adam anyway."

And to be candid, I did kind of want to see where the police car was headed. I kind of had a taste for crimes and mysteries and solving them. The way the car had been speeding, I was sure that whatever had gone down must have been serious, and I wasn't above some rubber necking.

Maybe I could even give Ryan a bit of a helping hand. I had experience with police matters, after all. I wouldn't exactly say the small town police force was incompetent at their jobs...exactly. Some of the force, like Ryan for instance, was smart and perceptive. But others weren't entirely on the ball. I'd only been in town for two months and thus far, I'd solved two murders before the police managed to even arrest the right suspect.

But surely this police car, traveling out of the center of town, wasn't heading toward anything as serious as a murder scene.

My craft shop was in the center of Pottsville, the central business district, so to speak. Rents were relatively high as it was a popular street and Pottsville was a well-known tourist town, especially for artistic types and those interested in antiques and crafts.

But outside the main part of town, the rents were much lower, and for a good reason: they didn't get the foot traffic or the tourist love. It was hard work trying to rent a shop outside of town and a lot of these fading store fronts sat empty and the ones that did make a go of it struggled.

The police car was stopped in front of a craft store. One of my rival stores, I supposed, though I never worried too much about Julie and her store, stranded all the way out here. Two blocks out of town in Pottsville was the same as being two suburbs out, if Pottsville had been a city.

"What's going on?" I asked a man standing beside me as I looked at all the broken glass covering the pavement.

"What does it look like? Some lowlife broke into the shop." The man shook his head. "Not that there'd be anything much of value in a craft shop."

I ignored that rude comment and moved away to someone a little more pleasant. I whispered to the tall woman with the red rimmed glasses that was peering into the craft store. "Do you know what's going on?" I asked her. She smiled and was about to respond, but then, to my utter dismay, Jasper jumped up onto her white trousers, leaving behind brown dirty paw prints.

"Oh my goodness, I'm so sorry!" I said, mortified as the woman gasped and backed away, telling me to get my dog under control.

Well, we were all out of friends at the crime scene.

Looked like we were just going to have to find out ourselves. I stepped gingerly over the pavement, avoiding the broken glass and making sure that Jasper's paws didn't get anywhere near it.

I stuck my head in through the broken glass. The lights in the shop were off so it was a little hard to see, especially since the dark clouds hiding the sun weren't helping me that day. I could see, though, that the cash register was open and there were items—beads, paper, scissors—scattered all over the ground, as though the robber had been caught and hurried to get away. I let out a slightly disappointed sigh. I supposed I wanted something a little more interesting than just a run of the mill robbery, as terrible as that sounded.

"Come on, Jasper. It's just a break-in," I said, wanting to get away before we made any more enemies. The woman with the dirty white pants was muttering to someone else nearby, pointing at the two of us.

The crowd started to disperse when they realized they weren't going to get much more of a show. A little broken glass, a few stolen items... With the wind and storm brewing, people needed more than that to keep them outdoors and away from their cozy fires.

Suddenly there was a scream from the back of the store. We all turned our heads and stared at each other. "What was that?"

Jasper pulled so hard that his lead escaped my grip and he was free. He sprinted in the direction of the screams, through the window and over the spilled items on the ground. "Jasper!" I screamed, running after him.

The shop was dark and I almost tripped as I raced to try and get my unruly dog back. I banged straight into the wall at the back of the shop. Jasper leapt up against it and clawed at it wildly, barking and trying to get through the other side.

There was a door. I opened it.

I probably shouldn't have.

There was Ryan, kneeling over something white on the ground—a sheet covering up something—while a blonde woman I didn't recognize, wearing a police uniform, stood over the same thing with an expression of shock.

Ryan turned around sharply, his face shocked and angry when he saw me. "George, get back," he said, holding his hand up.

"Please, control your dog," he shouted.

Talk about embarrassing.

Jasper ran all the way up to whatever the sheet was covering and grabbed the corner between his teeth before Ryan or I had a chance to stop him.

He yanked the sheet back to reveal the unthinkable.

A dead body. A woman, with marks around her neck like she had been strangled.

Ryan stood up and grabbed Jasper's leash, handing it to me. "George, get out of here," he said fiercely. "And take Jasper with you."

* * *

Jasper trotted along beside me on the pavement, his tail between his legs. If I'd had a tail, it would have been hanging in a similarly downtrodden way. I didn't think there was much chance of Ryan and I going out for that drink any time soon.

And, considering the way the woman with the ruined white trousers had shaken her head and muttered toward the others as we'd left the crime scene, I didn't think there was much chance of making friends in Pottsville any time soon either.

"I guess it's just you and me again Jasper," I said, laughing a little. Oh well, maybe it wasn't such a bad idea to give up on making human friends, and it was probably a very wise choice to give up on men. I mean, did I really need to add yet another husband to the list?

I laughed again as I thought about Adam, shaking my head as I bent down to pet Jasper, who was wagging his tail again. "You would have liked Adam," I murmured, looking up at a gap between the dark clouds. "He always loved dogs as well, as I recall..."

I'd been young, in my early twenties, and sure I knew everything about the world. Sure that I knew everything about love. Sure that if I got married, it would last forever. But Adam, as bright as sunshine as he was on the outside, had a side that was dark and grey. When I'd left, it was because those clouds had come in and covered the brightness completely. I'd had no choice.

I shivered a little. "Let's go home," I said decisively. Brenda could close up the shop. I needed to be by the fire with a glass of red and forget about everything that had happened that day.

Jasper suddenly started barking frantically.

"Not again Jasper," I said, frustrated. "What has gotten into you today—"

I stopped.

There, standing right in front of me, absolutely, completely, one hundred percent was Adam.

Chapter 2

He was a little grayer, but his hair was still as thick and curly as it had been in his early twenties. Darn it. For some reason that annoyed me more than anything else at that moment. Aren't men supposed to be balding by the time they hit their forties? The wind flicked the dark, salt and pepper-streaked curls around his face and it reminded me, just for a second, why I had fallen in love with him in another lifetime.

Jasper was desperate to run over to him, like he was trying to greet an old friend.

"Sit, Jasper," I commanded, making him behave. He sat, but he was still whimpering and I knew if I gave him the all clear, he would leap into Adam's arms. I shook my head. Dogs were too trusting. Far too easy to win over.

"Don't I even get a hello?" Adam asked, holding his arms out as though I might run into them, given the chance.

I shook my head in slow disbelief. "A hello? More like a what the heck are you doing here, Adam?" I said.

"It's your birthday tomorrow, isn't it?" he said with

an easy grin, as though that was the most normal explanation in the world. "Forty-one, is that right?"

I silently groaned. He'd never missed a chance, when we were married, to point out that he was a year younger than me. I wondered how he'd react when he found out that the young man I had a flirtation with was fourteen years younger than me. Not that I cared about making Adam jealous. As soon as I found out what he was doing in Pottsville, I intended to bid him farewell—for good.

"Right. So after sixteen years, you just happen to turn up to wish me a happy birthday? I didn't even get a card from you for the last sixteen."

Adam shrugged again, irritating me with the causal confidence that had once been so attractive to me. "It's always good to celebrate with an old friend."

Friend?

I shook my head.

"What are you really doing here, Adam?"

He picked up a knapsack that had been laying on the ground, which I hadn't even noticed up till that point. I also hadn't noticed that people had slowed down, stopping to look at our conversation, and suddenly realized, with my angry tone and look of confrontation, that I was only providing grist for the gossip mill.

"Do you have somewhere I can rest up for a while?" Adam asked with a wide grin. And, hating myself for a second while I said it, I invited him back to my home.

* * *

Jasper wouldn't stop barking. "I know, I know, there's a stranger in the house. Well, don't worry. He definitely won't be staying the night here." I threw a bone out onto the lawn and while Jasper sprinted to get it, I closed the glass sliding doors.

I composed myself before I turned around, taking a deep breath. *He'll be gone soon. He'll be gone soon.*

"There are plenty of motels and B&Bs in town," I said, trying to smile. I could feel my red lipstick cracking as I made the effort. "This is a tourist town so you won't have a problem finding a place to stay."

"Actually, I'm kind of out of cash," Adam said. He was already sprawled across the sofa, getting comfortable as he picked up the TV remote.

I sighed. "Of course you are." No big surprise there. "Well, there's always the empty field near the lake. That's free. Even though you aren't technically supposed to camp there without paying. But I'm sure one night won't hurt..."

I walked over, took the remote out of his hand, and turned off the TV. I'd already given him a drink of water and allowed himself to make a sandwich from the leftover food in the fridge. "I think you've more than outstayed your welcome," I said, pulling him off the sofa.

"George..." he pleaded as I tried to push him out the front door. On the other side of the open-plan room, Jasper jumped up against the glass and scratched at the window. He didn't want his new friend to leave. "Come on, let me stay for just one night. I won't make a peep. You won't even know I'm here."

When I still showed no sign of relenting, he said, "Come on, you're not really going to make your ex-husband sleep in the dirt, are you?"

"I can lend you a sleeping bag," I said flatly. "You can return it in the morning on your way out of town."

He titled his head to the side and pleaded with me, using those puppy dog eyes which I now hated as much as I used to love.

"Fine. One night only. And I don't want to hear a sound, Adam. Not a sound."

* * *

Oh, goodness. How can it be morning already? I glanced at the clock. I had to open the shop doors in twenty minutes.

"Jasper?" I called as I climbed out of bed and threw on my silk robe. He was usually at the end of my bed first thing in the morning, looking for some attention and food.

I rolled my eyes when I heard the sound of Adam and Jasper playing together downstairs. "Good boy!" I heard Adam call and as I descended the stairs, I saw Jasper running around the living room after his new favorite person.

I pouted a little as I watched them playing. For some reason, it really irked me to see them getting along so well. I thought Jasper was a better judge of character than that. Couldn't he sense that Adam was bad news? That his intentions, his motivation for being in town, couldn't possibly be good.

"Good morning," I said loudly as I moved through to the kitchen to make a cup of coffee. Jasper didn't even look up. I tried not to be too insulted.

"Morning, George," Adam called out with a grin. "Happy birthday! You don't look a day over forty." I could see from the mess he'd made on the sofa and coffee table that he'd already made himself totally at home. The cushions and blankets made it look like a well slept in bed and the table was strewn with the remnants of a late night snack. And the crumbs. Jasper ran to the coffee table and started licking at the plate and leftover scraps.

I poured myself a coffee and Adam asked where his was. "You can make one yourself," I said. "I see you already know your way around the kitchen."

I mean, it wasn't like he hadn't had his good qualities. If he hadn't, I'd never have married him in the first place. He was charming, and good looking, and kind of dangerous in an attractive way, and the perfect sort of boyfriend to have in your early twenties. I'd just made the mistake of marrying him, instead of keeping him as just a boyfriend.

I opened the sliding glass doors and let my other

beloved dog, a small white terrier named Casper, inside after doing her business. At least Adam had been thoughtful enough to let her out. Or maybe it was just another example of how at home he was making himself...

"Well, at least you're keeping a level head," I said, kneeling down to pick up Casper, who, unlike her brother, was little enough that I could easily scoop her up. She was far more cautious and had been hiding behind my ankles ever since Adam had shown up uninvited and, basically, unwanted. Unwanted by everyone except Jasper, that was, who was still excitedly jumping up and clawing against Adam's chest.

"I guess you won't be coming in to work with me today, Jasper?" I called. I raised my eyebrows at Adam. "Well, if you're going to be my unwanted houseguest, you can at least dog-sit for free."

* * *

There was a strange vibe in town, and it wasn't just due to the strong winds that seemed to blow the wrong way. Everyone was looking at everyone else with suspicion. *Are you the one who did it? Are you the one who killed Julie Williams?*

"No dog today?" Brenda asked. She'd already opened the shop for me. I'd been fairly naive to think that I was capable of getting myself dressed, made up, and into town in under twenty minutes. But one hour later, I was there. "Good. I am starting to think I am allergic, you know. And it isn't good to have a dog on the premises all the time. It isn't professional."

I hung up my coat and tried not to roll my eyes. Brenda wasn't allergic. She just enjoyed complaining, and getting the final say about everything related to the store, even though I was the one who actually owned it and paid the rent, not her.

"It's just for one day," I said flatly. "Jasper will be back with me tomorrow. After..." I didn't finish my sentence. I didn't need Brenda in my business any more than she already was.

"It's terrible news, what happened yesterday, isn't it?" Brenda murmured, trying to sound casual when she knew the subject was anything but. "I was there at Julie's Craft Shop when it happened, you know."

I spun around to face her. "What do you know, Brenda?" I asked.

She was curling ribbon for gift-wrapping and there

was a little smug smile on her face that she was trying to suppress. "Oh, wouldn't you like to know?"

"Yes. That's why I asked." I sighed and pulled the ribbon right out of her hands, causing it to lie flatly on the glass counter. "Come on, spill."

"The police already have a suspect," she said, her nose suddenly in the air. "Thanks to me and my keen eyes. And I can't say I'm surprised at who it is either. He's a real good for nothing..."

"Who is?" I asked.

Brenda shook his head. "You're still too new in this town, aren't you, Georgina. You ever hear of the name Gem Dawes?"

The name wasn't familiar. I shook my head.

"Of course you haven't," Brenda replied far too smugly. "But his name—the Dawes name, especially— is infamous in this town. If you were a real resident, you would know all about them." She picked the scissors and ribbon up and went back to work.

I groaned. She really loved rubbing in how 'fresh' and out of place I was in this close-knit community. Well, I wasn't going to let her lord it over me again right then. "Fine, if you don't want to tell me, don't. I'm not even interested."

Unsurprisingly, that got her to spill everything. Brenda loved hoarding information, but she also hated not feeling like the most important, most knowledgeable person in the town. And if not the town, at least the shop.

"The Dawes are a family that have lived here in Pottsville for generations, unfortunately," Brenda said right as a big gush of wind blew the front door shut with a bang. She barely even looked up, or noticed, she was so eager to continue her story. "They're one of the founding families; they first settled here in the eighteen-seventies during the gold rush." Brenda let out a shrill, judgmental laugh. "They were thieves and scavengers then and nothing has changed."

"What do you mean?" I asked.

"Just that half the family has been to prison and the other half are on their way there," Brenda said with a heavy judgmental tone. I didn't want to have to remind her that she had a family member who was on her way to prison—for murder, no less. I literally lived in a glass house, and I know not to throw stones. I wasn't sure Brenda knew not to from her metaphorical one.

"They all live up the hill together," Brenda

continued, shaking her head. "No one with an ounce of class would choose to live up there. The land was sold off for cheap decades ago and the Dawes snapped it up. People say those hills are haunted, you know."

I sighed and tried to ignore that part. "What about this Gem Dawes you mentioned? Why him?"

"Gem is the youngest brother of the lot. I suppose we all held out some hopes for him. He was a good kid at school, attended the same high school as my nephew. He'd be about twenty-four, twenty-five now. Gem wasn't like the rest of them...or at least, so we thought." Brenda raised her eyebrows. "Soon after he turned twenty, he began committing petty crimes like the rest of his family. I guess that kind of thing is bred."

Brenda's expression turned even more serious, and even more judgmental. "And now he's graduated from small petty crimes to murder. He should have been locked up years ago."

Something about the whole tale perturbed me. "Is there any real evidence that Gem is the one to blame?"

"I saw him at the scene of the crime!" Brenda said, as though that was it, case closed, gavel banged down on the bench, sentence handed out.

"That's it?" I asked in disbelief. "Brenda, people's

eyes can be mistaken. You can think that you see something, or someone, and be totally wrong."

Brenda looked at me with narrowed eyes. "And what about that person you thought you'd spotted yesterday? Did that turn out to be who you thought it was? Or were your eyes mistaken?"

My cheeks felt a little flushed. "That was...that was...okay, yes, that did turn out to be who I thought it was, I'm very dismayed to report."

Brenda raised an eyebrow. "And who is this mysterious visitor who has got you so flustered, Georgina?"

"That's none of your business." And I meant it to. Only problem was, I was bursting to tell someone and friends in Pottsville were still hard to come by.

"Fine, if you don't want to tell me, I don't care. I'm not interested," Brenda said, lying as she threw my own words back at me.

"He's my ex-husband," I blurted out.

Brenda's mouth opened wide, presented with a bit of this juicy piece of gossip. "Which one?" she asked.

"My first." I shook my head. "It was a long, long time ago." I actually smiled as I started to tell the story, about how Adam and I had first met while on vacation on Greece, how I'd been in my final year in college and he—having never attended college—was there on a holiday visa that had long ago expired. When I'd returned to the US, he'd come with me and, much to the dismay of both sets of parents, we'd gotten married when I was just twenty-one and Adam just twenty. "But we made it work. At least, for a little while."

But Brenda wasn't interested in listening to me reminiscing, or gabbing about old relationships.

"Don't you think his timing is a little suspicious?" Brenda asked, butting in while I was still talking.

Well, I thought a lot of things about Adam's sudden reappearance in my life was suspicious, but I hadn't given that much thought toward the timing. "What are you getting at, Brenda?" I asked, narrowing my eyes. She was always working some kind of angle. I just had to find out which one.

"He turned up the same day that Julie was killed." She thought about it for a second. "In fact, he must have arrived in town right before she died."

Now it was time for my mouth to drop right open. "You have got to be kidding me, Brenda." I really, really hoped she was.

But she shrugged and picked up her stupid ribbon again, the sound of it scraping against the scissor blade getting right on my last nerve.

"So it's just a coincidence, is it, that the same day as your no-good husband turns up—"

"Ex-husband."

"The same day your no-good ex-husband turns up is the same day an innocent woman is killed?"

I threw my hands into the air. "Five minutes ago, you were sure that this Gem Dawes person was to blame! Brenda, I believe that you just like to think the worst of people," I shouted before storming to the front door. "Make up your mind before you go blaming every last innocent person in this town. And one other thing—get some actual reliable evidence!"

I stormed out the door and down the road. I was so mad at Brenda that I couldn't even stand to be in the same room as her. She always had a way of winding people up, but usually I could laugh her manner off. Usually her rudeness and judgmental nature was like water off a duck's back to me. Brenda was always harmless enough. Or so I'd always thought.

Why am I taking this accusation so seriously? I wondered as I stomped my way down the pavement.

Why am I taking it so much to heart?

But as I continued to storm my way out of town, I realized I was heading straight back to my house and I knew exactly why Brenda's accusations had irked me so much.

Because they echoed my own fears.

I needed to ask Adam a few questions of my own.

* * *

The pink-frosted monstrosity in front of me had two candles sitting on top of it. A 4 and a 1. Below the candles "Happy Birthday" had been piped in large white bumps. "I know you said it's not a big birthday, but I know you can't resist a slice of cake," Adam said, grabbing a knife from the knife block. He really had made himself at home. "And I know you don't like pink but this is the only birthday cake that the cake shop had."

I thought Adam didn't have any money?

I sighed as I looked down at the cake. "I don't feel much like celebrating," I said, folding myself up into a seat at the table. Jasper finally remembered that he

340

loved me and that I was the one who fed him and he came and curled up at the legs of the chair.

"You always loved celebrating your birthday," Adam said, looking concerned.

"It's been a long time since you were in any position to say what I 'always' love doing," I said wryly. "I've changed, Adam." But had he?

Adam pushed the cake to the side and sat down next to me. "I know that your love of cake must have remained the same. You couldn't have changed that much."

I pushed the cake even further away, just to one-up him. My appetite had totally soured. "Forty-one isn't even a big birthday. It's not worth celebrating."

"Sure it is," Adam said, refusing to take the hint. He'd always been like that though, self-absorbed, happy-go-lucky when things were going his way and then a petulant child when things weren't so rosy for him.

"You know a woman was killed yesterday, don't you?" I asked. "It seems in bad taste to break out the cake and balloons."

I watched Adam's face carefully while he answered.

"Yes, I know, George. It's a terrible thing to have happened."

"Terrible that it happened right as you arrived in town, isn't it? Must make you think that this isn't quite the quaint small town you must have assumed it was."

"I try not to make assumptions about places," Adam answered. "All towns and cities have their dark secrets."

Yes. And so did the people in them.

"I'm just saying. It seems funny timing, you arriving right as Julie was killed." I paused for a second, wondering if I should say what I was thinking or bite my tongue. "Especially considering what happened sixteen years ago."

Adam's face turned white as he leaned back and pushed his seat back from the table. "I had nothing to do with what happened sixteen years ago, George. Wow." He shook his head and picked up the cake. As he walked away with it back to the kitchen, I almost thought he was going to throw it in the trash, but he changed his mind and it landed on the counter with a small thud as he let it drop.

Adam had always maintained his innocence. And even though I'd left him and filed for divorce, I'd always believed deep down that he was innocent. I had to. I couldn't let myself believe that I had really, once upon a time, married a murderer.

But now, I wasn't so sure.

Chapter 3

Jasper whimpered at the bottom of the hill and pulled on his lead, trying to pull me back toward home. "I know, boy, I want to go back too." Though I wasn't too eager to go home. I just didn't want to be at the foot of the Pottsville hills, with their eerie shapes that seemed to move and blend in with the clouds, and the shadows that seemed to dart around, only visible out of the corner of my eye. Maybe there really were ghosts up that way.

But Jasper had never been scared of ghosts before. Whatever was up that hill must have been really scary to make Jasper want to turn back.

"Come on now, boy," I said gently. I wanted him with me for safety reasons, if nothing else, even though I'd made a vow not to let Brenda's prejudices about Gem and his family influence me. It was a little hard, now that I was there and I realized how stranded I was. The hills lay to the east of the town, far away from the center, and the few properties that lined the road that led me there lay abandoned. I felt totally removed from society even though I'd only walked for fifteen minutes from my craft shop to here.

laugh when Jasper licked his cheek. Jasper looked back at me excitedly, wanting me to join in the fun as well. I hung back for a moment.

I still had to wonder if Jasper really was the best judge of character. First Adam, now Gem Dawes. But he was just a dog after all, wasn't he? They tended not to judge, but to love everyone, no matter what they might have done.

"We were just wandering through the...neighborhood," I stated. Though 'neighborhood' didn't seem the right way to describe the enclave of haphazardly built houses and cottages and the old shells of cars and trucks that lay abandoned in the fields.

"No one just wanders up this way," Gem said, straightening up. He immediately looked a little less boyish and a little more intimidating. "People tend to stay away from these parts. Smart people, anyhow."

"Well, maybe I'm not so smart." I grinned at him. "And I don't mind walking where others don't dare to tread."

Gem shrugged. "I still think you've got to be brave to come up this way so late in the afternoon, right before the sun sets..."

Okay, that kind of creeped me out a bit. I tried to shrug it off. Maybe it was just a compliment, not a warning.

"Can we chat a few moments?" I asked with another smile. "I'm kind of an outsider in this town as well."

Gem thought about it for a second but shrugged. "Sure," he said. "Why don't you come inside for a cup of tea?"

I hadn't really expected to be invited inside and the question caught me off guard for a moment. I wasn't entirely sure I should be alone in his house with him, even with Jasper there to protect me. I wasn't sure how much protecting Jasper would even be doing. He was still jumping all over Gem and ignoring me. If anything went down between the two of us, Jasper would probably be on Gem's side.

"You're not scared to be alone inside with me, are you?" Gem asked.

I shook my head. "No, of course not." I smiled and followed him inside, clipping Jasper's leash back on to his collar and pulling him closer to me as we walked through the front door.

For some reason it surprised me to see that Gem had modern appliances and a brand new electric kettle that he used to boil the water with. I was surprised the cottage even had electricity. That was probably terribly judgmental of me, and I gave myself a silent lecture. I was there to find out the truth, not to judge Gem and his family the way everyone else in the town had.

I sat a little nervously while Gem made the tea. "Is English Breakfast okay by you?" he asked. "It's my favorite."

I replied that it was fine and tightened my grip on Jasper's leash.

"I've only been in town such a short while," I said, wrapping my hands around my tea cup, trying to steady myself. "And I've already seen so many remarkable things."

"Have you?" Gem asked, sitting down with me. I was hoping he'd ask me, 'such as what?' but he wasn't going to make this easy for me. Was there going to be any easy way to ask him if he'd killed Julie, though?

"How's the tea?" Gem asked.

"Perfect," I said and took another sip.

Well, there was no point in making any more small talk about tea. "Did you hear about what happened in town yesterday?" I asked Gem.

He stared back at me with a dark look. "I didn't just hear about it," he said in a flat tone that made me uneasy.

I took a sip and then put my cup back down. "Some people are saying that they saw you at the scene of the crime."

"I was at the shop, so what?" Gem asked. He turned away and stirred two full spoonfuls of sugar into his tea. "I like to go there sometimes. Is it that hard to believe that I am into crafting?"

I tried not to look too surprised. "I've never seen you inside my shop," I said. "I own a craft shop too, a bigger one than Julie's in fact."

Gem didn't look impressed at all. "If it's one of those fancy places in the center of town I usually stay away," he said drolly.

I never would have referred to my shop as a 'fancy place,' but I tried not to look too amused at his description.

I glanced around his small tin house. "You're not the usual demographic for a crafter," I answered carefully, trying to look for any clues that he was telling the truth. I didn't see any scrap books, or yarn, or carving tools anywhere. The house was sparsely decorated in fact, even though I'd expected it to be cluttered with junk. But it was neat and tidy and there were few items on a bookshelf that I noticed was full of well-thumbed fantasy novels.

"Yeah, well, people tend to judge."

"They do," I mused and stared into my tea cup. "Especially in a small community like Pottsville. Don't worry, Gem, I can relate..."

I spotted a brand new sewing machine, still in its box, in the corner of the room and quickly averted my eyes. Too late. Gem caught me. "I bought that," he said defensively. "I paid for it and everything. Do you want to see the receipt? I think I've still got it around here somewhere."

I shook my head quickly. "No, it's okay..."

"You think I stole it, don't you?" Gem asked, shaking his head. "I just told you, I am into crafts. I like sewing and making leather-wear."

He stood up and grabbed my half-finished tea cup and took it over to the sink, pouring the rest of it out. "I think you'd better leave."

It looked like I couldn't even make friends with a suspected criminal in this town.

I stood up and spoke gently, wanting to reassure him.

"It's okay, Gem. I believe you."

He stomped over to the door and opened it for me. "Take my advice," he said. "You really want to get away from these hills before it gets dark."

* * *

I looked at my prized possession in the shop—a pricey spinning wheel that sat in the corner. I spun the spinning wheel around and watched the spokes whirl until they became invisible.

Brenda's voice broke through the daze I'd fallen into in the back of the shop.

"So, you came back alive?" she called out.

I spun around and nodded.

If I wasn't imagining things, Brenda actually seemed relieved to see that I'd arrived back from the hills unharmed.

"It wasn't as scary as you made it out to be. I wasn't even worried," I lied, tidying up the shop for the night, ready to close up. The sun had already started to set and I was eager to get home before it was entirely dark. Gem's words had unsettled me and now it wasn't just the hills that seemed scary, but the entire town.

"So what did you find?" Brenda asked. She usually insisted on being out the door right on the dot, not wanting to work for a second longer than I was paying her for. But tonight she was lingering, wanting to know every detail.

"Nothing..." I said unconvincingly as I turned the sign around to 'closed.'

Brenda raised her eyebrows. "You did find something," she whispered excitedly. "Come on, I'm the one who told you where to go. You have to tell me what you found. It's only fair."

I told her about the sewing machine, brand new and still in the box, that I had spotted in the corner.

I hesitated a moment before I asked her. "Do you know if that was one of the items that was stolen from Julie's store?"

Brenda shook her head slowly. "I might know a lot of things, but I'm afraid I don't know those details. You might have to speak to that boyfriend of yours." I was confused for a second, thinking that she was talking about Adam.

Right, she meant Ryan. "I doubt he's talking to me after I let my dog destroy a crime scene," I muttered.

Brenda tutted and shook her head. "I've told you before, you need to leave that dog at home."

"Brenda, can you focus on the important details? When he offered to show me the receipt, I refused, but now part of me wishes I had..." Should I go back and check? If just to put my mind at ease?

"I'm one hundred percent sure he stole it," Brenda said, setting her lips in a firm line.

Okay, now I suddenly wanted to give Gem nothing but the benefit of the doubt—and nothing but faith. Maybe Brenda was the kind of person who demanded to see a receipt, but I didn't want to be that sort of person.

"He'd have to be pretty stupid to steal something from the crime scene and display it in his home, wouldn't he?" I asked.

"Those Dawes boys are not exactly known for their high intellect," Brenda answered. "He's probably stupid, and arrogant enough to display it."

"I didn't get that impression of him," I mused

quietly. "He didn't seem arrogant at all. He just seemed like a shy young boy, lost almost."

Brenda shook her head. "You are being taken for a fool, Georgina."

"No, I am just using my gut," I said, hoping that Brenda was wrong and that I wasn't being taken for a ride, acting like the idiot I'd been once upon a time, when I was younger. When I'd first been married...

"I don't believe he did it," I said firmly. "There's a killer loose in this town, Brenda, and no one benefits if we are chasing the wrong guy."

"Believe what you want," Brenda said. "But that doesn't change the truth. And the truth is that Gem Dawes was at the shop yesterday. And he wasn't alone when he left either."

I stopped at the door, my coat in my hands. "He wasn't?"

Brenda shook her head. "No. He was with a man I didn't recognize. Looked much older than him though, about your age, Georgina. With curly, dark, greying hair. Sound like anyone you know?"

Chapter 4

I ran down the road, having overslept by three hours, hoping that Brenda wouldn't lord it over for me for the entire day. The still violent wind didn't work in my favor either, pushing me back as I struggled against it.

"Careful there," a voice called out. "You'll blow away."

I straightened up and pushed the hair out of my face. "Ryan," I said with a bright smile. "Gosh, I am terribly sorry about that inconvenience the other day." I waved down at the empty space at my ankles. "As you can see I am trying to let Jasper be more independent these days." I frowned. "Or maybe it's me that needs to learn how to be more independent."

Ryan raised his eyebrows in surprise and laughed. "I never thought you had any problems being independent. I would have said the opposite was true. I always thought you needed to learn to be less independent."

Oh, Ryan. He was so young. Probably too young for me. I wondered if this 'independence' he was talking about was really just because he was only twenty-six and women his own age knew their own minds less and were probably a little more clingy.

"Anyway," I said, trying to sound breezy and casual, even though I was feeling anything but, being pushed around by a terrifying wind and wondering, in the back of my mind, if I was living with a killer. I'd barely seen Adam the night before. Nor the morning. He'd been out, taking Jasper for a walk when I'd slipped away, three hours late to work. "How's the investigation going?"

Ryan took a sip from the paper coffee cup he was holding. He laughed. "You always try your luck, don't you?" He lowered his voice a little. "To tell you the truth, not so well," he said, looking a little troubled. "We're dealing with a witness who can't stop sticking her nose in and telling us what we are doing wrong."

I raised my eyebrows. "Oh, let me guess who that is." I shook my head. "Sorry about that," I said as I started walking again. "I'll try to keep her busy today so she doesn't have time to bother you."

Ryan waved at me as I left. "I'd appreciate that."

"Woah," I said, walking into the shop. The two aisles were so full with customers I had to squeeze past them to even hang my coat up. Looks like I wasn't going to have any problem keeping Brenda busy for the day.

I heard the cash register ding as Brenda rang up yet another item.

"Are we having a sale that I forgot about?" I asked Brenda, spinning around, confused. I couldn't see any red or yellow dots on anything, and there were no signs up in the window. Unless Brenda was running a secret sale she hadn't told me about, I was at a loss to explain this sudden rise in popularity.

"I guess now that our competition has closed down, we're the place that people are flocking to."

I froze. Was Brenda right? Were we suddenly benefiting from Julie's craft store being closed?

Were we benefiting from her death?

The idea made my stomach churn. I wanted to be a success, but not at the expense of someone's life.

But I didn't get much of a chance to let the guilt overtake me. All day, I was busy running backward and forward, tending to customers and getting stock out of the back to refill shelves. By the time the clock hit five o'clock, I was exhausted and my feet were aching. But it was a good kind of exhaustion. I realized I was also grateful to have had my mind taken off all the things spinning around in my head.

But now that the shop was empty, those thoughts had started to creep back in.

"Huh," Brenda said, counting the money after we had finally closed for the day.

"What?" I asked, sitting on the floor. I leaned against the counter, too exhausted to stand.

"It's just funny, isn't it?" Brenda replied.

I rolled my eyes since she couldn't see my face. "What is?" I asked.

"It's just funny that Julie dies, and you are the beneficiary of her misfortune."

I suddenly jumped back up to my feet and confronted her.

"So what are you suggesting now? You think that Adam killed Julie just so that my craft store could do better business? That's insane, Brenda."

She opened her mouth so say something, but I had had enough of her nonsense. I wasn't ready to let her have her say until I had had mine. "Do you really think, after sixteen years, my ex-husband turned up out of the blue, like some crazed knight in shining armor, to kill off my crafting competition? I know there have been some insane motives for murder in this world, Brenda, but that would really take the cake."

Brenda just stared at me in bemusement, and the more angry I got the more bemused she looked. When I finally stopped to take a breath, she had the last word.

"No, Georgina. I'm suggesting that you are the one that killed Julie."

* * *

"That's it!" I said, pacing across the tiles of my living room, while near by, Adam lay splayed causally on the sofa with Jasper curled up on him, both acting like they didn't have a care in the world. Well, they'd just been chilling out all day, playing in the park and eating food from my fridge, not dealing with a barrage of customers and a co-worker accusing them of murder. "I have had it. First thing in the morning, I am firing Brenda!" I stopped for a breath and to take a long gulp of the red wine I'd been holding so fiercely it was a wonder the stem hadn't snapped in my grip.

Adam pondered this and took a sip from his coffee mug. No wine for him, he always said it gave him a headache. "This Brenda seems like the sort to sue for wrongful dismissal."

"Oh, this is not wrongful dismissal!" I shot back, shocking even myself at how wound up I was getting. "The woman accused me of murder! And get this, Adam—this is not even the first time she has done this!" I resumed my pacing, or rather, stomping. "And I've put up with her, written her off as some harmless old biddy, but this..." I shook my head and finished off the last of my wine. "This is too much. I'm not putting up with this from an employee any longer."

Adam grinned and I had to ask him what could possibly be funny at that moment.

"It's just that this is the George that I used to know all those years ago. The one I married." His grin grew even wider. "I knew she was still in there somewhere, underneath all this new bright jewelry."

"Yes, well, that was all a long time ago." I sat down next to Adam on the sofa. For just a moment, I longed to be back in those simpler days. Before everything had crumbled and fallen to dust, that was. Before the police came knocking and asked to see Adam, asked his whereabouts on that Monday night that our neighbor had been killed.

"Do you remember that night?" I asked Adam softly.

"What night are you talking about?" Adam asked.

I looked down at the wooden floorboards. "You know the night I'm talking about," I said quietly.

"Of course I remember it. I remember the way you protected me," Adam said, sitting up straighter. "Told the detective that I'd been home all night, even though, as per usual, you'd slept like a log and..."

"And wasn't even sure if I was lying or not," I said, finishing his sentence for him. I looked up at him, into those deep hazel eyes that had once been so familiar to me. "It's not as though I could have testified against you, anyway."

Adam shrugged. "You could now, though. We haven't been married for sixteen years."

"Let's hope I don't have to," I said with a little nervous laugh. I was sure that it couldn't have been Adam that Brenda saw with Gem when Julie was killed. I was telling myself that she'd just gotten the idea in her head that it was Adam when she'd learned he had arrived in town that day, and was now fixing the evidence to support it. She was letting her judgements cloud reality. Her 'memories' were probably entirely fabricated.

Adam edged a little closer to me on the sofa.

"I'm not sure you fit in in this town, George. You always belonged in a big city. Where people are a bit more open-minded. More like you. You're getting stifled in this town with all the small-minded prejudices."

I looked at the floor again, wondering if maybe he was right. There was no way I wanted to give him the satisfaction of saying so, though.

I sat up straight and folded my hands in my lap. "Some people in this town are all right. They're not all small-minded," I said. "I've even made a couple of friends. One of the police detectives, for instance, has his wits about him." I smiled as I thought about Ryan, one of the few people in the town I'd managed to forge a connection with. "He's intelligent as well, and caring. And he doesn't judge people, he takes the time to get to know them. He's an old soul in a way..." I mused, leaning against the back of my sofa with my elbow, my feet suddenly tucked up underneath me.

"Sounds like you have a thing for this guy," Adam commented. "Are we talking about your next future ex-husband here?"

I stood up and walked over to the kitchen counter

and poured myself another glass of wine. "I'm done with all that," I said firmly.

There was a knock at the door.

"Oh, I ordered some Mexican takeout," Adam said, looking at the time. "Took long enough to get here."

"Yeah, well, there are about two takeout shops servicing the whole town. It tends to be slow," I said as I grabbed my wallet. "Don't worry, I've got it. In both senses," I said wryly as I walked to the door. It would be far less embarrassing for all of us if I just paid for the food and saved Adam from having to make excuses.

"Ryan!" I said, straightening up as I answered the door. Hmm, did I want him there in my house with my ex-husband in the room behind me? It did seem a little strange, for several reasons. I mean, geez...Ryan was basically the age that Adam had been when I was married to him.

"Um, it's actually not the best time for me right now," I whispered, leaning forward. "I'm just about to eat dinner, then I'll be getting to bed early."

"I'm not actually here to see you, George," Ryan said, taking his hat off. "At least, not right now."

"Oh, okay. Who are you here to see then?" I asked.

Ryan scratched his head. "I hope this isn't too awkward," he said. "But I'm here on official police business. I hear that you've got a lodger staying with you?"

I pulled away from the door. "You're here to talk to Adam?" I asked. Suddenly I had flashbacks from that night seventeen years earlier and I could feel a cold sweat breaking out.

"George?" Ryan asked. "Are you all right? You look a little pale."

I nodded quickly. "I think I'm just hungry," I said, looking over his shoulder. I laughed nervously. "I'm just waiting for a food delivery... They always take so long, don't they? I mean, geez, sometimes I think I'd be better off closing the craft shop and opening a takeout restaurant, I'd probably make a killing..." I stopped talking when I reached the word 'killing' and realized I'd been awkwardly rambling.

Ryan cleared his throat and took a step forward. "Can I come inside?"

I chugged down another glug of wine while I listened to the two of them talking. The entire bottom half of my house was open plan so there wasn't another room I could go to even if I'd wanted to. And I didn't. I wanted to hear every last detail, no matter how terrible it was.

Why on earth would Ryan think that Adam had anything to do with Julie's death? How would Ryan even know about Adam at all?

I already knew the answer, though.

Brenda had opened her big fat mouth. Of course she had.

"Mr. Thornton," Ryan started to say. I hadn't heard Adam referred to like that in a long time. And it had been even longer since someone had called me "Mrs. Thornton." To this day, Adam's was the only last name I ever took. After our divorce, I reverted to my maiden name and kept it even throughout my subsequent marriages. "When did you arrive in town?" Ryan continued, ready to jot the answer down on his notepad.

"Wednesday morning," Adam answered. He seemed calm enough as he spoke, but I knew him too well and I could see from his mannerisms, by the way that he kept moving his hands around, that he was nervous.

"And how did you arrive in town?"

"Bus." Adam's answers were short and to the point.

"And was anyone else on this bus with you?" Ryan asked.

"Yes," Adam replied.

Ryan looked up from his notepad. "Anyone you know? Anyone who can confirm?"

Adam shook his head. "No one that I knew. I didn't speak to anyone during the journey. I slept for most of it. I only woke when we arrived in Pottsville."

I tried to read Ryan's face. He kept it pretty straight, but I couldn't help feeling like he wasn't buying Adam's story. "Where did you go when you got off the bus?" Ryan asked.

It took a long time for Adam to answer. I was starting to get nervous. "I went into a cafe, in, erm, in the middle of town." He coughed and cleared his throat. "It was a long bus ride. I was hungry."

"And I guess no one saw you go into this cafe," Ryan said wearily.

"I'm not sure."

I tapped my fingernails nervously against my wine glass. *Just cut to the chase, Ryan.*

He did.

"I have to ask you," Ryan said. "Where were you between the hours of midday and three pm on Wednesday afternoon?"

Adam looked up at me, a slightly pleading look in his eyes. "I was with George. Wasn't I, George?"

Great, I thought, trying to catch my breath. *I'm really back here. I'm seventeen years in the past.*

Both men stared at me as they waited for my answer.

"Yes," I finally said, making the same mistake twice. "Adam was with me the whole time."

By the time Ryan left, the Mexican food that had arrived halfway through the interview had gone cold and I had lost my appetite anyway.

"Thanks, Georgie..."

I turned my back on Adam and called Jasper to come and sleep at the foot of my bed this time. "You're not staying downstairs tonight, Jasper." I shot a look over my shoulder at Adam. "And this is the last night you're staying here, Adam. In the morning, you need to be out of here."

Adam nodded sadly and trailed off to the sofa, flicking the lights off, and I was left standing, in a daze, at the top of the stair case.

What had I done?

And what did Adam have to hide?

Chapter 5

"I have to talk to you," I said to Brenda as soon as I stepped through the doors. I threw my purse onto the counter with so much force that it knocked over a carton of buttons, scattering them everywhere.

"Well, you're just going to have to wait," she said through a tight, forced smile while she tended to another customer. "And in the meantime, you can clean up the mess you just made."

I did no such thing. I stomped to the back of the shop and found my checkbook, where I began to write out Brenda's pay slip. Two week's severance seemed fair enough; she was lucky she was even getting that.

Twenty minutes passed before she was finally free and the shop was briefly empty. I handed her the check and she just stared at it for a moment, her mind working overtime to work out what was happening.

The penny finally dropped.

"You can't fire me!" Brenda screamed in outrage. "Not after all my hard work. I have been the one managing this place, covering for you while you sleep in and run all around town, chasing after men..."

"I do no such thing!"

Brenda shoved the check back into my hands and stood stubbornly. "I have been the model employee. I have never done a single thing wrong!"

"You've been talking to the police," I said. "I had a visitor last night, asking for Adam. Asking him where he was when Julie was killed. You're the one who started the whole rumor that he was involved. So the only conclusion I can draw is that you are the one who has been running your mouth."

Brenda crossed her arms. "You can't fire me for speaking to the police," she said smugly. "I will have a case for unfair dismissal."

Darn it, she was probably right.

I looked at the check in my hands. Suddenly it was starting to feel more like a bribe. I quickly shoved it in my pocket.

"Why are you trying to make trouble for me, Brenda?" I asked in disbelief.

"I'm a good, law-abiding citizen of this town," Brenda replied. "And I only told the police what I saw. I told them that a person that I recognized and knew very well was walking away from the scene of the crime."

"You don't even know it was Adam!" I practically shouted. "And you hardly know him 'very well.' You've never even met the guy."

Brenda's face was full of confusion. "What are you talking about?" Brenda asked. "It wasn't Adam that I told the police I had seen."

I was speechless. "Then who did you see?"

Brenda shook her head. "I didn't want to have to do this, Georgina, but your actions gave me no other choice. I wanted to be loyal, and I was torn, but at the end of the day I had to be honest about what I saw."

"What are you talking about Brenda?" I said, just about ready to grab her by the shoulders and shake the information out of her if she didn't hurry up and come clean.

"Georgina, I saw you walking away from the scene of the crime."

* * *

"She's really gone too far this time," I said to Adam

as we hurried along the pavement that was about to come to an end when we reached the edge of town. "She's not just making accusations now, she's going to the cops with her half-thought out theories." I was walking so fast that the wind, still pushing against me, was no longer a match for me. It didn't slow me down at all.

We were headed back to Julie's shop. I knew that the answers—or at least something that could save Adam and I—must lay there. There must have been clues I missed the first time I was there, thanks to Jasper and his inquisitiveness.

"I don't understand," Adam said. He was breathing heavily as he practically jogged to keep pace with me. "How could she have seen you at Julie's store that day?"

I shook my head. "She couldn't have. I didn't leave work that day. I was at the store the whole entire day up until..."

"Until what?"

"Until I saw you." I stopped walking and gasped for breath. "Oh no..." I said, remembering. "I did leave for a little while. For ten minutes to get lunch and go to the bank. Well, it was actually twenty minutes." I started walking, but slower this time.

"You saw me?" Adam asked.

I nodded, lost in thought. I stared down at the bright beads I was wearing around my wrist and used the other hand to twist them. "This isn't good, is it?" I murmured. "Both of us out and unaccounted for during those important minutes..."

Adam laughed uneasily. "I know you didn't do anything, George." He cleared his throat for a moment. "But do you know the same of me?"

I stopped and stared at Adam. "Do you know what kind of trouble I can get in to, for lying for you like I did? What if Ryan finds out?"

Adam glanced around and told me to keep my voice down. He was right. The street wasn't crowded, but there were a few stragglers and I was panicked, talking far too loudly.

"Why did I need to lie, Adam?" I asked. "Tell me what you are really hiding."

He began to walk again, slowly. "Nothing," he said, burrowing his hands in his pockets. "I just know how bad it looks that I have no real alibi for that time."

I pulled on his arm and made him stop again. "Just tell me something, Adam. Do you have anything to hide? Just be honest with me. If I am covering for you, at least let me know what I am getting myself into." I placed a hand on my hips. "I don't want a repeat of what happened seventeen years ago."

He looked into my eyes and shook his head. "I promise you, George, that I did not hurt Julie. I never even saw her or met her. If you showed me a picture of her, I wouldn't even be able to recognize her. I didn't even go anywhere near that part of town after I got off the bus."

"Well, that is where we're headed now." I watched for any change in his eyes. If he'd really never been there, he shouldn't look worried.

He didn't seem concerned at all. I wasn't sure if I was relieved or disappointed. "Let's go then," he said. "I'm as eager as you are to find out what really happened. It took me a long time to throw off my reputation last time I was questioned for murder. I don't want it happening again..."

We walked in silence for a few minutes, the only noise the sound of the wind whipping all around us.

"Hey, it's kind of nice, don't you think?" Adam asked.

I couldn't possibly see what he was referring to at

that moment. The fact that we were both being accused of being murderers? The wind that was blowing so hard it felt like a hundred tiny knives against the skin? "What is kind of nice?" I asked in disbelief.

"Us two, back together like this, us against the world," Adam replied.

I shook my head. Maybe Adam was having a fun time reliving old times, but I just wanted to get the whole thing cleared up so that Adam could get out of town and I could get my old—new—life back.

Adam grabbed my arm. He even gasped a little. "George—" He pointed ahead. There was a real look of fear in his eyes. He looked positively spooked.

With a shaking voice, he whispered, "Who is that?"

* * *

Okay, now I really had seen a ghost.

"We gotta get out of here," I said, tugging on Adam's arm so we could get the heck out of there.

But Adam was rooted in position, like a tree that had stood there for a thousands years.

"Adam!" I said, turning away so that I couldn't see the person up ahead.

"Don't you want to find out who that is?" Adam whispered.

I shook my head. My answer was firm. "No. It is bad luck to see your doppleganger. Do some research, Adam! Seeing your doppleganger means you are about to die!" I wanted to move, but it was like I was paralyzed.

"The George I remember wouldn't be scared so easily," Adam said with surprise. "She would have walked straight up to this woman and asked what on earth she was doing, impersonating her."

Is that what the woman was doing? Impersonating me? I had a thousand thoughts flooding my head and most of them were too scary to dwell on.

I knew how stupid I was about to sound, but I said it anyway. "But what if this woman is not flesh and blood?" I whispered. "What if it really is an apparition? I mean...how can someone who looks exactly like me have just walked around the corner? When I am clearly standing right here?"

"Why don't we go and find out?" Adam asked. Then, without warning, he placed his hand in mine and began to pull me toward the mysterious imposter. And suddenly, the thought of confronting a ghost was the least of my concerns. I yanked my hand out of his grip, just about ready to slap him across the face with it.

"You don't get to do that," I snapped. "You don't get to hold my hand."

"Sorry, sorry," Adam said, holding his hands up in remorse. "I was only trying to..."

"Oh, I know what you were trying to do," I said, wrapping my shawl around my shoulders as I hurried off. Adam tried to run after me but I raced ahead, no longer waiting for him as I closed in on the woman. "Go back home, Adam!"

The wind whipped at me while I tried to run. The woman was fast and I had to hurry so that I wouldn't lose sight of her.

She was headed toward the hills.

Great.

Knowing it was best to catch her before she headed up their spooky slope, I increased my pace to a jog.

"Wait!" I called out breathlessly, but the wind swallowed my words. I stopped to catch my breath and this time shouted, "Stop!"

The woman froze and spun around.

I froze as well, a mirror of her in more ways than one.

After a few seconds, I finally released the breath I had been holding.

She had the same short, still blonde but with streaks of silver, curly hair that flew out a little wildly from her head. And she wore the same bright beads around her neck and wrists. I narrowed my eyes and squinted at the blue and yellow bracelet, trying to figure out if it was in fact one of my own designs.

"Who are you?" the woman asked, stunned.

But looking closer at her, there were some differences as well as the striking similarities. Up close, we had entirely different noses—hers a short button, mine longer and more European. And she had freckles where I had none.

I let out yet another long sigh of relief. She wasn't my long lost twin. And she wasn't a ghost. She was, indeed, flesh and blood. Just a curious look-a-like.

"My name is George," I said, taking a step nearer to her. "I'm a little new in town, so I don't know many people. I just thought I'd say hello."

"So your way to make new friends is to chase them through the woods, shouting at them to freeze?"

I laughed a little. "I'm not always the most socially apt," I said with a little wink. "It just struck me how similar we look to each other." I looked her up and down. "I thought it was a little curious, that's all."

"Yes, it is a little curious," the woman said, flipping her hair back out of her face, returning the same curious stare back at me.

"Your name isn't George too, is it?" I asked with another small laugh.

The woman shook her head. "No. It's Caroline."

She was a little short with her words. She also looked like she was ready to run away at any second. I couldn't blame the poor woman. After all, I had just chased her through the woods. And I did look almost exactly like her.

But if she was going to run, there was only one way to head—straight up the hills.

"I have to ask," I said, nodding at the hills. "This is an area of town that most people tend to avoid. What are you doing here?"

The question was a little direct, and I knew it was

really none of my business. But hey, that had never stopped me from asking questions before. I had a habit of sticking my nose into matters that were none of my business.

Caroline glanced behind her at the hills, which again seemed to move out of the corner of my eye, only maintaining their shape when I stared straight at them. Her answer surprised me. "To be honest, I'm not really sure myself. Now that you've stopped me, I think I might have lost my nerve altogether."

"Sorry," I said, walking over to her. We stood side by side and stared up the hill together, looking at Gem's small cottage at the top. I gasped a little when I saw a face peep out from behind the curtain for just a second, before the curtain was quickly pulled back.

"Looks like we're being watched," I said.

Caroline nodded. "It was stupid of me to come here. I almost want to thank you."

Time to be direct again. "Were you here to visit someone? It's not such a great day for a casual walk through the most dangerous part of town."

Caroline nodded. "Yes. Well, not visit exactly. The person I was visiting isn't a friend of mine. I don't think I've ever spoken to him."

I waited a second before I asked, "Is that person one of the Dawes?"

"Yes." Caroline took in a deep breath and shivered inside her coat. "Gem Dawes."

Okay. That was interesting. "Why have you come to visit Gem Dawes?" I asked. Okay, I have to admit, I jumped to the worst conclusion first. I thought maybe Caroline was somehow caught up in one of Gem's schemes. Maybe she was buying stolen good from him? I glanced down at the beads that looked so familiar.

They really do look like my creation, I thought, but I didn't remember Caroline ever coming into the store to buy them. And there was no way that I would have forgotten serving a woman who looked exactly like me.

Caroline shivered even more as she finally answered. "I wanted to ask him a few questions. About the death of my sister, Julie."

Chapter 6

"It is uncanny," Caroline said as she stared at me from across the other side of the restaurant table. She sat her glass of white wine down and shook her head. "How long did you say you've been in town?"

A waiter sat Caroline's plate of pasta in front of her and the smell of the creamy white sauce, hot and fresh and filled with chopped herbs, made me wish I'd ordered that instead of the crab salad that the waiter sat before me.

"About two months now," I answered as I chomped down on a mouthful of salad, still dreaming of pasta. Was it too late to switch my order? Caroline and I definitely weren't genetic twins of any kind if she could regularly eat creamy pasta and keep her figure.

Caroline swirled her fork in the noodles. "I suppose it's a little strange that we haven't run into each other before," she said. "But I travel a lot for work. I sell medical supplies. I only came home this weekend because of...well, you know," she said quietly before she took a long sip of wine.

"I'm sorry about your sister," I said, placing my fork

down. Truthfully, it was for more reasons than one, but it wasn't the right time to tell Caroline that both myself and my ex-husband, who was living with me, were being accused of her sister's murder. She might very well lose her appetite at hearing that.

"So you only arrived in town after your sister...died?" I asked, trying to choose my words at least somewhat carefully.

Caroline looked a little startled at the question. "Yes," she said quickly. "Why on earth do you ask that?"

I picked up my knife and fork again. "No reason. I apologize." I offered her a wide smile. "Were you and Julie close?"

Caroline nodded. "Extremely."

I took a sip of my own wine, though mine was red. "I have to ask. What did you intend to do if and when you actually knocked on Gem Dawes's door?"

Caroline laughed and went back to her pasta. "I'm not even sure," she said, shaking her head as she slurped on a long noodle. "I don't know what I was thinking. Taking matters into my own hands like that. I probably would have lost my nerve even if you hadn't turned up."

I poked around at my salad. "Do you think Gem Dawes had something to do with your sister's death?"

Caroline folded her hands. "Do you mean do I think he killed her?" Okay, so it seemed that Caroline was someone I could—and should—be direct with.

"Yes," I answered. "Did he know Julie at all? Is there anything you have to go on besides his reputation?"

Caroline looked a little unsure. "Not really, no. But a witness did say that she thought she saw him at the scene of the crime."

I let out a very low laugh. "Yes, well, a witness also said she saw ME at the scene of the crime, when I was nowhere near it." I shook my head and laughed again, louder this time. "Maybe it was just someone who looked exactly like..." I suddenly stopped. Both speaking and laughing. It didn't seem funny anymore.

Well, that was awkward. I suddenly become very interested in my salad hoping that Caroline either didn't hear what I had said or would choose to politely ignore it in the name of forging a new friendship.

"I just told you," Caroline said icily. So, not ignoring it then. "I only arrived back in town after my sister's death."

I nodded quickly. "I didn't mean anything by it. I really didn't mean what I was saying. It was a joke." I tried another laugh. "Maybe it was a third mysterious woman who looks like both of us." Okay, that was stretching believability a bit.

Caroline's fork scraped angrily against the bottom of her plate. The noise made me shudder involuntarily. "I think perhaps this witness was just mistaken."

"About Gem Dawes too?" I asked.

Caroline looked up at me warily. "You're very interested in this Gem Dawes person," she said. "I'm surprised you even know who he is." Caroline narrowed her eyes. "How did you even know he lived in the hills, anyway? How did you know what I was doing there?"

I placed my cutlery down. "Because I went to visit him yesterday. Because, Caroline, I am also investigating the death of your sister."

* * *

"I don't think I've ever made a friend and lost a friend so quickly," I said, checking the time on my watch. "All within the space of half an hour."

Adam seemed to find this funny while he sat the table. To make his earlier behavior up to me, he'd offered to cook. I almost wanted to hug him when I'd arrived home and discovered he'd made pasta.

Almost.

"It is a little strange though, isn't it?" Adam asked as he petted a very eager Jasper, who was climbing all over him and licking his face. "You would have thought she'd be grateful that someone was trying to figure out who killed her sister."

"Yes. Unless she has something to hide."

"And you think she does?"

Jasper jumped onto the table and stole a bread roll.

I sighed. "Brenda did say she 'saw me' at the scene of the crime. What if it wasn't me she saw—which, well, I know it wasn't—but Caroline instead?"

"Didn't you say that Caroline said she was out of town at the time?"

I threw Adam a look. "But people do tend to lie about where they were at the time of the crime."

Adam sat the food down heavily in the center of the

table along with the serving spoons. "You still think I'm hiding something?"

I didn't want to answer. I poured us each a glass of wine and quickly drank mine.

I finished the glass and groaned as something hit me. "So does this mean I have to apologize to Brenda?" I could think of nothing worse. "I mean, technically, she did think she actually saw me. She thought she was doing the right thing."

Adam shook his head. "No way! She should be the one apologizing to you! She accused you when it was clearly not you!" He sat up straight and Jasper bounced away. "Don't let her off the hook for this one, Georgie."

I shook my head, unable to help the little smile that crept onto my lips. This was the Adam I had fallen in love with all those years ago. The one I had married. The one who always had my back and was always on my side. It had always been us against the world.

"You're right," I said firmly. "Well, I don't think I'll have to push the issue. When Brenda finds out the truth, I am sure she will do the right thing and apologize first!"

* * *

"I saw what I saw!" Brenda said stubbornly, the following morning. "You won't hear an apology escaping my lips." She stomped her foot. "In fact, Georgina, it is you who should be apologizing to me!"

"Well, I am certainly not apologizing to you!" I shouted as I stomped to the back of the shop. I felt like I was being held hostage in my own store. We couldn't go on working like this. As I hung my coat, I seriously started to consider my idea of selling and opening a takeaway shop instead.

Jasper jumped out of his bed and ran over to where his leash was hanging on the door. So he wanted to escape as well, even though we had only just gotten there.

I grabbed my coat straight back off the hook.

"Let's go, Jasper," I said as I stomped past Brenda again. Then I loudly added, so that she could hear me loud and clear: "I want to go look at some empty real estate down the street. So that I can sell this shop and start a new business!"

Brenda glared at me as I walked past, her cheeks so

full and red she looked as though she might explode. Then, she did the unthinkable. She pulled off the apron she always insisted on wearing and then ripped off her name tag that said 'Assistant Manager' and threw it down onto the counter.

"Good luck running your 'new business' without me!" Brenda shouted as she raced to get her windbreaker, beating me to the door while I stood there speechless. "And good luck running this business on your own as well!"

* * *

I heard something loud and wooden hit the floor at the back of the shop with a loud crack.

The long line of customers in front of the counter all turned their heads to look at the back of the store, craning their necks to see what had made the almighty noise. One old lady turned her nose in the air. "You shouldn't have a dog running around inside here!"

It looked like I could get rid of Brenda, but I couldn't get rid of her sentiments, nor her judgements. "I'm sorry," I said, stepping past the line, anxious to see what the noise had exactly been. "What have you done, Jasper?" I called out, wondering for a moment whether he might have knocked into the wall and cracked the actual foundations of the building.

What I found was almost worse. My prized item, laying broken on the floor, with a very remorseful Jasper sitting beside it, his ears and tail low like he knew that he was in big, big, trouble.

"Oh, no, the spinning wheel!" I cried out. By far my most expensive item in the store. I couldn't afford to have it crack right through, no matter how good business was at that moment; it sold for close to a thousand dollars and I only ever stocked one at a time.

Jasper whipped around and lay down, ready to be yelled at. I didn't have the heart to do it, no matter what amount of money he had just cost me. I leaned down to pet him. "It's okay, boy, I know you were only playing..."

"Ahem!" a voice called out. It was that same lady who'd told me off about having Jasper in the shop. "We are waiting for service, you know! You should put that dog outside!"

I stood up and forgot for a moment that the customer is always right. "It is blowing a gale out

391

there!" I said. "He is safe inside. And he is more than welcome inside, thank you very much."

I swished back to the front counter with my head held high, but it wasn't long before more trouble presented itself.

"The lady who usually works here put the item aside for me yesterday," a mousy woman with glasses stated. "She promised I could come back and get it today."

"Oh, er, just let me check," I said, getting flustered as I leaned down behind the counter, trying to find the location that Brenda apparently stashed all these 'on hold' items. "Just a second!"

The woman shook her head. "I suppose you must be new here, then."

I stood up quickly and pushed the hair back out of my face, the blood rushing to my head. "Actually, I am the owner of this store," I said, taking some offense. "And the woman who served you will no longer be working here, I am sorry to inform you."

After another three customers had come up and asked for their on-hold products—and I still couldn't find them—I was at my wit's ends. "You'll just have to come back tomorrow!" I eventually said, throwing my hands up. Meanwhile the line was getting longer and longer and Jasper, relieved at not getting yelled at earlier, was running around like he was possessed, knocking over everything in his path. The disgruntled customers stormed off, telling me they would go elsewhere if I couldn't find the things that Brenda had hidden. "Maybe you should call her," one suggested unhelpfully before storming out.

Fat chance of that happening.

Just when I was about to give up and ask everyone to clear out for the day, someone equivalent to an angel made an appearance.

"Oh, thank goodness you're here," I cried out in joy as Adam walked through the door.

"You haven't been so happy to see me recently," Adam said with a little laugh. "I just thought I'd pop in to see how you were doing—"

"Do you know how to use a cash register?" I asked, pushing him in the direction of the counter. I didn't even give him a chance to answer. "Great! Thank you!"

I ran around trying to clean up after Jasper while Adam took care of the customers. He had natural charm, and was better at it than I was.

I picked up the spinning wheel, trying to see if it was salvageable at all, but it wasn't just cracked up the center up the center of the stand, the entire wheel was cracked with large shards of wood sticking out. It gave me a splinter when I touched it, as though, like Sleeping Beauty, I had just touched the pointy end of a needle. I yelled out and shook off my bloodied finger. Adam was so busy—and the store so noisy—that he didn't even notice, or look up if he did.

"Guess what I heard through the grapevine?" Adam said when we finally got a chance to speak. I was busy searching through a drawer in the back for a bandage.

"What did you hear?" I asked. "And can it help me to stitch my finger back together?"

He shook his head. "Nope. I think your instincts were right about Caroline. Word on the street is that Julie was in a feud with her sister right before she died."

I wasn't sure I wanted to hear this little 'tidbit.' And I wasn't sure I entirely trusted Adam's motives in telling me. I stood up straight, a bandage in one hand and my other one extended toward him, the splinter still in my index finger.

"And how do you know this, Adam? How do you

even know what the word on the street is? From one of the many friends you have here in town?"

"A friend did tell me actually," he replied.

I looked at him suspiciously. "You're not just saying this to get yourself off the hook, are you?"

Adam rolled his eyes a little. "No. Scout's honor."

"I doubt you were ever a scout."

Adam took the bandage away from me and took my other hand in his. "Hmm," he said, peering down into it. "You need to get the splinter out before you put a bandage over the top of it," he said, reaching into the front pocket of his jacket and producing a Swiss army knife.

I guess he was always prepared.

I winced and turned my head away as he flicked the knife out and used the end of the blade to remove the splinter. "There," he said, squeezing on some antibiotic ointment and putting on a bandage. "Now you won't get an infection."

"Thank you," I said. And I meant it. I watched as Adam flicked the blade back into the knife and placed it back in his pocket.

"See? I'm always here when you need me!" Adam

said, waving around the shop. "And I always know just what to do."

"Well then, you really have changed," I said. "Because the Adam I married wasn't exactly the most reliable." And I wasn't quite ready to believe that he could have changed so much, even if sixteen years had passed. Was I really ready to give him a second chance to enter my life again?

I was still nursing my swollen finger when I saw the look of hurt in Adam's eyes. "But you are here now, and I suppose that is what matters," I said gratefully. "I couldn't have gotten through this morning without you."

I walked to the front of the shop, ready to count the cash in the till and see if the profits we had made could cover the loss I'd take on the spinning wheel, when I stopped dead in my tracks.

"It's Caroline!" I gasped, taking off my apron. It was early afternoon and nearing my busiest time of the day, but right then I wasn't thinking about that. If Adam's 'word on the street' was right, then I needed to talk to Caroline. And I needed to take my chance. I wasn't exactly her favorite person in the world right then.

"Where are you going?" Adam called out. "Are you

crazy? You can't leave me alone with all this!"

But this was his chance to prove himself, to let me see if I actually could rely on him. And in that moment, I had total faith, because I had to.

"You'll be fine, Adam! I believe in you! All the best!" I yelled out, grabbing my coat as, for the second time that week, I chased my lookalike down the street.

As I flew out of my shop, I never could have imagined the carnage I'd return to later that night.

* * *

Maybe it wasn't the best thing to call out, but I yelled, "Stop! Freeze!" down the street, loud enough to make Caroline, as well as about a dozen or so passersby, stop in their tracks.

I apologized to the innocent bystanders and headed toward my target in a bee-line.

"Caroline."

She crossed her arms. "Georgina."

Only Brenda ever called me by my full name like that. It got my shackles right up, but I decided that

Caroline had no way of knowing.

I cleared my throat. At least she hadn't run away. She almost looked open to listening to what I had to say. Almost. "I know we didn't get off to the greatest start the other day."

Caroline surprised me. Her face even softened a little. "Actually, I was hoping to apologize to you for that."

"Oh." I was a little caught off guard. I'd assumed I would be the one groveling and I'd assumed she would be the one punching me in the face.

"I shouldn't have stormed out of the restaurant like that, without even paying the bill," Caroline said.

I shook my head. "It was nothing," I said. "I can cover the cost of a plate of pasta and a bowl of salad."

"Still, I shouldn't have gotten so angry with you," Caroline said. "I should have been grateful that you are investigating Julie's death." She nodded at me and there was a look of sincerity in her eyes, which were the same green as mine. "At least someone else cares. And I'm glad you're looking into her death. Julie was very dear to me. I'm just a little emotional."

"Of course you are." I took a few seconds to collect

my thoughts. Could Adam's source have been completely off base? If Caroline truly had been in a feud with her sister, the last thing she would want was me poking around. Or talking to her.

Caroline went one step more than just talking and invited me to a late lunch, reminding me that I hadn't had a chance to eat yet. "This time, I'll pay," she said with a friendly smile. "You know, Georgina, it would be nice if you and I could be friends. I don't have many in this town either."

* * *

This time, I did what I wanted and ordered the creamy pasta. "This is amazing," I said, digging in. I asked the waitress for some extra parmesan on top and extra cracked pepper—even better.

But this time, Caroline ordered the salad. And she pushed it around the plate, soaking the lettuce leaves in balsamic vinaigrette while staring at me. For someone who wanted to make a new friend, she was being standoffish.

I needed to tread carefully. I didn't want a repeat of

last time, when Caroline had overturned her plate and stormed off, leaving me with a very red face and a double bill to pay.

"Caroline, were you and Julie..." I stirred my fork in my pasta, hoping the right words would come. 'In a terrible feud right before her death' didn't seem like the right choice. "Close? Before she died?"

I let out a small sigh of relief. I hadn't totally blown it yet.

"Julie and I were incredibly close," Caroline said, choking up a little as she spoke. She apologized and grabbed a tissue from her purse. "I'm sorry. I don't usually get so emotional," she said, before dabbing at her eyes and then blowing her nose.

"Well, this is a very emotional time for you," I said. "Your sister has just died." I reached across the table and patted her hand.

Caroline pulled her hand away and sat up straight. "But I have to be practical now," she said. "There are things to take care of. There is a business that's been closed for days. It needs to re-open at some stage. My family needs to keep the money coming in. A closed shop can't make any cash."

Huh. I didn't know there were plans to keep Julie's

shop open. I tried not to show my look of disappointment. It was wrong of me to be disappointed anyway. And I should have known that my own increased business was an anomaly, not something to get used to.

Looks like I'm gonna have to find a way to cover the cost of that spinning wheel.

By the time I looked back up at Caroline, she had completely composed herself and half of her salad had disappeared from the plate. "Enough crying," she said in a clipped tone. "I intend to look toward the future now, not dwell on the past."

Caroline did have a certain coldness about her, but I wasn't sure if it was due to a lack of true emotions and remorse, or whether it was just a defense mechanism, a way of surviving such difficult times.

But she was already closed off. "How about when you and Julie were growing up? Were you close as young girls?" I tried to ask, but Caroline just glared at me and reminded me that the past was the past and that was where it should stay.

"When was the last time you saw...?"

"Drop it, Georgina, please. If we are going to have a pleasant lunch or any chance of a friendship."

Caroline's salad was totally gone and she asked the waitress for a dessert menu. "Now, onto more pleasant matters," she said to me, her hands folded in front of her.

There were pleasant matters at that moment?

"I've heard the rumors about you, Georgina," Caroline said, a little twinkle returning to her eye, proving to me that she was human, after all, not a robot. She ordered a caramel cheesecake from the dessert menu, but I had to decline after the full plate of pasta I'd only just managed to get through.

"What rumors are those?" I asked with a little laugh, trying not to sound nervous. *Gosh, what has she heard?*

Caroline arched an eyebrow. "I heard that you're involved with a younger man."

Great. So she knew about Adam. "He's not that much younger, he's only forty. And, anyway, I am not involved with him. He's my ex-husband!" I said, feeling myself getting a little flustered, before I reached for my glass of ice water.

Caroline looked a little bewildered. "No, I am talking about that hunky young policeman."

"Oh. You mean Ryan?" I had to laugh at that. "How

did you know about that? Never mind," I said, finishing off my glass of water. "That little dalliance is dead and buried. Whoops, poor choice of words," I said, sitting my glass back down.

Caroline didn't seem upset about the unfortunate word choice. "That's a shame," she said. "I was hoping to live vicariously through you. Or at least hear a little bit of gossip."

"Oh, I've got plenty of gossip, don't worry about that..."

Then, I heard the police sirens. I turned my head to see the car speeding past.

"There goes your boyfriend," Caroline said with a little knowing laugh.

Yes. Fantastic.

What on earth could have happened now?

Chapter 7

"Yikes!" Caroline called out, backing away from the shop front. "Good luck, George. I'm afraid I'm going to have to love you and leave you, though."

I spun around to look at her briefly, my mouth wide open. Oh, she meant it. She was already practically making skid marks, the speed at which she was fleeing the scene.

But the scene of...what exactly? I wondered as I stepped gingerly into the shop. There were no more customers, and we were technically past closing time, but the sign was still turned to 'open.' There was no sign of Adam anywhere.

I honestly couldn't believe what I was looking at. My shop, abandoned, not even locked up, and the cash register open with all the day's takings just sitting there.

"I'm lucky I wasn't robbed!" I said out loud as I hurried through the aisles to push the till shut. *I'm going to kill him.*

Then I saw that something even more important and valuable had been left out in the open.

"Jasper!" I cried. Jasper ran up to me in distress. "I'm so sorry, boy," I said, kneeling down to comfort him. "I can't believe that Adam would just abandon you like this. Oh, you are such a good boy to stay put and not run away," I said as I wrapped my arms around him.

Though, from looking at the contents of the shop, I could see that even though he might not have run away, perhaps 'good boy' was pushing it. He had knocked three shelves completely clean and ripped apart an entire aisle of yarn and string. It looked like he had attempted to make a very large, multi-colored nest to sleep in out of the destroyed materials.

But it was not Jasper I was angry at in that moment. It was a human that was the object of my fury. One who should have known far better than to leave a shop— and a dog—unattended.

He is just as unreliable as he was when I was married to him!

I stood up and took a few deep breaths. First I just had to make sure all the money was still there. Then I could lock up. Then I could kill Adam. Then I could throw him out of my house.

Cleaning up took far longer than I expected and

after half an hour, I had only managed to make the shop look worse. I also had no idea what I was supposed to do with all the ruined and broken items. I didn't know where I was supposed to store them, if I could write them off, send them back to the manufacturer... I ended up just filling up a trash bag and collapsing down beside it while Jasper tried to comfort me.

Where is Brenda when I need her?

For the hundredth time that day, I considered phoning her for help, then just as quickly reminded myself not to stoop that low. I couldn't bear to give her the satisfaction, nor could I bear to swallow my pride.

As I cleaned up the remainder of the mess, I vowed that no matter how desperate I got, I wasn't going to call her to ask her to come back to work.

But when my own cell phone rang while I was sweeping up, making me jump, I hoped, just for a second, that it was Brenda calling me. Maybe she would be the one swallowing her pride.

It wasn't. It was a voice asking if I would accept a call from the Belldale Police Precinct.

"Yes?" I said nervously.

There was static on the other end of the line, and a sinking feeling in my stomach. "You're my one phone call," Adam said. "I can't believe I'm asking you this again, George..."

I hung up the phone without even giving him my answer, I was in such a daze. But I grabbed my coat anyway, and my checkbook, and hurried out the door.

"I guess that's why he left in such a hurry," I said, calling Jasper to come with me. This time, I actually locked the door.

* * *

It took everything I had in my savings to bail Adam out of the tiny cell he was being held in. "You'd better not leave town," I said as we walked out of the station two hours later. "I can't believe I actually just said that..." Wasn't leaving town precisely what I'd wanted him to do all this time?

"I'm surprised you didn't just let me spend the night," Adam said. "It was free room and board after all. And probably more comfortable than spending a night sleeping in the field."

"You don't have to sleep in a field tonight," I said with a sigh. "Although the thought of making you do so is terribly tempting."

"I appreciate it," Adam said. "Even though the sofa is getting a little hard on my forty-year-old back," he said.

Don't push your luck.

"Do they really think you did it?" I asked Adam softly.

Adam shoved his hands in his pockets and looked up at the moon. Uh oh. He looked worried. Adam never looked worried. "My prints were at the crime scene," he said.

I stopped walking. We were still in the parking lot of the station. "So you were there," I said. It wasn't a question. Somehow I'd known it all this time.

"George, I know how it looks," Adam said, rubbing his brow. "I was looking for you! I'd found out that you ran a craft store in Pottsville. When I got here, I asked for directions. I asked this young kid I met when I got off the bus."

"Gem," I said, shaking my head.

"Yes," Adam said guiltily. "I asked him where the best craft shop in town was. He said he could show me, so he walked me over to Julie's."

I tried not to take offense at Julie's being called the best craft shop in town. It wasn't the time nor the place.

I shook my head. "So Brenda was right..." I muttered. "She did see you and Gem there. So, what, you were there right when it happened?"

Adam shook his head slowly. "I walked in through the doors. I was a little nervous, thinking I was about to see you for the first time in sixteen years." A little smile danced on his lips. "But when I walked in, obviously you weren't there. There was a woman with dark hair behind the counter. I asked her for the owner. She got a little annoyed with me and told me that the owner was busy right then, and could I help her."

"So it wasn't Julie?"

Adam shrugged. "I don't know who it was. I just realized I had the wrong shop. And that maybe you owned the second best craft shop in town."

"Hey!" I said, giving him a playful little whack on the arm. "You can't trust Gem Dawes's opinions on this matter," I said.

"I guess not," Adam replied glumly. "But I didn't know any better right then. Anyway, I left, and the brunette woman closed the shop right away, which I thought was a little strange. And I tried to find the right shop. Gem wasn't interested in coming with me."

"So Gem stayed behind?" I asked.

Adam nodded and shrugged. "I suppose so. The break in, and the murder, must have happened right after I left." He stared into my eyes. "But I could hardly have told anyone this, could I? Who was going to believe I was innocent? A newcomer, at the scene of the crime, with my only alibi the town crook."

"But you touched items while you were there?"

Adam nodded. "Yes, the door...and while I was inside, I was so nervous I probably picked up a dozen different items and placed them back down again. I don't remember. I was kind of in a daze. Then I probably leaned against the counter..."

It was kind of touching that he'd been so nervous to see me that he'd totally forgotten what he was even doing. But that probably wasn't the right thing to focus on right then.

I let out a long sigh. Adam was right. It didn't look good for him. "Plus some people have this crazy idea that I am benefiting from Julie's death," I said, cringing. It wasn't that crazy, actually. I was benefiting from it. "But, I mean, you wouldn't have killed Julie just to help out my shop, right?"

I laughed, but Adam didn't. He just stared at me. "I would do anything to help you, Georgie."

"Come on, Adam. You're scaring me a little." I backed away from him. Suddenly, I had visions of him entering Julie's shop, realizing that I was, in fact, not the owner of the 'best craft store in Pottsville' and offing her so that I could claim the number one spot.

Adam laughed. "Of course that is crazy," he said. "I got out of there as fast as I could. I wouldn't hurt anyone."

I nodded and let out a sigh of relief. Of course he wouldn't.

"I don't believe you're guilty, Adam," I said softly.

It took a long time for him to answer. "Of this?" he finally asked. "Or what happened seventeen years ago?"

"Both," I answered. It was what I had to believe. I could see Ryan glancing at us through the window of the station.

411

"I just want this very long day to be over," I said, walking over to untie Jasper from the poll he had been patiently waiting at. "So let's get out of the line of fire, please."

* * *

"You know, you really should get a car," Adam said. "It's not safe for a woman to be walking alone here at night."

"You just don't like walking," I pointed out. "You always were a little lazy, Adam."

He shook his head. "Seriously. I'm worried about you."

It was almost nine o'clock and I felt like the longest day of my life was never going to end. I didn't want to admit it, but a car would really have come in handy right then.

"I can protect myself," I stated with confidence. Jasper jumped up a little as if to say, 'hey, I am pretty good protection too!' "Besides, Pottsville is a safe, small, loving community..."

Adam laughed. "Small? Definitely. Safe? Come on,

Georgie. And loving? Don't make me laugh. I've been here four days and already somebody has been killed, and we've both been accused of being the murderer."

I wanted to defend the community that I'd somehow come to love, even though it had done its best to ostracize me and make me feel like an outsider. I felt like I'd just started to chipmunk my way through, though. I thought, with communities like Pottsville, it was about sticking it out. Making yourself a fixture, putting down roots, showing that you're there to stay, even when people don't want you to.

And, anyway, Adam was even newer than I was. He didn't have the right to judge the town when he was so fresh. He hadn't put down any roots yet.

"It's not always like this," I said defensively. Even though that wasn't entirely true. "You can't judge an entire community from one incident. I feel perfectly safe walking the streets."

"What about what people say about the hills? After dark?" Adam asked, glancing up at the sky.

I stopped walking. "How would you know about those tales?" I asked him. Unless he really was friends with Gem Dawes. Had they really said goodbye at Julie's shop and left it at that? Was that really the only time they had interacted?

Adam shrugged. "People talk."

We were about to leave the center of town to take the road that would lead us home and Jasper was already pulling forward, on autopilot, knowing exactly where he wanted to go. Home. To where his food bowl was.

"Let's just walk past the shop," I said, changing my mind, and my course, at the last minute. "I've just got this funny feeling—probably paranoid, I know—that I didn't lock up properly."

Jasper looked up at me, wagging his tail wildly. Hmm. That was interesting. "Look, Jasper agrees. I trust his instincts more these days." Or maybe he was only picking up on my own uneasy vibes.

Adam shook his head and gently placed his arm around my shoulder, trying to lead me back in the other direction. "Come on, Georgie, you're just being silly. It's out of the way. And it's late. You just said how tired you are. I'm sure that you would have remembered to lock up."

I shrugged his arm off me. I was insistent. "No," I said, a little annoyed. "I just want to check. Are you coming with me or not?"

I couldn't quite read the look on his face. He seemed positively distressed at the idea of adding five minutes to our journey. "It's fine," I said. "You can go home and I'll check on my own."

But with a reluctant sigh, he agreed to come with me.

But by the time we reached the top of the street, I glanced down and my heart started to settle a little. "Oh, you're probably right after all," I said to Adam. "The street is perfectly still, and sleepy."

Adam looked relieved. "Just like you are. Just like I am, actually. Come on, let's—"

Jasper suddenly pulled so hard on his leash that he almost made me fall forward onto the pavement. "Jasper!" I admonished him as his leash slipped out of my hands. "Come back!" I shouted as he raced as fast as he could toward my shop, a blur of black and white as he dashed through the empty street.

I chased after him, not noticing that Adam hung back and didn't follow.

Jasper was barking like a dog possessed at the window of the store. I had never seen him like that before, snarling and practically frothing at the mouth.

That was how I knew it was something serious. He wouldn't behave that way unless he was trying to protect me, or alert me, or both.

It only took me a few seconds to join him at the front of the store. I stopped, my heart racing so fast I felt like I was about to pass out.

The front window was smashed.

A figure, holding a brand new box with a brand new sewing machine inside it, stepped furtively through the window, unaware at first that it wasn't just a dog who had disturbed him.

I didn't think I'd ever felt so disappointed in my life.

"Gem?" I asked. "Oh, Gem. What have you done..."

Chapter 8

I threw a ball across the park for Jasper to catch and return.

While he chased it and picked it up in his mouth, he wasn't so good with the 'returning' part, and instead decided to keep it to himself, sitting down and gnawing on it like it was a bone.

I shook my head. "You still need a little bit of training, don't you, boy?"

One of these days, when I had the time and the money, and Jasper didn't have such bad separation anxiety, I intended to send him to puppy training camp, even though he was a bit older than a pup. Apparently, there was a camp nearby that took dogs of all ages.

But until then I was just going to have to train him as well as I could, on my own.

"What do you think, Jasper? Do you think either of these men I know are truly innocent?" I was sitting on a log with my knees tucked up against me. The wind was a little gentler, but it still made my jewelry jangle and whipped my hair into my eyes every now and then.

But I didn't feel like being inside, not at home, right

then.

I was starting to wish I'd never bailed Adam out of jail.

All I could think about was how reluctant Adam had been to check the shop, how he'd tried to drag me back home.

"Did he know that Gem was going to be there?" I asked Jasper when he finally brought the tennis ball back to me and placed it at my feet. "Did he give Gem the all clear that the shop was going to be empty?" Were they in it together? I mean, someone had to be helping Gem, right?

The wind suddenly died down completely for the first time in days and the park was totally still and quiet. And finally I was starting to be able to get my thoughts clear.

Jasper sat and looked up at me in earnest.

"Hmm, you're right, boy," I said, nodding. "Adam was only able to make one phone call from jail, and he made it to me. How could he have possibly told Gem that the shop was going to be empty?"

I just didn't know what to think. My gut, usually something I could rely on to get me through these situations, was all over the place. First of all, my instincts told me that Adam must be innocent. That he was not capable of murder. But they also told me he was hiding something, and that he knew more about Gem's schemes than he was letting on.

"Come on," I said to Jasper, standing up. "It's just you and me again now."

When I got home, the place was empty. I was thankful and took the chance while I had it. I placed a couple of hundred dollar bills down on the counter along with a note, letting Adam know that I had already called up and checked that there was a room free for the night at the near-by Flamingo Inn.

"Please be gone by the time I get back."

* * *

It was finally time for that drink.

"Wow, with new joints like this popping up, Pottsville is going to become positively cosmopolitan," I commented, glancing around at the interior of the flashy new bar. "Though it is a little too red for my tastes." The walls were red and the lights were red, and with the black bar and tables, I think it was supposed to have a romantic atmosphere. But to be honest, it was a little creepy.

"Do you want to try one of these cocktails?" Ryan asked, handing me the menu for me to peruse. "Looks like they switch them around every week."

"Hmm, they all sound tempting, and delicious," I said. "Especially the espresso martini. I could do with the shot of caffeine right now..."

"But?" Ryan asked knowingly.

"But, you know that I can't resist my glass of red," I said a little apologetically. "Does that make me terribly unadventurous?"

Ryan laughed. "I don't think the drink a person orders is a very good indication of how adventurous they are," he said with a wink. "Because that's certainly not the word I would use to describe you. You seem to change every time I see you."

"It's funny, because my ex-husband doesn't seem to think that I've changed at all."

Ryan declined the offer of a cocktail as well and ordered one of the bar's specially brewed boutique beers.

"And how is it going, having your ex-husband stay with you?" Ryan asked after his beer had arrived and he'd taken a few healthy gulps.

"He's not. Not any longer," I replied simply.

I could have sworn Ryan looked very pleased to hear that news. "Things didn't work out then?"

"Got a little awkward after he was arrested for murder last night," I quipped back. Then, in a less amused tone, "Kind of brought up some old, bad memories as well."

I looked away, hoping that Ryan would change the subject. He picked up on the cue. "Man, this beer is...different tasting. More floral than I was expecting. Though I guess this place does do things differently."

"Well, I think this place is just perfect," I said, clinking my glass against his bottle. "And I'm glad that you finally called me. It was a pleasant surprise to hear from you last night. Believe me. I needed a pleasant surprise."

"Sorry it took so long for us to catch up again like this," Ryan said. He laughed a little nervously and tore at the corner of the label of his bottle. "And sorry for..." He cringed a little. "...everything that happened with Adam."

"It's fine," I said, waving my hand as though it was all truly nothing. It was definitely awkward, though. How could it not be?

"I know things have been a little weird between us," Ryan said.

"I have to ask you something," I said, cutting him off. "Because it's really been troubling me."

Ryan frowned and pushed his beer aside. "Well, that's no good. You can ask me anything that's on your mind."

"Why haven't you arrested me?"

Ryan looked a little startled. "Excuse me?"

"For Julie's murder. Or at least, why haven't you questioned me? Brenda told me that she'd been to the cops to tell them I was as the scene of the crime."

"Oh, that..." Ryan threw his head back and laughed before picking up his beer bottle again. "We stopped taking her seriously after the third suspect she came forward with," Ryan said. "Besides, no one else saw you at the scene and your prints weren't there." He shrugged. "We can't take every thing Brenda says to us too seriously, or we'd never be able to conduct our own investigations."

"I see." My voice sounded a little flat.

Ryan took another sip of beer and raised his eyebrows. "Why does that not seem like the answer you wanted to hear?"

I laughed a little. "I don't know... I'm just being silly." I fluttered my eyelashes a little bit in an over-exaggerated fashion. "I suppose I was hoping to hear that you had so much faith in me that you couldn't possibly believe I was capable of murder."

"That too," Ryan said carefully as he sat his empty bottle down and ordered another. I shook my head as he offered me another drink. My wine glass was still surprisingly full.

"And how is that working out for you, George?" Ryan asked.

"Huh?" I asked, realizing my attention had drifted a little.

"Having faith that people can't possibly be capable of murder?"

I stared into my pinot noir and swirled the glass, forming little waves of red to splash inside like a violent ocean. "I think anyone is capable of anything, really."

* * *

Ryan had promised to call me the following day, but I was too old to believe lines like that and so was hardly waiting by the phone.

But when he did text me, just to say hello, the next morning while I was making my morning coffee in peace, it was another pleasant surprise. *See? This is a man who you can actually rely on.*

We texted back and forth for a few minutes. I told him how amazing it was to have the house to myself again and not to wake up to a pile of dirty dishes on the coffee table.

Uh oh, I texted. **There's a knock on the door. That is never good news.**

Oh no, Ryan quickly replied. **I hope it's not your houseguest.**

I decided that if it was Adam standing there, I was going to call Ryan up and tell him that Adam was threatening to leave town so he could throw him back in jail. But it was someone even worse.

Brenda.

"I was just out for a walk," she said. "Now that I have more spare time, I've taken the opportunity to get plenty of exercise."

I smiled at her, not wanting to give her the satisfaction of letting her know that she was getting on my last nerve. "Wonderful morning for a stroll," I said cheerily. "I trust you're enjoying the cold air, so I'll let you get back to it."

I tried to shut the door but she stood in front of it. "Really, I wouldn't want to get in the way of your exercise," I said.

Brenda looked worried. "Georgina, I need to tell you something... What is that scratching noise?" she asked, nosily poking her head through the door.

"It's Jasper trying to get in through the glass doors," I replied drolly. "He always knows when there's an unwanted guest here."

Brenda straightened up. "Do you want to hear what I have to say or not?"

I shrugged casually. "You can say whatever you want, it's a free country. That doesn't mean that I have to listen to it. Or even hear it."

Brenda was growing more and more annoyed. Hey,

better her than I, right? "Georgina, I've been down to the police precinct to try and tell them something, but they refuse to take me seriously." She was practically wringing her hands with worry. "And you know how much I care about this town. I am only trying to help."

I stared at her flatly. "Help? Or make everyone in the town look—and feel—guilty?"

"Georgina. If the police aren't going to listen to me, then I have to turn to you," she said. "Believe me, I didn't want to come here. But I know who did it. I know who killed Julie."

"I'm going to have to take the lead of the police force here," I said. "And stop taking you seriously after the third person you accuse of murder. You're the boy who cried wolf, Brenda. Sorry, the middle-aged woman who played wolf."

Brenda crossed her arms in offense. "I am younger than you are, Georgina."

That fact always surprised me.

"My point still stands," I said, starting to close the door.

"Fine. But you're ignoring me at your own peril!" Brenda cried. "Because I know who killed Julie. It was her sister."

* * *

Eager to prove to myself that I didn't need the help of either Adam or Brenda, I opened the shop, on time, and worked the full day on my own. Every time a customer came in and asked for their layaway goods, I informed them that we no longer offered that service and offered to refund their money.

"I'll be heading back to Julie's store as soon at it reopens!" a few customers grumbled.

Well, I was just going to have to cross that bridge when I got to it.

If Caroline was arrested, then there would be no chance of the shop ever opening again. I could have a monopoly in this town.

I had to push that thought out of my head. I couldn't let greed cloud my judgement. And I certainly couldn't listen to Brenda.

The house seemed eerily empty when I got home and Adam's things were no longer sprawled out on the sofa, and there were no more dirty dishes strewn across the coffee table. Call me crazy but for a second, I almost missed them.

Even Jasper seemed to notice the absence. "Don't worry, boy," I said, walking to the pantry to fetch him a treat. "I will play with you just as much as Adam did."

But he seemed a little despondent as he crouched down on the floor, his ears down low. He was sulking.

"Well, don't blame me!" I said, standing up with my hands on my hips.

He looked up at me with his large puppy dog eyes as if to say, "Do something about it then."

I shook my head. "You don't give me the commands, Jasper. I give them to you." Not that he ever listened.

I couldn't stand that sad look on his face for a minute longer. I sighed. "Fine. You win."

The sun was already setting, but I was heading back to the hills.

Chapter 9

I'd had to bribe Jasper with treats to get him this far, and even that was barely enough to get him to move from the foot of the hills. I couldn't help being mildly annoyed. "It was your very effective guilt trip that got me to come all the way out here in the first place, remember?"

If the hills had been mildly spooky during the day, they were downright terrifying at night. As I moved along the steep path, I could have sworn I saw a pair of bright red eyes staring at me from behind a tree. I turned to look, my heart beating quickly, but the eyes had moved, or disappeared.

"Or they were never there in the first place," I said out loud as I tried to drag Jasper up the slope.

If there had really been someone in the woods then Jasper would have wanted to run after them, I told myself. But he didn't want to go anywhere near them. So that meant that they were empty...right?

I never thought I'd be so relieved to see Gem Dawes.

He pulled the door back and the light inside his cottage was a beacon inviting me in from the dark.

Well, Gem wasn't exactly inviting me in. He was guarding the door with his arms crossed.

I tried smiling. Always my best bet in situations like this. "I thought it was customary to be a little more contrite to the person you just robbed."

Gem lowered his arms.

"You shouldn't be here."

"I didn't think there was any law against me visiting the person who stole from me," I said with a shrug. Though, maybe there was. Was I really supposed to stay away from him until after the court date? Ryan had said that it wouldn't be for months. There were more important things for the police and the courts to deal with. Like open murder cases.

"I don't mean that," Gem said, lowering his voice. He stepped aside and waved me in through the doors, though he seemed a little reluctant to do so. "I mean that you shouldn't be walking up the hills after dark."

"Oh, not that again," I said dismissively, unhooking the leash from Jasper's collar as I stepped through the door. I hoped that I wasn't still shaking. That might give away the fact that my laissez-faire attitude right then was all a put on.

"You can be dismissive, but that doesn't mean it's not real," Gem said as he quickly tidied his kitchen table. He grabbed a sheet of paper off and quickly hid it in the pocket of his red checked coat. I narrowed my eyes, trying to think of a way to get a look at what he was trying to hide. *Maybe if he gets warm, I can grab the coat and go through the pockets.*

But the cottage was freezing cold, with no fire or heater for warmth that night. "How about some of that amazing tea you made me the last time I visited?" I asked warmly. "And make it extra hot." Hey, it was my best shot at getting him to remove the coat.

With my cup of tea in my hands and the lights shining brightly, I suddenly didn't feel so terrified about being in the so-called haunted hills. In fact, it all seemed very silly indeed, the way I had been jumping at shadows.

"No fire tonight?" I found myself commenting. It seemed a little strange, considering we were surrounded by trees. "What, is the forest running low on timber?" I asked with a little laugh as I took a sip of tea.

Gem didn't find it funny at all. Okay, maybe it wasn't.

"It's a full moon. We don't go chopping down wood under a full moon. We can't do anything to disturb the woods at all. They don't belong to us, you know," Gem said quietly.

"They—they don't?" I said. "I thought your family owned all the land up here."

Gem looked at me like I was quite dense. "I mean that there are creatures that live in there that are better left alone."

"Like...coyotes?" I asked.

Gem rolled his eyes. "Sure. If that's what you want to call them." He shook his head in frustration. "But the things that my family have seen sure don't look like coyotes to me. Do coyotes live for hundreds of years? Do they stalk the woods and walk on two legs?"

"Those are just fairytales," I said.

"And you don't think that fairytales have any basis in reality? Rumors usually do have some fact to them."

I stared into my cup. All I could think about was the fact that I still had to walk back home alone after this visit. I was happy to talk about something, anything, else.

Gem stood up and took his coat off, throwing it over

the back of his chair. So, the tea had worked like a charm after all.

This is it. This is my chance.

Well, almost. He was still sitting on the chair so it would take some considerable skill to reach on my behalf to reach into the pocket unnoticed.

"I'll be back in a second," Gem said, standing up. "Just using the bathroom."

I couldn't believe my luck. As soon as he was out of sight, I reached over and grabbed the coat, searching the pockets. I must have checked the wrong one first, because it was empty. In my anxiousness, I dropped the coat on the floor and by the time I had picked it up and found the right pocket, Gem had already walked back into the room.

"What are you doing?"

I dropped the coat. "I'm sorry," I said. "I saw you put something in the pocket before I sat down."

"So you thought it was your right to see what it was?"

I stared at him. "No. But I had to wonder what you might have to hide from me."

"I can't have privacy in my own home?" he asked,

storming over to take the coat from me. He put his hand in the pocket and produced the slip of paper that he had stashed in there.

"This is what you wanted to see," he said, waving it around in the air. "And I don't just mean today."

"What do you mean?"

"Here," Gem said, handing me the receipt. "See, I did pay for that sewing machine I got from Julie's."

I glanced over it. It was definitely a receipt for the price of the sewing machine. I placed it down on the table. "Why were you hiding it from me?" I asked.

He let out a petulant little scoff that reminded me he wasn't much older than a teenager, despite his world-weariness. "I didn't want to give you the satisfaction."

I could relate to that.

"And what about the sewing machine you stole from me? Do you have the receipt for that?"

Gem's face turned red. He sat down and shook his head.

"I'm sorry, George," he said. "I never should have stolen from you."

"Why did you do it?" I asked, leaning forward. "I thought we connected the other day, Gem... I actually trusted you."

He let out a heavy sigh. "You wouldn't understand," he muttered.

I raised my eyebrows and shook my head. "No. I don't understand stealing at all. Please, if there is more to the story then let me know."

I sat and waited for his reply, wondering if I was going to get a heartfelt confession that explained everything—his life of poverty growing up, his attempts to better himself in a town that couldn't let go of prejudices, which led him to repeat the cycle of crime over and over again.

Gem shrugged. "I just really love crafting." His answer was flat and heavy with sarcasm.

I sighed. No heartfelt confession, then.

I leaned forward and looked Gem square in the eye. "I'm not here about the robbery at my shop," I said. Gem just stared back at me in disbelief. "I know, I should be, but that matter is for the police and courts to decide on now." I leaned back again.

"So what are you here for then?" The note of

defensiveness had crept back into Gem's voice. No longer such a cocky little kid.

"I wanted to talk about the day that Julie died. You were there," I said. "And not just to buy crafting items. My husband, my ex-husband, said you walked there together and he left you there alone, right before Julie died. You must have seen something."

"Why do you care so much anyway?" Gem asked.

"Someone I care about looks like he might be guilty," I said.

"Who?" Gem asked, with a little note of hope that broke my heart a little bit.

"Adam," I said. "I need to know, Gem, if he really left before anything happened. You were there with him. Did you see him leave?"

"Oh," Gem said, in the same flat tone of voice I had used when speaking to Ryan.

"Are you okay, Gem?"

He shrugged. "Must be nice to have someone care if you are guilty or not," Gem said in a sad tone.

I looked up at him. "I do care whether you are guilty or not, Gem," I said with a heavy sigh. "Believe it or not, I quite like you, even though you have given me absolutely every reason not to."

Gem looked away, ashamed.

"Please let me help you, and my ex-husband. Gem, did you see anything at the crime scene? Anyone who might have known Julie, or had a reason to hurt her?"

Gem nodded slowly. It seemed to pain him to answer. "Yes. But you're not going to like the answer, George. Because it was that ex of yours. I never saw him leave that day."

* * *

The bright lights coming up the hill were blinding me. I held my hand up and shielded myself, but as soon as I opened them, all I could see was stars.

And Ryan.

I'd been dreading a walk home down the hills all alone, but this wasn't the ride back to town that I had been hoping for.

Ryan's face looked crushed as he stepped out of the car and delivered the news. "I'm sorry, George," he said. "But I'm going to have to ask you a few questions about the afternoon that Julie Williams was killed."

I shook my head. "Not you too, Ryan. Tell me you haven't turned against me as well."

He dropped his head. "I'm sorry. I didn't want to have to do this. New information has come to light."

And so I was wrong. That time I'd caught Gem stealing from me was not the most disappointing moment of my life.

This one was.

Chapter 10

"So what do you say, Jasper?" I asked him as we walked out of the parking lot of the small Belldale Police Precinct for the second time that week.

He looked up at me, his ears pricked.

"Are you ready to skip town with me? Up for a life on the lam?" We could be like Thelma and Louise, only one of us would be a dog.

But Jasper wasn't listening to me. He only wanted to go home, and I didn't really blame him. I was lagging behind, still considering my new scheme of just making a run for it and skipping town for good. I tugged at one of my curls, musing as I imagined what I would look like as a redhead.

I sighed. If I was going to run away—with two dogs, no less—I was going to need a car.

"Okay, boy, I'm on my way," I called out to my frantic dog who was impatiently waiting for me at the house.

Jasper was barking wildly at the front door.

Thinking he was just hungry or eager to get to his

water bowl, I told him to calm down and quickly fetched my keys from my purse.

But the front door was already unlocked.

I froze. Someone had broken in.

Last time I was at the police station, Gem Dawes took the opportunity to break in to my shop.

Had he really betrayed me again? I couldn't put it past him at that moment.

Jasper shot through the front door, straight down the hall to where the sounds of footsteps on the floorboards made my blood run cold.

I crept quietly after him, trying to find something to grab so that I could defend myself from the intruder. My house is kind of minimalistic, though. I don't leave baseball bats just laying around in the hall. I don't even own a baseball bat.

I spotted a blue and white vase with a floral print. I'd hate to have to smash it against someone's head, it was expensive, but I edged toward it just in case.

Footsteps quickly headed toward the hallway where I was still crouched, reaching out for the vase.

I screamed, sure that I was coming face to face with the burglar.

"Adam," I gasped, clutching at my chest. "I know that I am only forty-one, but I think you just almost gave me a heart attack."

"I'm sorry," he said, taking a step forward. "I assumed you'd be home. The door was open..."

Oh dear. I did have a terrible habit of forgetting to lock the door.

"I might be a scatterbrain, Adam, but that does not mean that you can just let yourself into my home after I asked you to leave."

Adam's brow was creased. "You look terrible, Georgie,"

"Thanks."

"Where have you been?"

"If you really must know—" I popped the cork from a bottle of red and poured it right to the brim of a wine glass that I didn't even bother to rinse. "I was at one of your favorite places in town. The police precinct."

Adam nodded slowly like this didn't come as a surprise to him at all. "So they've turned on you now, have they?"

"Who?" I asked once I had finished gulping down my wine and could finally take a break to breathe and

441

speak.

"This town," Adam said knowingly as he leaned forward against the counter.

"What are you talking about?" I asked.

"They don't like outsiders here."

I shook my head and rinsed my empty glass before placing it in the dishwasher. A second glass was tempting, but it would only make me even drowsier. Jasper jumped up on my legs and I remembered I needed to feed him. "I don't need your help," I said to Adam when I saw him walking toward the cabinet where I kept Jasper and Casper's dry food.

He held his hands up. "Suit yourself. Just looks like you've had a rough night."

I poured food for the two hungry pups.

"What I need from you is to give me an explanation. What are you doing here, Adam?" I stood up straight and looked him up and down. "What happened to your alternative accommodation? Did the money I gave you run out already?"

"I was staying with a friend," Adam said, digging into his pocket and handing over the same hundred dollar bills I'd left for him a few days earlier. "So you can have this back."

I pocketed the money. "Which friend?"

"It doesn't matter," Adam said softly. "I just came by to check on you before I..."

Jasper began barking wildly at something outside on the lawn and I jumped a mile. "For crying out loud, Jasper!" I said, almost collapsing against the sink. I caught Adam looking at me in concern. "I've just had a trying day," I explained. "I'm not usually this jumpy."

Adam had that same knowing look on his face. "You never used to be...until you moved here."

"This house has nothing to do with it," I said, pulling out the top shelf of the dishwasher to load it properly. I shook my head when I saw that Adam had clearly made himself a meal before I'd gotten there, going off the plate that was covered with ketchup and mayonnaise that wasn't mine. At least he put things in the sink this time, I supposed.

"Isn't there a reason you were so scared when you walked into the house tonight?" Adam asked. "You were about ready to jump and attack me."

I just stared at him blankly. "Yes. There is a reason. You broke in."

Adam sighed. "You know deep down that this town isn't safe, no matter how much you try to defend it as a cozy, little loving community."

The dishwasher made a loud howling noise that I was grateful for in that moment, because it allowed me to ignore what Adam was saying. I tried to find more chores to busy myself with—usually I hated cleaning, but I had a sudden urge for it—but Adam just trailed me around the kitchen as I opened doors and pulled out paper towel and sprays.

"And this town is not safe in more ways than just the one, George."

"What do you mean?" I spun around, holding the bottle of counter spray like it was a gun.

Adam held his hands up. Don't shoot.

"It's not a safe environment for you, George, for your individuality. I know you, and you need space to be yourself. Can you really tell me that Pottsville honestly gives you that opportunity?"

"It does." I tried to speak confidentially, but even I could hear the note of uncertainty in my voice as I scrambled desperately to find evidence. "It's a community for artists, for crafters, for writers...for people who want to express their creativity."

Adam let out a soft scoff. "Maybe in theory it is. But I've seen these people up close. They are judgmental and small-minded."

"You've met Brenda," I said. "They aren't all like her."

"And what about your policeman friend? Is he as caring and supportive as you thought he was?"

For the first time I had to wonder, seriously wonder, if Adam was jealous of Ryan. That was insane though, right? Adam and I hadn't even seen each other, much less been married, for over sixteen years. If he was acting jealous, surely it was just an alpha male thing. He couldn't still have feelings for me. I was sure of it.

When I didn't answer, Adam shook his head.

"Do you want to know the real reason I came to Pottsville?" Adam asked. His voice was soft now, and there was a twinkling in his eyes. Just for a second, I felt like I was twenty-one again, back in Greece, when we were young, and happy...and incredibly foolish.

I shook my head. "I'm not sure I do, actually. I think there are a lot of things I don't want to know about you, Adam."

Then he said something that truly shocked me.

"I am still in love with you, Georgina."

All I could think to say was, "No one calls me that." I was too shocked to think of a proper response. I shook my head and slunk away from him. Maybe if I just pretended he hadn't said that, the words would dissolve like smoke and be gone by the time I woke up.

"George? Where are you..."

I shook my head and backed away up the staircase. "You can stay here for the night," I said. "On the sofa."

* * *

It wasn't until the next morning that I discovered Adam's true reason for breaking in the night before. He had come to say goodbye.

"You're leaving?" I asked, looking at his packed bags.

Adam stood up straight and stretched, and I heard the bones in his neck crack. Looked like neither of us were so young anymore. "Not sure I can handle another night on the sofa."

"But...but I don't understand." I said, shaking my head. This was too much before I'd had a chance to have a coffee.

"Don't worry," Adam said. "I'm no longer an active suspect so you won't lose your bail money."

"That's not what I am concerned about," I said, although of course it had been a bit of a concern.

Adam finished tying his knapsack and looked up at me. "What are you concerned about then, George?"

I wrapped my silk robe around me. "I'm...I'm concerned about you just leaving with no money to your name, for one thing," I tried to say as firmly as I could. "How are you even going to afford to travel?"

"I've got enough for a bus fare," he said. "And I've always gotten by before."

Were there tears springing to my eyes? I tried to fight them off as I spoke. "How can you just leave after what you said last night?" I said, trying to control the shake in my voice. I was angry as much as I was upset. In fact, I was downright furious. "How can you just drop a bombshell like that and then walk away from the carnage? Honestly, it is so typical of you, Adam..."

He sat his bags down and walked over to me. "I had

to see you. Say those things to you before I left," he said gently. "Or I never would have been able to live with myself if I didn't at least find out..."

"Find out what?" I whispered.

"Come with me, George," Adam said, brushing a strand of hair across my cheek. "We can start over. It can be just like it was twenty years ago. George, I never met anyone else that I loved since I was married to you. Come with me."

* * *

"Am I crazy to actually be considering it?"

Caroline had straightened her hair before our meeting this time. I wasn't sure if it was a deliberate attempt to differentiate herself from me, or whether she just happened to be trying another style. Either way, it worked. We no longer looked exactly like twins. And I noticed she no longer wore the same bold, brightly-colored jewelry that I did.

Caroline shrugged at me over her coffee. "No, I don't think so. It sounds like nothing but trouble has found you ever since you arrived in Pottsville."

"That's an understatement." I picked up my coffee and mused over it. "When I first moved here, I was duped into buying a house that someone had been killed in. Then the first friend I made here in Pottsville was killed." I took a sip of my coffee. "And that's pretty much set the tone for everything that's happened since!"

I really had to laugh. Adam had a point, didn't he? "In fact, I think I had a less tumultuous life when the two of us were married. And I never thought I'd say that."

Caroline tilted her head to the side like she was sizing me up, but she spoke with the warmth and fondness of an old friend. "To be honest, George, it sounds to me like you have a taste for adventure. Isn't that what attracted you to Adam in the first place? And isn't that what makes you want to stay in Pottsville now?"

I bit down on my lip a little as I considered this, staring out the window of the diner to the main street outside that looked so quiet in that moment, so still, now that the wind had started to settle. But I knew it was only a mirage, this stillness. When I'd moved to Pottsville, I'd told myself it was for a sea change. Or, well, you know, a forest change. A chance to leave my wild past behind. Convinced myself that was what I wanted.

And when life in Pottsville had turned out to be surprisingly wild itself, I'd pretended to be appalled. 'This isn't what I signed up for!' I'd shouted. Inwardly, if not to anyone else.

But deep down, maybe I'd been pleased. Thrilled, even.

Was this one of the reasons I couldn't leave now?

I shook my head. "Well, leaving with Adam would be a different kind of thrill," I pointed out to Caroline. "Though I'm not sure it's the kind of adventure I want now. It would be like re-living an old adventure, and that's never the same, is it?"

Caroline shrugged. "I suppose it depends. You two don't know each other that well any longer. Maybe it would be like starting over. Perhaps there will be new adventures to come?"

But I wasn't sure I wanted any new adventures with Adam. Adventures with him weren't always the fun kind. Sometimes they were the dangerous kind.

"I've never told anyone in Pottsville this," I said, stirring another sugar substitute into my coffee. It seemed extra bitter right then. "But the reason that Adam and I split up sixteen years ago was because he was the suspect in a murder."

Caroline's mouth fell open a little. "Another one?"

I nodded. "Our neighbor was killed. A woman, in her thirties. She was a decade older than us at the time. We never had much to do with her, but some people started these rumors that she and Adam were involved...and he had no alibi the night she was killed." I shook my head as I recalled the whole thing.

"And did you believe he was guilty?" Caroline asked. She leaned forward eagerly like I was about to impart a juicy piece of gossip and she couldn't wait to gobble it up. She almost knocked her coffee over in the process.

"At the time, I wasn't sure," I answered. "Well, I wasn't confident in myself like I am now that I am a bit older and wiser. And the rumors about Adam and the woman clouded my judgement. Of course, I had to believe deep down that he was innocent. But my parents got inside my head. They told me that I couldn't risk it, could I? Living with a murderer. Being married to one. I needed to get out of there."

Caroline still looked shocked by the entire story. It was reactions like this that usually kept me from telling it to people. They always thought that Adam was guilty.

I shook my head. Like usual, I jumped to defend him. "I suppose the thing that I keep coming back to, is, how could I have married him and not seen that side of him, if it was there all along?"

Caroline scoffed. "People can surprise you though, George. You can believe, with all your heart, that they are good, that they would never do anything to break the law, anything that could hurt someone else..." She stared at me. "And then they do something that shocks you to the very core."

I nodded. I didn't know who she was talking about, exactly, but I agreed that the sentiment was correct. "I stupidly believed that Gem Dawes wouldn't do anything to hurt me."

Caroline looked up at me sharply. "You should never have trusted that boy."

I nodded. "Maybe I do need to get away from this place."

Caroline shrugged and looked down. "I mean, half the reason I do the job I do is so that I can escape this town half the time."

I frowned. "Why don't you just move away, then?" I

asked. "There are plenty of other towns and cities that you could base yourself out of."

"My family needs me here," she said. "My sisters need me."

"Sisters?" I asked, confused. I placed my coffee down and stared at her.

"Well, just sister, singular, I suppose."

Oh, right, she had just made a mistake. She just meant Julie.

"But now you don't have any sisters here, right?" I asked, a little tactlessly. Didn't quite come out how I meant it. "I only meant, you have no ties, now."

Caroline narrowed her eyes at me. "No, I still have my other sister, Sophie."

My blood froze in my veins for a second. "I didn't know that you and Julie had another sister..."

"Yes," Caroline said coolly, sipping her coffee. "She worked at the shop with Julie on occasion."

I gulped. "Was she working there the day that Julie died?" I asked quietly. "Does she happen to have brown hair?"

Caroline sat her coffee down, her face made of

stone. "Drop it, George. If you know what is good for you." She pushed back her seat and stood up. "Maybe you should take your ex-husband's offer. Get out of town."

Chapter 11

"Adam," I called out, jogging toward the bus stop. "Please, stop! Don't get on the bus!"

I stopped when my ankle almost gave out beneath me. "I don't think I've run this much since we were married," I said breathlessly. I was practically breaking out in a sweat.

Adam dropped his bags and walked toward me with a wide grin on his face. "George, does your being here mean..."

Oh. I realized he must have thought I'd chased him down at the bus station to tell him I was going with him. He thought I was going to profess my love for him, say that my feelings for him had never faded, and that I wanted to run away with him. I kinda couldn't blame him for jumping to that conclusion, given the scene I was making.

"Um, Adam. I think you might have misunderstood." I shook my head. "No. I can't leave town with you."

His face fell. "Then what are you doing here?" he asked defensively.

"I found out something about Caroline and Julie... I

can't believe I am saying this, but Brenda was right. Julie was killed by her sister. I thought...I thought you might want to..."

Adam nodded. "Right. So now that you've realized I'm not guilty after all, you've come to find me? Is that it?"

I shook my head. Although I wasn't entirely sure he was wrong. "I thought you might want to help," I said. "I thought you might want to help me catch the real killer. I still care about you, Adam, even if I can't skip town with you. What do you say, for old time's sake?"

Adam hung his head sadly. "I hope this all works out for you, George. Not just this mystery, either, but your life here. But if you don't want me to be a part of it, then, well..." He picked his bags up again and glanced over his shoulder in the direction of the waiting bus.

I nodded, biting my lip and trying not to show the emotion. I understood why he had to leave.

"Goodbye, Adam."

* * *

"I thought you might like a little help," a familiar

voice called from several feet behind me.

I spun around. "Gem," I said with a soft smile. "You don't know how glad I am to see you here right now." I waited for him to catch up to me. "And yes. I could use some help," I said warmly. Then I shivered a little as I glanced at the police station that loomed large about a yard away.

"Gem, are you finally ready to be honest?" I asked him. "I spoke to Adam. I know that he didn't do it. Why did you say that he did?"

He was back to being a petulant kid. "Of course Adam just wants to protect himself..."

I cut him off. "I spoke to Caroline too. Tell me, Gem, why you wanted Adam to look guilty. Why were you protecting Sophie?"

"I wasn't," he mumbled. "I was protecting myself." He shrugged. "And Julie, I guess," he said, a little sadly.

I had come to a complete stop. Before I headed inside to see Ryan, I needed to hear this. "Protecting Julie?"

Gem stomped his foot on the ground and stared at the sky. "I suppose I may as well tell you now. I'm already in for it. Julie and I... We had a deal going on.

She would give me big ticket items to sell for her, black market, and then she would write off the items so that she could take a loss, tax-wise."

I just stared at him. "Are you sure about this?"

Gem rolled his eyes. "Why would I make this up? We'd had the same setup for years. She always printed me off a fake receipt so that if I ever got caught with a hot item, I could claim I bought it."

I narrowed my eyes. "So you aren't in to crafting, then."

Gem shook his head sheepishly. "No. I'm sorry. I'm sure it's great and all..."

"So what happened?" I asked him. "Was Sophie involved as well?"

"No. Sophie used to work at the shop. Julie kept it a secret from her, but one afternoon, she over heard us discussing a 'deal' and, well, she lost it."

"Lost it?" I asked.

Gem nodded. "Sophie wanted to buy into the business. Julie had lied to her, cooked the books to show her it was making more of a profit than it was. Sophie felt betrayed. That day, Adam and I were there..." Gem stopped speaking and gulped. "I saw

Sophie do it, George. I'm sorry. I should have said something. But I was involved too and Adam was there..."

"And he was an easy person to lay the blame on," I whispered.

Gem nodded. "None of this has been easy for me," he said. "How do you think I make a living now?"

"That's why you stole from me?" I asked.

Gem nodded. "I'm sorry."

"Caroline must have been trying to protect Julie as well..." I murmured.

Gem shoved his hands in his pockets. "I knew that if I came forward that I would be in big trouble."

"But you didn't kill Julie," I said firmly. "And you need to help the person who did be brought to justice."

Gem nodded. He looked terrified.

"I didn't want to do it, at first," he said. "But Julie offered me a larger and larger cut until I agreed. And she told me that if I helped her out, then she might be able to offer me a legitimate job, working in the shop. I never had one of those, you know."

I nodded. "I understand, Gem. I don't approve, but I

understand." I started walking again, hurrying toward the station. I needed Gem to come with me and repeat all of this to Ryan.

"It was tough for Julie to make the rent of her shop, seeing as she was so far out of the central business district," Gem said, almost tripping over his untied shoelaces. We didn't have time to stop, though.

"I always wondered how she stayed open there," I said, "when almost all the other shops had closed down."

The darn wind had picked up again. It pushed against us as we made our way down the street. Was it a sign that we should turn back?

Gem stopped a few feet away from the precinct. "Gem, what are you doing?" I asked.

He shook his head. "I can't do it," he said, before he turned and ran away.

"Gem!" I screamed after him. But he was gone with the wind.

I shook my head and started running after him.

* * *

Gem had already disappeared from sight by the time I arrived in front of Julie's shop.

I gulped as I looked up at it. Something drew me toward it. *Is this where Gem is hiding?*

Turn back, George, I told myself. *You can always go to the cops with what you already know. You don't need Gem.*

But reason didn't win out that time, and I took a step inside the empty, still-closed-for-business shop.

"Gem?" I called. When I heard footsteps, I breathed a sigh of relief. "It's okay, Gem. You just freaked out for a moment. I'll come with you for moral support when you tell your story to the police. You can tell them everything you know about Julie and Sophie, and I can back you up."

It wasn't Gem who stepped out of the shadows, though.

"Caroline!" I gasped. "What are you doing here?" I took a step backwards, but it was dark and I banged into one of the aisle shelves, causing a bucket of random buttons to scatter to the ground. When I tried to run, I skidded on them and Caroline got to the door

461

ahead of me.

"I can't allow this secret about my sisters to get out," she said, standing in front of the door.

"Caroline..." I said, trying to reason with her. "You're one of the suspects in Julie's murder. There's no sense in you taking the blame for what happened. Who does that help?"

She moved away from the door, resigned, and leaned against the now empty shelf. "It helps Julie," she said, shaking her head. The emotion was finally showing in her voice. "I don't want anyone to know that she was involved with this dodgy scheme." She looked up at me. "And Sophie is my baby sister," she whispered. "I can't turn her in."

"Don't worry, I'll do all of the turning in," I said, actually trying to be helpful, but Caroline's face was dark, not grateful.

"I can't let you do that," she said in a low tone. She grabbed a vase—a blue and white floral design, just like the one in my home—and held it up, her eyes glaring down at me.

"Caroline..." I said, backing away with my hands up.

It looked like Sophie wasn't the only one of the

William's sisters who was willing to kill to keep a secret.

We both gasped when the back door opened and a woman, familiar looking yet foreign to me at the same time, walked into the store.

So. There was a third woman that looked like both of us, after all.

Sophie had slightly longer hair, and it was a little darker than mine and Caroline's, but with the curls and bright jewels, she could easily have been mistaken for our double. Or would that be for our triple?

There's still no way I'm going to apologize to Brenda for any of this.

Gem had made the unknown things, the eyes that hid in the forest, seem like the scariest thing. But it was the real, tangible threats, the ones that walked toward you with a crowbar, that are truly the scariest.

"Sophie," I said, holding my hands up as I walked away. I already knew what she was capable of. She'd killed her own sister. And I was a perfect stranger. Maybe reason would work. It was worth a shot. "You don't want to add another murder to your list," I pointed out. "You'll never get out of prison in this lifetime."

With a crazed look in her eyes, she smiled at me and then her smile fell. A sadness took over her face and for just a second, I thought she was going to lower the crowbar. Instead, she lunged toward me and aimed for my head. I barely moved out of the way in time. Thankfully, instead of the crowbar hitting me square in the head it came down hard on my shoulder, knocking me to the ground. I cried out in pain as I scrambled to move away from her.

The crazed look and smile was back as she inched toward me. Suddenly my back hit something. I looked behind me to see that I had backed into the wall. There was nowhere else for me to go. I covered my head as she took a step toward me and I tried to brace myself for the blow. I let out a scream as I sensed her arm coming toward me.

I heard the noise, but it didn't register at first what it was. I looked up to see Sophie lying on the ground in front of me. Caroline was standing behind her, shaking and holding part of vase—the rest of it shattered on the ground around Sophie's head.

It took me a minute to command my body to move. I was still terrified and my arms wanted to remain plastered over my head to protect it.

Caroline looked down at her sister and stared at her with a bitter expression washing over her face. She bent over and checked Sophie's pulse. "She's breathing just fine," she said in a morbid tone that drifted away as she spoke.

But the vase had not gotten away so unharmed. It was split right up the center of its blue and white floral center and chipped into a hundred pieces that glue was never going to be able to put back together.

"Looks like we won't be able to sell that," Caroline said flatly.

* * *

"I'm not going to say I told you so," Brenda said. "Because you never even gave me a chance to tell you so. But maybe if you had listened to me, you wouldn't have almost died..."

I had barely even gotten a chance to turn the sign to 'open' before Brenda had turned up to definitely not tell me she told me so. She'd clearly already heard everything.

"You can have your job back," I said, cutting her off.

"You're good at your job and our customers like you." I glanced around at the mess that seemed to have grown worse during the couple of days I'd had to close up while I was babying my badly bruised shoulder at home. "And you seem to have a system that works better than mine does." I even managed a small smile. "Maybe you could even show it to me some time."

She tried to speak, but I still wasn't done.

"But, Brenda, I won't have you talking to me the way you have been. I have to put my foot down. I am the boss, and you are the employee. You have to treat me with a little respect."

Her mouth dropped open like she was about to object.

But I knew she wasn't going to turn down the chance to come back to work. And I was right, she didn't push it. She just silently walked to the counter, picked up her apron, and tied it around her waist.

She didn't say much for the rest of the day, but she couldn't help needling me just a little.

"So what happened to this other business you were going to buy?" she said. "Did you realize that was a stupid idea?"

"Not stupid. Just not for me, at the moment."

"And what about this town?" Brenda asked. "I thought you were going to throw that in as well. Run away. People talk, you know, George."

Oh, I knew.

"I decided to stay put," I mused while I fiddled with a flower display in the window. "I have a couple of friends in town now. So, I think I'll be sticking around."

Epilogue

With her new red hair, Caroline was almost unrecognizable.

"I was wondering recently what I would look like with red hair," I said to her as I entered her shop, nodding my approval. "Quite good, as it turns out. Maybe I will have to give it a try," I said, a little teasingly.

"Don't even think about it," Caroline warned.

I laughed. "Okay then. At least not until we're living in different zip codes."

"I take it you're not going to leave town any time soon then?" Caroline asked.

I shook my head slowly. "Not for now. I decided it was time for new adventures. Not old."

Caroline laughed. "It's a new adventure for me too. Looks like I'm the only sister left standing now, so I've gotta make this business work."

"It looks good in here," I said to Caroline. "I'm impressed by how quickly you're getting things cleaned up." I nodded. "And all the new light fixtures make the place look a lot more modern."

"And it's going to be an honest operation from this point forward," Caroline said firmly.

Caroline was going to give up life on the road. She was going to try settling in Pottsville, and I was going to try it with her.

"I just hope you're up for the competition," Caroline said. "I heard that you took most of our customers while we were closed. You're going to have to get prepared for us to poach some of them back."

I nodded and smiled at her. "I like a good bit of healthy competition," I said.

* * *

I didn't like living with regrets, which was why I found myself back at the bus station the day after I had said goodbye to Adam.

I might have given up my chance to go with him, and I didn't regret that, but I did regret the way things had ended.

"Back again?" the heavy-set bus driver asked as he

stepped out of the coach. He must have recognized me from the scene I'd made a day earlier. "I'm afraid I'm not making another trip out of here till tomorrow, ma'am."

Ma'am? I was at least a few years younger than this man, I was sure of it.

But I decided to be charming. "I was looking for one of your passengers. My ex-husband, Adam. Do you remember him?"

The driver nodded. "I do."

"I don't suppose you could tell me, at least, what station he got off at?" I asked with a sad smile that I tried to make bright. "He never even left a forwarding address."

"I'm sorry, ma'am, I can't."

I wasn't sure I was more annoyed by the use of the term ma'am or the fact that bus drivers had such strict driver/passenger confidentiality.

"Oh come on," I said. "Asking for the name of a bus station is hardly a huge breach of privacy."

"No, you misunderstand, ma'am." There was that term again. "I can't tell you which station he got off at because he never got off the bus."

I was utterly confused. Was I just exhausted or was this bus driver talking in riddles? I shook my head. "What, he just stayed on the bus?" I asked. "Till which town?"

The drive shook his head. "Mr. Thornton never boarded the bus," he said. "Or, rather, he did, but he got right back off. And I couldn't offer him a refund, which annoyed him a little."

"What? Then where is he?" I asked in shock.

The bus driver shrugged. "Beats me, ma'am."

When I got home, my front door was open. I shook my head as Jasper jumped up onto his hind legs, eager to get off his leash and into the house to greet his favorite house guest. Because I already knew who was waiting for me on the other side of the door.

"Hi there, George."

"Hi, Adam."

I walked inside and shut the door behind me, wondering what adventures lay ahead.

Thank You!

Thanks for reading the *Bakery Detectives Cozy Mystery Boxed Set (Books 7 - 9)*. I hope you enjoyed reading the stories as much as I enjoyed writing them. If you did, it would be awesome if you left a review for me on Amazon and/or Goodreads.

If you would like to know about future cozy mysteries by me and the other authors at Fairfield Publishing, make sure to sign up for our Cozy Mystery Newsletter. We will send you two FREE books just for signing up. All the details are on the next page.

If you haven't read the first six books in the Bakery Detectives series, be sure to check out the *Bakery Detectives Cozy Mystery Boxed Set (Books 1 - 6).* It is available on Amazon for a special low price.

amazon.com/dp/B01MRRVABU

At the end of the book, I have included a preview of the first book in the Glock Grannies Cozy Mystery series from my friend Shannon VanBergen. Check out the preview then get your copy on Amazon at:

amazon.com/dp/B06XHKYRRX

And I have one more special surprise - I'm also including a preview of the first cozy mystery from my friend Miles Lancaster, *Murder in the Mountains*. Check out the preview then get the book on Amazon at:

amazon.com/dp/B01DSKLY62

FAIRFIELD COZY MYSTERY NEWSLETTER

Make sure you sign up for the Fairfield Cozy Mystery Newsletter so you can keep up with our latest releases. When you sign up, **we will send you TWO FREE BOOKS!**

FairfieldPublishing.com/cozy-newsletter/

Now, turn the page and check out the previews.

Preview: Up in Smoke

I could feel my hair puffing up like cotton candy in the humidity as I stepped outside the Miami airport. I pushed a sticky strand from my face, and I wished for a minute that it were a cheerful pink instead of dirty blond, just to complete the illusion.

"Thank you so much for picking me up from the airport." I smiled at the sprightly old lady I was struggling to keep up with. "But why did you say my grandmother couldn't pick me up?"

"I didn't say." She turned and gave me a toothy grin—clearly none of them original—and winked. "I parked over here."

When we got to her car, she opened the trunk and threw in the sign she had been holding when she met me in baggage claim. The letters were done in gold glitter glue and she had drawn flowers with markers all around the edges. My name "Nikki Rae Parker" flashed when the sun reflected off of them, temporarily blinding me.

"I can tell you put a lot of work into that sign." I carefully put my luggage to the side of it, making sure not to touch her sign—partially because I didn't want to crush it and partially because it didn't look like the glue had dried yet.

"Well, your grandmother didn't give me much time to make it. I only had about ten minutes." She glanced at the sign proudly before closing the trunk. She looked me in the eyes. "Let's get on the road. We can chit chat in the car."

With that, she climbed in and clicked on her seat belt. As I got in, she was applying a thick coat of bright red lipstick while looking in the rearview mirror. "Gotta look sharp in case we get pulled over." She winked again, her heavily wrinkled eyelid looking like it thought about staying closed before it sprung back up again.

I thought about her words for a moment. She must get pulled over a lot, I thought. Poor old lady. I could picture her going ten miles an hour while the rest of Miami flew by her.

"Better buckle up." She pinched her lips together before blotting them slightly on a tissue. She smiled at me and for a moment, I was jealous of her pouty lips, every line filled in by layers and layers of red.

I did as I was told and buckled my seat belt before I

sunk down into her caramel leather seats. I was exhausted, both physically and mentally, from the trip. I closed my eyes and tried to forget my troubles, taking in a deep breath and letting it out slowly to give all my worry and fear ample time to escape my body. For the first time since I had made the decision to come here, I felt at peace. Unfortunately, it was short-lived.

The sound of squealing tires filled the air and my eyes flung open to see this old lady zigzagging through the parking garage. She took the turns without hitting the brakes, hugging each curve like a racecar driver. When we exited the garage and turned onto the street, she broke out in laughter. "That's my favorite part!"

I tugged my seat belt to make sure it was on tight. This was not going to be the relaxing drive I had thought it would be.

We hit the highway and I felt like I was in an arcade game. She wove in and out of traffic at a speed I was sure matched her old age.

"Ya know, the older I get the worse other people drive." She took one hand off the wheel and started to rummage through her purse, which sat between us.

"Um, can I help you with something?" My nerves were starting to get the best of me as her eyes were focused more on her purse than the road.

"Oh no, I've got it. I'm sure it's in here somewhere." She dug a little more, pulling out a package of AA batteries and then a ham sandwich.

Brake lights lit up in front of us and I screamed, bracing myself for impact. The old woman glanced up and pulled the car to the left in a quick jerk before returning to her purse. Horns blared from behind us.

"There it is!" She pulled out a package of wintergreen Life Savers. "Do you want one?"

"No, thank you." I could barely get the words out.

"I learned a long time ago that it was easier if I just drove and did my thing instead of worrying about what all the other drivers were doing. It's easier for them to get out of my way instead of me getting out of theirs. My reflexes aren't what they used to be." She popped a mint in her mouth and smiled. "I love wintergreen. I don't know why peppermint is more popular. Peppermint is so stuffy; wintergreen is fun."

She seemed to get in a groove with her driving and soon my grip was loosening on the sides of the seat, the blood slowly returning to my knuckles. Suddenly I realized I hadn't asked her name.

"I was so confused when you picked me up from the airport instead of my Grandma Dean that I never asked your name."

She didn't respond, just kept her eyes on the road with a steely look on her face. I was happy to see her finally being serious about driving, so I turned to look out the window. "It's beautiful here," I said after a few minutes of silence. I turned to look at her again and noticed that she was still focused straight ahead. I stared at her for a moment and realized she never blinked. Panic rose through my chest.

"Ma'am!" I shouted as I leaned forward to take the wheel. "Are you okay?"

She suddenly sprung to action, screaming and jerking the wheel to the left. Her screaming caused me to scream and I grabbed the wheel and pulled it to the right, trying to get us back in our lane. We continued to scream until the car stopped teetering and settled down to a nice hum on the road.

"Are you trying to kill us?" The woman's voice was hoarse and she seemed out of breath.

"I tried to talk to you and you didn't answer!" I practically shouted. "I thought you had a heart attack or something!"

"You almost gave me one!" She flashed me a dirty look. "And you made me swallow my mint. You're lucky I didn't choke to death!"

"I'm sorry." As I said the words, I noticed my heart was beating in my ears. "I really thought something had happened to you."

She was quiet for a moment. "Well, to be honest with you, I did doze off for a moment." She looked at me, pride spreading across her face. "I sleep with my eyes open. Do you know anyone who can do that?"

Before I could answer, she was telling me about her friend Delores who "claimed" she could sleep with her eyes open but, as it turned out, just slept with one eye half-open because she had a stroke and it wouldn't close all the way.

I sat there in silence before saying a quick prayer. My hands resumed their spot around the seat cushion and I could feel the blood draining from my knuckles yet again.

"So what was it you tried to talk to me about before you nearly killed us?"

I swallowed hard, trying to push away the irritation that fought to come out.

481

"I asked you what your name was." I stared at her and decided right then that I wouldn't take my eyes off of her for the rest of the trip. I would make sure she stayed awake, even if it meant talking to her the entire time.

"Oh yes! My name is Hattie Sue Miller," she said with a bit of arrogance. She glanced at me. "My father used to own most of this land." She motioned to either side of us. "Until he sold it and made a fortune." She gave me a look and dropped her voice to a whisper as she raised one eyebrow. "Of course we don't talk about money. That would be inappropriate." She said that last part like I had just asked her when she had last had sex. I felt ashamed until I realized I had never asked her about her money; I had simply asked her name. This woman was a nut. Didn't Grandma Dean have any other friends she could've sent to get me?

For the next hour or so, I asked her all kinds of questions to keep her awake—none of them about money or anything I thought might lead to money. If what she told me was true, she had a very interesting upbringing. She claimed to be related to Julia Tuttle, the woman who founded Miami. Her stories of how she got a railroad company to agree to build tracks there were fascinating. It wasn't until she told me she was also related to Michael Jackson that I started to question how true her stories were.

"We're almost there! Geraldine will be so happy to see you. You're all she's talked about the last two weeks." She pulled into a street lined with palm trees. "You're going to love it here." She smiled as she drove. "I've lived here a long time. It's far enough away from the city that you don't have all that hullaballoo, but big enough that you can eat at a different restaurant every day for a month."

When we entered the downtown area, heavy gray smoke hung in the air, and the road was blocked by a fire truck and two police cars.

"Oh no! I think there might have been a fire!" I leaned forward in my seat, trying to get a better look.

"Of course there was a fire!" Hattie huffed like I was an idiot. "That's why Geraldine sent me to get you!"

"What?! Is she okay?" I scanned the crowd and saw her immediately. She was easy to spot, even at our distance.

"Oh yes. She's fine. Her shop went up in flames as she was headed out the door. She got the call from a neighboring store owner and called me right away to go get you. Honestly, I barely had time to make you a sign." She acted like Grandma Dean had really put her in a bad position, leaving her only minutes to get my name on a piece of poster board.

Hattie pulled over and I jumped out; I'd come back for my luggage later. As I made my way toward the crowd, I was amazed at how little my Grandma Dean— or Grandma Dean-Dean, as I had called her since I was a little girl—had changed. Her bleach blonde hair was nearly white and cut in a cute bob that was level with her chin. She wore skintight light blue denim capris, which hugged her tiny frame. Her bright white t-shirt was the background for a long colorful necklace that appeared to be a string of beads. Thanks to a pair of bright red heels, she stood eye to eye with the fireman she was talking to.

I ran up to her and called out to her. "Grandma! Are you okay?" She flashed me a look of disgust before she smiled weakly at the fireman and said something I couldn't make out.

She turned her back to him and grabbed me by the arm. "I told you to never call me that!" She softened her tone then looked me over. "You look exhausted! Was it the flight or riding with that crazy Hattie?" She didn't give me time to answer. "Joe, this is my daughter's daughter, Nikki."

Joe smiled. I wasn't sure if it was his perfectly white teeth that got my attention, his uniform or his sparkling blue eyes, but I was immediately speechless. I tried to say hello, but the words stuck in my throat.

"Nikki, this is Joe Dellucci. He was born in New Jersey but his parents came from Italy. Isn't that right, Joe?"

I was disappointed when Joe answered without a New Jersey accent. Grandma Dean continued to tell me about Joe's heritage, which reminded me of Hattie. Apparently once you got to a certain age, you automatically became interested in people's backgrounds.

He must have noticed the look of disappointment on my face. "My family moved here when I was ten. My accent only slips in when I'm tired." His face lit up with a smile, causing mine to do the same. "Or when I eat pizza." I had no idea what he meant by that, but it caused me to break out in nervous laughter. Grandma Dean's look of embarrassment finally snapped me out of it.

"Well, Miss Dean. If I hear anything else, I'll let you know. In the meantime, call your insurance company. I'm sure they'll get you in touch with a good fire restoration service. If not, let me know. My brother's in the business."

He handed her a business card and I saw the name in red letters across the front: *Clean-up Guys.* Not a very catchy name. Then suddenly it hit me. A fireman with a brother who does fire restoration? Seemed a little fishy. Joe must have noticed my expression, because he chimed in. "Our house burned down when I was eight and Alex was twelve. I guess it had an impact on us."

Grandma Dean took the card and put it in her back pocket. "Thanks, Joe. I'll give Alex a call this afternoon."

They said their good-byes and as Joe walked away, Grandma Dean turned toward me. "What did I tell you about calling me 'Grandma' in public?" Her voice was barely over a whisper. "I've given you a list of names that are appropriate and I don't understand why you don't use one of them!"

"I'm not calling you Coco!" My mind tried to think of the other names on the list. Peaches? Was that on there? Whatever it was, they all sounded ridiculous.

"There is nothing wrong with Coco!" She pulled away from me and ran a hand through her hair as a woman approached us.

"Geraldine, I'm so sorry to hear about the fire!" The woman hugged Grandma Dean. "Do they know what started it?"

"No, but Joe's on it. He'll figure it out. I'm sure it was wiring or something. You know how these old buildings are."

The woman nodded in agreement. "If you need anything, please let me know." She hugged Grandma again and gave her a look of pity.

"Bev, this is my...daughter's daughter, Nikki."

I rolled my eyes. She couldn't even say granddaughter. I wondered if she would come up with some crazy name to replace that too.

"It's nice to meet you," Bev said without actually looking at me. She looked worried. Her drawn-on eyebrows were pinched together, creating a little bulge between them. "If you hear anything about what started it, please be sure to let me know."

Grandma turned to me as the woman walked away. "She owns the only other antique store on this block. I'm sure she's happy as a clam that her competition is out for a while," Grandma said, almost with a laugh.

I gasped. "Do you think she did it? Do you think she set fire to your shop?"

"Oh, honey, don't go jumping to conclusions like that. She would never hurt a fly." Grandma looked around. "Where's your luggage?"

I turned to point toward Hattie's car, but it was gone.

Grandma let out a loud laugh. "Hattie took off with your luggage? Well, then let's go get it."

Thanks for reading a sample of *Up in Smoke*. You can read the rest at:

amazon.com/dp/B06XHKYRRX

The Preview for Murder in the Mountains begins on the next page. I hope you enjoy that one too.

Preview: Murder in the Mountains

Screams were not a normal part of the workday at Aspen Breeze. When Jennifer heard the anguished cry of the maid, she ran around the desk and sprinted out the door. Clint, not through with his breakfast, followed at her heels. The door to the room had been left open. The maid stood on the thick burgundy carpet in front of the unmade bed and pointed at the hot tub.

Water remained in the tub, but it wasn't swirling. The occupant, a red-haired, slightly chubby man whose name Jennifer had forgotten, was face down. His blue running shorts had changed to a darker blue due to dampness. Reddish colorations marred his throat. Another dark spot of blood mixed with hair around his right temple. Pale red splotches marred the water.

For a moment, she felt like the ground had opened and she had fallen into blackness. Legs weakened. Knees buckled. She shook her head and a few incoherent syllables came from her mouth. Clint's arm grasped her around her waist.

"Step back. It's okay," he said.

It was a silly thing to say, he later thought. Clearly, it was not okay, but in times of stress people will often say and do stupid things.

He eased her backward, and then sat her down on the edge of the bed. He walked back and took a second look at the hot tub. He had seen dead bodies when he covered the police beat. It wasn't a routine occurrence, but he had stood in the rain twice and on an asphalt pavement once as EMTs covered a dead man and lifted him into an ambulance.

By the time he turned around, Jennifer was back on her feet and the color had returned to her cheeks.

She patted her maid on the shoulder. "Okay, it's all right. We have to call the police. You can go, Maria. Go to the office and lay down."

"Yes, ma'am."

She glanced at Clint and saw he had his cell phone out.

"...at the Aspen Breeze Lodge," he was saying. "There's a dead body in Unit Nine. It doesn't look like it was a natural death." He nodded then slipped the cell phone in his pocket. "They said the chief was out on a call but should be here within fifteen minutes."

He nodded weakly. "Yeah, Bill's been a friend of mine for years."

"I remember you from when you checked in yesterday, but I'm sorry I can't remember your name."

"Dale Ramsey."

Ramsey had a thin, pale face that flashed even paler. There was a chair close to him and he collapsed in it. He had an aquiline nose and chin but curly brown hair. His hand went to his heart.

"Sorry you had to learn about your friend's death this way, Mr. Ramsey," Jennifer said. "I regret to say I've forgotten his name too."

"Bill Hamilton."

Jennifer turned back to Clint. "Do you think we should move the body? Put it on the rug and cover it with a blanket?"

Clint shook his head. "I think the police would prefer it stay right where it is, at least for now."

Jennifer nodded. A steel gaze came in her eyes. She looked at Ramsey, who almost flinched. Then he shook slightly as if dealing with the aftermath of a panic attack.

"Mr. Ramsey, I am the owner of this Lodge and obviously I am very upset someone used it as a place for murder. So I trust you won't mind if I ask you a few questions - just to aid the police, of course."

Ramsey swallowed, or tried to. It looked like a rock had lodged in his throat. "Of course not. I...I do will anything I can to help," he said.

"Six single individuals checked into my lodge last night. That's a little unusual. I was commenting on that to Clint just last night. Now it turns out that you knew the deceased. Do you know the other four people who checked in?"

"Yes...I...yes."

There was a pause and Jennifer noted the look of sadness in his eyes.

"I realize you are upset, Mr. Ramsey, so just relax and take your time."

"We are all members of the Centennial Historical Society. All of us are history buffs," he finally answered.

"Why did you all check in here?"

Ramsey shifted in his chair. "This may sound unbelievable."

"Let's try it and see," Jennifer said.

"About a hundred and twenty-five years ago there was a Wells Fargo gold shipment in these parts. An outlaw gang headed by a man nicknamed The Falcon stole it. He got the name because he liked heights and the Rocky Mountains and had actually trained a falcon at one time. Rumor is, the gang got about a hundred thousand worth in gold, coins and bars. What's known is the gang drifted apart and a few members got shot, but the gold was never found. We believe it's buried very close by, up in the Rocky Mountain National Forest."

Jennifer nodded. The entrance to the forest was less than five miles from Aspen Breeze. All drivers had to do was turn left when they left the lodge and they would hit the entrance in about ten minutes.

"The Rocky Mountain National Forest is a huge area, thousands of miles there of virtually unexplored wilderness. You better have a specific location or you'll spend your lifetime looking and never find anything," she said.

'We have researched this gang for years. We think we know approximately where the gold was buried. It's more than just recovering the gold. This would be a historical find of enormous significance. We were going up there today to try to find the site."

"Maybe someone didn't want to share," Clint said.

Ramsey shook his head. "I doubt it. I've known these people for years. I don't think anyone would kill Bill. Besides, whoever it was would have to kill all of us too if he wanted to keep the gold to himself. Bill was in the high tech field, lower management, but he also liked the wilderness. He knew this forest better than any of us. We were counting on him to help find the site of the gold. He had searched the forest a number of times during the past five years.

I came out with him a few times. He thought he knew where the outlaws had hid their stash. He shared his opinions with us, but he was the one with the most expertise. Eddie, Eddie Tercelli, one of our group, is the second most knowledgeable about the location. He was out a few times too with Bill searching. But it would be tough for him to find the place on his own."

A blue light waved and flickered in the room. They heard a car door open and then slam shut. They looked up as the officer walked in. He wore a fine, crisp blue uniform with a bright silver badge. He had a slight paunch over his belt, but it didn't make him look old or slow. The intense gray eyes under the rim of the black police cap took in everything. His revolver was clearly visible on his right hip.

"Chief Sandish," Clint said, nodding.

Thanks for reading a sample of my first book, *Murder in the Mountains*. I really hope you liked it. It is available on Amazon at:

FairfieldPublishing.com/murder-in-mountains

Or you can get it for free by signing up for our newsletter.

FairfieldPublishing.com/cozy-newsletter/